Dark Vet

CJ Hannon

Dark Vet

Print Version
ISBN 978-1-9162737-5-7

1
Melody

The Defender pitches, rises. Outside: real bonnet-denting, headlight-blurring rain. Inside: "Red Red Wine" by UB40 plays on the digital radio, calm. Dapper's farm is irksome to find at the best of times. There, the turning. She takes it and bounces along the single-track road, running along the fold between two South Down hillocks.

Farm lights draw outlines: the corrugated sheeting of the hay barn roof, the boxy tractor, the broad farmhouse. It's as if the house, barns, sheds and outbuildings were built on separate slopes and slid down, gathering on this sternum of flat land. The Defender's already in 4 x 4 mode, and even then, doesn't so much as stop as slide to a halt in the mud. Dapper should get it gravelled, though he never will.

Despite the mud, the rain, the job at hand, it's a good reason to get away from the practice. Out of *his* orbit.

The light is brightest from the cow shed. Doors yawn open. A figure in silhouette waves. Melody splashes through the puddles, and ducks into the shed.

Dapper motions to one of the cows. 'Took your time. She's over there.'

There's a little stab of defiant pride that Dapper still calls on her. Kitteridge's is an urban practice in affluent Hove, tending, by and large, to over-preened domestic pets. Large animal work forms just ten, maybe fifteen, per cent of their business. Typically, it's the domain of the checked-shirt, bearded-man vet, like Martin. Except Martin prefers the glamour and sterility of the operating theatre, pumping hands with owners in the doggie salon, and upselling luxury pet food.

Here, in the mud with the big beasts. This is her domain.

Farmers don't normally expect a woman, though she must be doing something right to be called back during calving and lambing year after year. Though it's bittersweet. Instead of seeing animals, Dapper sees assets.

This is her role: to protect his assets by staying the hand of death.

Her own hand is now inside the cow in question. The animal is jittery. In pain. Immediately, by smell alone, she knows the news will be bad.

The calf comes out backwards, dead and stinking, already part rotten. Dapper covers his nose with his arm.

Melody has a strong constitution, but doesn't begrudge his reaction; death is an odour that goes bone-deep. Dapper calls to someone to drive the scoop over.

She soothes the mother, stroking her snout.

'It's over now.'

Dapper, handkerchief held over his nose, inspects the calf with a stick. 'Heifer too. Just my bloody luck.'

After tending to the mother, she inspects the four newborns farther down the shed. Three of them are coughing.

'Are they eating yet?'

'Not properly. This one's off food completely.'

Melody takes the temperature of the worst-looking one, nods. It's thirty-nine and a half Celsius. Too high. She scrutinises the barn.

'George, we spoke about this. You need to improve the ventilation in here, pneumonia thrives in stuffy places. It's not about the cold.'

'And I told you last time, don't need you telling me how to run my bloody farm!'

'It's a false economy. Surely you–'

'Just give them something for it, that's what I pay you for, isn't it? And you're hardly cheap.'

'Unlike yourself.'

Dapper mutters something, arms crossed while she administers drugs to bring down the cows' temperatures, and gives them antibiotics. 'Don't be surprised if you lose one or two, even with the medication.'

'What's the point in paying you for all this then, woman?'

'There's nobody to blame but yourself.'

Dapper grunts. 'Are you finished?'

'I'm serious, George. It'll cost you a lot more lost stock in the long run. Get the ventilation sorted or find yourself another vet.'

Dapper waves her away, muttering expletives. He strides out into the rain, yells something to the farmhand driving the scoop. The calf leg hangs over the yellow lip, bouncing with each juddering movement.

Couldn't have been helped, that one.

Melody swings open the boot of her Defender. There are two bins in her boot; one for spent disposals, the other for clothes to be washed. The blend of blood, mud, dead calf and spent placental juices has infused her clothes, her hair, her skin. There's a change of clothes in the back, though she doesn't fancy getting changed in the icy wet rain or wrestling her clothes in the confines of her car. She strips off her gloves, cleans up. She's quick. Efficient.

A bath, hot to burn, with a splash of Dettol. She'd kill for it right now, but it'll have to wait.

She covers the driver's seat in a plastic covering. Climbs in. Rings home. No answer. Then the practice. No answer either.

Next, she tries Hugh, the receptionist, on his mobile. Background noise, men talking. A pub or wine bar.

'Hugh. I'm just finished at Dapper's.'

'I've finished for the day, Melody. What is it?'

'I'll give you the rundown tomorrow. Listen, was Martin still there when you left?'

'I think so.' A pause. 'Look. Melody… it's none of my business, but Martin…'

Melody turns on the engine. 'You're right, Hugh. It is none of your business.' She hangs up. Who does he think he is?

Half an hour later, Melody parks up outside the converted Edwardian townhouse. It's a cosy-bricked, handsome property with bay windows, high ceilings and a chessboard path leading to the entrance. An expensive brass sign above the door reads: The Kitteridge Veterinary Practice.

The entire ground floor is theirs, plus the little garden at the back. It is decorated sumptuously throughout in a two-tone minty Arsenic by Farrow & Ball, with a creamy Pointing also by Farrow & Ball; not mixing brands within a room keeps it colour-loyal and avoids texture clash. The property costs an absolute fortune in rent but "one must appear to be a success in order to be a success". A Martin axiom if ever there was one.

The house is lifeless. The only light on is at the front bay window – Martin's room – and the blinds are pulled down, like drooping eyelids.

She stinks. That bath would be wonderful, but she's here now. She runs a hand over her triceps on her left side, feeling a dull ache under her layers. The cold makes it worse. She dashes between the car and the entrance, splashing through puddles, and lets herself in.

Inside, an eerie quiet. Martin hasn't been in a suitable frame of mind to conduct surgery so there are no overnighters scrambling around in their kennels or cages. Reception is dark, brooding. A slanted rectangle of light bleeds from under Martin's door.

Knocks. 'You in there?'

She waits. Knocks again, louder.

'Martin? It's me.' She tries the handle. It's locked, but she has a key and lets herself in.

He's lying on the floor, passed out. It's a mess, papers everywhere, his *Vet of the Year* trophy under the desk.

She sighs, puts the trophy back on the shelf, picks up the papers and stacks them neatly on his desk next to the half-drunk bottle of Balvenie whisky. The bottle she takes to the sink and upends it. The amber liquid glugs and disappears down the thirsty plughole.

She prods Martin with her foot.

'Martin. It's me. Anybody awake in there?' She shakes him again, harder this time. Still, he doesn't stir.

'Martin?' She bends down, and rests a finger on his neck.

The flesh isn't cold. It's warm.

She waits. Nothing.

Then tries the wrist.

2
Astrid

Blue and white lights reflect in the pavement puddles. Behind a border of police tape, a few members of the public watch and gossip.

'Excuse me.' Acting Detective Inspector Astrid Van Doren ducks under the tape and holds it up for Detective Constable Collins.

Attending is an officer she doesn't recognise – a rookie? – and Tom Weston, a dyed in the wool patrolman she'd worked with six years or so ago. The rookie is scene guard, patrolling the tape, hopefully taking notes of the faces, getting names.

'Tom,' she says, unwrapping a white Tylex protective suit from its packaging.

'Astrid. Charlie.'

'Bloody hell, Tom. It's Baltic out here tonight,' Collins says, as if Weston controlled the weather.

Astrid zips up to her throat. 'What have we got then, Tom?'

'One fatality. Male. Martin Kitteridge, co-owner of this practice with his wife, Melody, also a vet. Wife found the body. Called it in just after half past eight.'

'Let's take a look at the body.'

'Through here, sarge. Or is it DI now? Did I hear that right?'

'Just Acting. Smithes is acting up, left a bubble behind him.'

'Good for you, Astrid. No ballsing it up from here on out then, eh?'

'With such political savvy, I'm surprised you're not Chief Constable now, Tom.' She snaps on latex gloves and clean shoe coveralls.

Inside it's classy, clean. The reception is frosted glass, the computer an iMac. God, she'd always wanted one of those. Rooms break off from the heart of the lobby; a pet salon, treatment rooms. The first room on the left has a band of tape across it.

Astrid ducks under into a vinyl-floored room split in the middle with a curtain. Gleaming metal table. Large digital scales. A few cupboards, a sink area. Beyond the curtain, an office or consultation area. It's here where the body lies.

Astrid approaches, bracing herself.

Male, late thirties, early forties. Stocky build, beard with dark curly hair flecked with grey. A lumberjack forced into dark blue vet scrubs.

The biggest surprise? There's no shock; it helps that there's no blood. It helps too that this is her fourteenth dead body. It was true what the old hats told you: it does get easier. Repetition hardens the nerves, desensitises. Still, she registers a little bump in her heart rate, as if aware of her own vitality in the presence of the other.

Collins takes in the various certificates and plaques on the wall. 'Cambridge University. Gold Pet Care Insurance's Vet of the Year last year.'

How does it feel, to die facing your accomplishments? Proud? Or ridiculous?

Astrid crouches by the body. The vet's eyes are a deep woody brown, lifeless and unseeing. She swallows to get some moisture in her dry throat. 'There's still a little colour in his cheeks. A fresh one. No blood visible on the floor.'

Collins is still not looking at the body. Spooked? She casts an eye over the desk. 'Another bloody iMac. Do you think we could conveniently lose it in evidence?'

She's trying to get Collins' head in the game. The gallows humour is a way to cope, to try and neuter the shock, and focus the mind.

'Big drinker.' Collins points to an empty bottle of Balvenie Whisky. 'No spent blister packs in the rubbish bin. No note on the table. Alcohol poisoning, heart attack...see what the coroner says.'

Astrid scans from the top of the vet's head, down his scrubs. A pen in his breast pocket, no note there either. Probably not a suicide, but you never knew. A bulge in his right pocket. A set of keys. Down the trouser leg and her breath hitches in her chest.

'Collins.'

'What?' He squats down beside her.

'There, look at those spots at the bottom of the trouser leg by the right ankle.' The dark blue scrubs hid the stain well. 'Blood?'

Astrid lifts the trouser leg up by the hem very gently with a biro, sliding it higher.

'Jesus H Christ,' Collins says. 'What are those… bites?'

Astrid counts six puncture wounds. Little pyramids, each with a red halo of inflammation.

'Slowly, very slowly, back out of the room.' She shuffles backwards, watchful for movement.

Collins clips the door shut; his eyes are like pinpricks.

'What did those bites look like to you?'

'Fang bites. A spider or snake?'

'I'm no expert but the size, the spacing…. my bet would be a snake.'

'We *are* in a vet's, maybe they had one on site and it got loose?' Collins offers.

'It could still be in there, or the building for that matter.' She thinks through what to do next. 'Let's split up, make sure all doors, windows, obvious escape routes are blocked off.'

'And if I see the snake?'

'Cuff it and read its rights? Just call out, okay? Let's move.'

Astrid enters a small sterile operating theatre, no windows, an air vent with a grille too narrow for even a mouse to squeeze through, but plenty of hiding places. Next, a cupboard full of cleaning materials.

The next room is a cloakroom. A hanging shadow gives her a start. A scarf. Just a scarf. She presses a palm to her heart. Feels the *thump thump thump* even through her forensic suit. The last room is a small bathroom, reassuringly white and well lit. She lowers the toilet lid. A few summers ago, she'd attended a flat in Kemptown where a python had appeared in the bathroom of an old lady; it had escaped from the local pet shop and somehow travelled through the plumbing.

They reconvene outside. She brings Weston up to speed.

'First things first, we need an RSPCA snake specialist to do a sweep and make sure the scene's safe. Nobody goes in until it's all clear, not the paramedic to certify the death, not the forensics teams, nobody.'

'Yes, guv,' Weston says.

'I'll call the Coroner, request a Home Office forensic pathologist to do an examination in situ. Collins, get a Crime Scene Manager in here, and the CSIs on standby.'

'Yes, Ma'am.' Collins steps away to call the control room with her wish list.

'Weston, have you talked to the neighbours yet?'

'Only tried the two flats above the practice. One is empty, the other has an elderly lady. TV blaring out, she didn't hear or see anything.'

'Rustle up support if you need to, door knock within half a kilometre, and urge everyone to shut all windows and doors as a precaution. No mention of the snake please.' Astrid runs her hand under her hair, feeling the bristles of her undercut. The wife. She would know about any snake kept on the premises.

Two patrol cars. 'Which car is the wife in, Tom?'

Weston clears his throat. 'Oh… her friend came. Drove her home in her car.' It's like he reads the displeasure on her face because he quickly adds, 'I took a statement, took a fingerprint with the mobile scanner. I've got her clothing in the forensic bag. She had a change of clothes with her, you see.'

'Christ! You let her go?'

'You'd have done the same.'

'No, Tom. I wouldn't have.'

'The poor thing absolutely reeked! She'd just lost her husband and come straight from delivering a calf over at Dapper's farm and was covered in… you know, blood and…. stuff.'

'Hold on, hold on, back up. Have I got this right? You let a key witness at an unexplained death, who is covered in blood, go home to wash it off before the lead detective *or* forensics got here?'

Tom's mouth opens and closes again.

'Tom!'

'There was no blood on the body, the floor! She stank!'

'We don't know what happened. That's the point of sending bloody detectives to the scene! When did she go? How long?'

Tom, ashen-faced, says: 'A half hour. Look, I still don't th–
'

'Just don't,' she warns him. She gestures to Collins and stabs a finger at their car.

'Sorry, what Ma'am?' He holds the phone to his chest.

'We need to blue light it to the wife's house. Now.'

3
Melody
Hastings 1990

There is a boy here already.

He has a name but names aren't worth much when you don't stay in places long, when you don't need to say them aloud. He tells her he has been here for over a year, he's older than her. He concentrates, tongue poking out the edge of his mouth. A quick hand could dart and catch it, like a frog catching a fly.

'You'll be my sister, I guess. I'd prefer a brother.' He is building something, a tower. 'My mum's a druggie and my dad's in prison. What about you?'

A druggie? What is that? It sounds like "doggie", but of course it can't be that. Prison though, she's knows what that is. Melody reaches for a piece of Lego and adds it to the building.

'That doesn't go there.' He snatches it away. 'It goes over here, see?'

She hugs her knees to her chest and watches, wary of making another mistake.

The lady is old. A hobbler. People drop food off for her in little crates. Vegetables mostly, but one day a skipping rope with blue handles arrives.

'For you,' the lady says.

She takes it, bunches the rope in her hand. All hers?

'Aren't you going to say thank you?'

In the yard, she holds the handles behind her shoulders and launches the rope, jumping forward with it. It catches on her shins with a whip. She tries again, and again. There's a rap on the window. The lady opens it a crack.

'Start with the rope resting on your heels, hands down by your sides.'

Melody does. Loops the rope in an arc over her head, and jumps awkwardly through once, twice, three times, then it catches.

'Feet together. The rope's thin as a cracker, there's no need to jump so high. Hasn't anyone ever taught you?'

It works, and she jumps lightly on her feet, her wrists twirling. The rope scuffs lightly on the ground and skims brickwork if she loses position. The sound is good, a repetitive, *thwack, thwack, thwack.*

A cat with a wobbly belly walks the tightrope of the fence top with casual grace, and pauses to watch her.

Hers is the bottom bunk. The carpet is brown, the walls a yucky banana colour. Maybe one day she could have a wall, just one would do, and paint it just the way she likes. It smells like moths, but it is nicer than the last place. The birds here shriek. Huge white and grey things who stamp and scratch the roof at bedtime.

'Sounds like a giant tapping his fingers on the roof tiles,' the boy says. 'Trying to tell if there's food inside.'

She pulls the covers up tighter to her neck.

'Do you know how to talk?' He appears upside down, hair electrified.

She nods.

'You don't have to. I don't care.'

Will a giant come, hinge open the roof and lick them off his finger like ants?

That night, she wakes up uncomfortable, her pyjamas damp, warm, and clinging to her skin.

Melody shakes the lady. She comes to, coughing and hacking. The bedside light blinks on, and she sips water.

'What is it? Oh… come on, let's get you cleaned up.'

At school, the other children are curious, asking her questions. The teacher asks her things too. She listens. Does her work faster and better than anyone else. A little sponge, the teacher calls her, sponges are squidgy and rough but it sounds like the teacher means it in a good way. She has drawn the cat in her garden and it hangs on a peg in the classroom with a yellow star stuck in the corner. It is by far the best drawing, the colouring neat and tight to the lines.

There is a woman she has to talk to, the one who brought her to the house. Big frizzy hair. She appears, usually with chocolate or sweets and lets her nod or shake her head to her questions.

Does she like living with the lady? A nod.

How would she feel about living somewhere else? A shake.

How does she get on with the boy? A shrug.

Does she like the school? A nod.

Is anybody mean or nasty to her? A shake.

Then she disappears again.

One morning. She is prodded awake.

'Pssst. Come on, Melody, wake up!'

She rubs her eyes. Weak light behind the curtains. Morning? It must be.

'Come and look.'

He places a finger over his lips. She tiptoes after him. This feels naughty and exciting. The staircase is old, creaks, but the lady is snoring, her door ajar. The kitchen is dark and quiet. The boy reaches up and turns the key, and beckons her.

The yard is damp. The cold soaked paving stones chill her bare feet. A snail hangs on the edge of the watering can. Dew drops on the handles of her skipping rope. It is cold, she wants to go back in. They shouldn't be out here.

'Look over there, can you hear them?'

Following his finger, there, against the fence, by the overgrown creeper, is movement.

She rubs her arms, bumpy gooseflesh. A step closer. Mewling sounds.

She gasps. 'Kittens.'

The boy is delighted. 'You spoke! I did it! I knew I'd get you to talk.'

Melody puts a hand over her mouth, like she's broken a rule.

'Do you want to help me name them?'

She nods and points to one with a two white socks. 'Socks.'

'This one can be Roger.'

She gives him a look.

'Like Roger the Dodger from the *Beano* comic?'

She shrugs, points at the next one. It's obvious. 'Snowy.'

The boy names the last one Plug, and the litter is named. Socks crawls onto her lap, the others fuss and play.

She gives Socks a squeeze, ruffles the head of Plug.

It is all she can think of. At school she draws them all, individually and together in various states of play. Maths problems are done in kittens. Four kittens divided by two are two kittens. In the morning, she is first up, and plays with them before breakfast.

After her porridge she clears her throat.

'Please could I give the kittens some milk?'

The lady stares. 'Of course,' she fetches a saucer, and some food scraps. 'They're getting milk from their mother but I suppose a bit extra won't hurt now, will it?'

Melody shows them how well she can skip. Counting up the tens into a hundred and beyond in her head. The kittens are playful, knocking over the watering can, tumbling off the little wall, squirming over one another.

The boy appears at the doorway.

'Cats are amazing. You know that they have a superpower that means they always land upright on their feet?' He gathers up Roger, stroking him. 'Watch this.'

The boy stands up on the brickwork of the raised bed, reaches to the top of the fence and posts Roger over. There is a damp thud on the other side.

'Did you hear that? No cry out in pain. Nothing. It just landed. Just you wait, in a couple of minutes it'll be back over here.'

It is the most amazing thing she's ever heard. Melody bends down and strokes Socks, and knows she has to try. The boy weaves his fingers together to give her a bunk, and over Socks goes. She listens for the sound, smiles in amazement. The boy is really rather clever to know this.

The boy posts over Plug, and she takes the last turn with Snowy.

The mother cat is unsettled, roaming about looking for her babies. The yard is suddenly very empty without them. Some time passes. The kittens don't reappear.

'You know… it's possible they haven't learned to climb yet.' The boy scratches his head. 'They might be stuck in next door's garden.'

This horrifies her, but just then, the doorbell sounds.

'Phew. I bet that's Mr Larry next door bring them back round.'

She races. The lady is there already. A man, grim, holds a shovel.

The kittens are in a mangled mess, heaped one atop the other. She tries to put them back in order in her head, like a jigsaw puzzle.

'Jesus, Mary and Joseph,' the lady says, and braces herself against the hallway wall. Melody hides behind her legs. 'Don't let the children see, Larry!'

'They should see, was them what did it!'

The lady turns.

'She did it.' The boy says, pointing at her. 'I told her not to.'

'Melody?'

The kittens are gone forever. She is dropped glass about to shatter into a hundred little bits.

4

Melody

Bubbles rise. The world above the film of water blurs and shifts. The ceiling spotlights are bright miniature suns. Surface. Her long black hair gathers on her shoulders. The ceiling could do with a freshen up. Something brighter, less creamy, maybe a Loft White by Little Greene.

The free-standing bath is decadent. Brass feet on oak flooring. Steam rises, the disinfectant, working slowly. The great purge. She sniffs her skin. A little more. The dead calf has impregnated every pore. Dead.

Martin is dead.

'Do you want a drink? Something strong? Mel?' Allison peeps around the bathroom door.

'Somebody should tell the staff, Ally. I should call them.'

'It'll keep 'til morning, let them have a good night's sleep at least. It's more than we'll get.'

'A Bloody Mary, then. But don't you make it, you won't do it right.'

'Teach me.'

'Hand me that towel.'

There is comfort in the ritual. Ice cubes smoke at the bottom of the glass, Grey Goose vodka, organic tomato juice, Worcester sauce, squeeze of lemon, quarter of a teaspoon of horseradish, twist of black pepper all mixed up into a red whirlpool with a crisp stick of celery. To finish, she laces the top of the ice cubes with Tio Pepe sherry, adds a little lemon zest, and pokes in a straw.

'Try it.'

Ally takes a sip, coughs. 'Holy cow! Let me go again,' takes another sip, 'Wow… yes.'

Melody tries it. It's strong. A pinch over-peppered, but fortifying. A real slap across the cheeks.

'Make me one.'

'You need to drive home.'

'Don't be stupid. I'll stay. Tristan can handle the girls.'

'You don't have to.' But she's already reaching for another glass.

Cleopatra slaloms between her feet, leaning into her flesh. Warm. Alive.

They clink glasses, a morbid toast to Martin. The Bose plays "Invisible Touch" by Genesis on her eighties playlist. Surreal. Like getting ready for a night out. He could almost burst in, take a sip from her glass and ask about their plans for the evening, passing imperious judgement on their restaurant options. 'The Oriental Palace? We had a take-out from there about a month ago, didn't we, Moody? Place has really gone downhill.'

'How do you feel?' Ally asks.

'Like I want to get drunk.'

Her phone rings.

'Don't answer it.'

Melody ignores her. It's Simon Bradshaw, a farmer near Pyecombe. Can she come?

'I'll be there as soon as I can.'

Ally stares at her. 'Tell me you're not serious, Mel?'

'I'm on call-out. Nature doesn't care about our personal lives. Bradshaw's got two in labour and one's brought her calf bed out.'

‘Not to state the bleeding obvious, but Martin’s just died! You could at least take more than an hour off work!’

‘What difference does it make? Come on, Al, there’s time yet for something good to come from today.’

‘Bloody supervet. I’ll put these in the fridge for when we get back.’

‘We?’

‘Please. You might be under the limit but there’s no way I’m letting you drive.’

Al pulls the Defender out of the drive and takes a right onto Church Road.

Melody pats her pockets. ‘Damn.’

‘What?’

‘I left my phone.’

‘Want me to turn and go back?’

Bradshaw sounded desperate. Wasn’t one to make a fuss unnecessarily. ‘No… I know the way, let’s just get there. Every second counts.’

An unmarked police car with blue lights on the dash shoots past them.

5

Astrid

Astrid presses her ear to the door, tries the bell. Then knocks again.

'Are you sure about the address? Medina Villas?'

She backpedals, squints at the top floor windows. Dark. No lights on.

'This is definitely the listed address for Martin and Melody Kitteridge.'

Astrid looks up and down the street. Perhaps the wife's done a quick run to the off-licence.

What a beautiful place to live. Victorian villas just metres from the seafront, very desirable. The innumerable estate agent signs all up the street attest to the normal fate of these villas; being carved up into apartments and studios. All except this one. A statement house. Must be worth well north of a million.

'No car in the drive, either,' Collins says.

Again, a difference. The only house she can see with an actual drive, albeit a stubby one. The rest of the street is crowded with cars. Are they resented by their neighbours? Seen as haughty and rich?

'Maybe she went to stay at her friend's?' Collins offers, blowing into his hands.

'I'm going to try her mobile again.'

The call connects, rings and rings and cuts through to an answer phone. Mrs Kitteridge's voice is brisk, no-nonsense. This time Astrid leaves a message asking to be called back.

She thumps the side of the car with her palm, takes a deep breath. 'Tom Weston. He knows better, Charlie.'

Collins jumps on the spot. 'Got an idea.' He rings Weston, asking if he'd taken a name or contact number for Mrs Kitteridge's friend. He shakes his head, hangs up.

'Urgh. Basics!' She stares at the dark house, helpless. 'What else can we do but wait for the RSPCA sweep?'

'I have a suggestion.'

'What?' she snaps.

'We could get something to eat. You're hangry.'

Collins chooses Nayeb's, an upmarket kebab joint. It's warm and close enough to the Kitteridge Practice, and that's good enough for her.

'Charlie!' the guy behind the counter says, and offers Collins a handshake. 'Good to see you, man. What'll it be?'

'Regular here, are we, Collins?'

He gives an embarrassed smile. A TV blares out in the corner, a foreign news channel. A group of four men in leather jackets sit at the back with plates of rice, salad, and meat, conversing loudly in Arabic. On the wall: photos of a palace, and a city underneath a snow-capped mountain. Tehran?

They take a table by one of the massive photo prints with their food and discuss a recent drug bust, right before she got called up to act as DI. It was a terraced rental with the carpets stripped out. Almost every inch of available floor space was dedicated to growing marijuana plants under heat lamps.

'Very entrepreneurial. You have to admire it, a little,' Collins says between mouthfuls, yoghurt and chilli sauce dripping out of the seam of the wrap.

The court case is in a week, just a formality, but it's one

she'll have mixed feelings about. On paper, a good bust, a street value of a few hundred grand. When she strips it back, it was a Vietnamese family of immigrants with no real connections to organised crime. Just a family business in a black market that had got big enough to blip on their radar. Of course, she couldn't say any of this to anyone – Jenna excepted – because it wasn't her role to judge.

'And what do you make of this snake circus with the vet? Food's good, no?'

Astrid takes a sip from her Coke. 'It's a weird one.' She dips the meat in yoghurt and spears lettuce. Bites, thinking. 'You first.'

'Mostly about the snake. What type, how'd it get there?'

'And was it the cause of death?'

Collins jabs a finger at her twice, 'Was it the ultimate cause of death?'

'And where is the wife?' She picks up her phone. 'And why the hell isn't she answering my calls or trying to get back to me?'

Her phone bursts into life, slips from her hands, and into a dollop of yoghurt.

Collins stifles a laugh.

'Don't.' She wipes it on a napkin. Answers. 'Van Doren.'

It's Tom Weston. Voice chastened, contrite. 'Ma'am, the RSPCA chap's just finished. The paramedic's certified the death and forensics teams are in there now.' Ma'am? He must be feeling embarrassed. 'Be there in ten.'

'Here.' Astrid offers the cardboard tray to the rookie.

'Thanks, ma'am.' She takes a coffee, a sugar packet, and a stirrer.

'Did you see the body, Constable?'

'Yes, ma'am.'

'And are you doing okay? First time can always be an experience.'

'Would you be asking me that if I was a man?'

'Oh, I like you.' She pats her on the shoulder. 'You're going to be fine.'

Astrid joins Weston, the Crime Scene Manager and Clive from the RSPCA, who'd also dealt with the Kemptown python. They each take a coffee, leaving a couple for the forensics team.

'Clive, we should really stop meeting like this. Find anything?'

'I swept every room twice. If I've missed it, then it would have to be in a very, very small space.'

'And it's definitely a snake?' Collins asks.

'Oh yes. I've seen the bites. The spacing suggests something at least medium sized, the head would have to be,' he holds his fingers a couple of inches wide, 'roughly this size at a guess. Whole thing is probably a couple of metres long.'

'Any way to tell what species?' 'Let's go in and chat with the pathologist. Between us I think we have an idea or two.'

Astrid climbs into new coveralls and gloves, and stretches on overshoes. Malone, the CSM, clears the forensics people and the scene photographer out of the room. The pathologist stands by the body and is on the phone, holding up a finger to give him a second.

'DS Van Doren,' he says, after ending his call. She doesn't correct him on her Acting rank.

'Dr Hall.'

'Just giving the lab a heads up. The blood sample's on its way.'

'Already?'

'Bike courier. It's golden hour. Time was of the essence.' He beckons them over. 'I understand we might have a snake on the loose, so determining the species seemed paramount.'

'Indeed. Clive here tells me you have an idea?'

'The inflammation around the bites themselves suggests venom, but also look here. See this slight puffiness around the eyes?'

She actually hadn't on her initial inspection, but now it had been pointed out to her, there did appear so be some thickness to the eyelids.

'Early stage of ptosis. It'll get worse, even after death. Then there's this.' He opens the mouth, and shines in a torch and feels the tongue. 'Swollen and stiff.'

Clive chips in, 'There are three main types of venomous snake, but these features are indicative of neurotoxic venom. Elapidae or elapids are the most likely family.'

'Elapids?'

'Black mambas, taipans, cobras and a lot of sea snakes. They tend to have shorter fangs, the puncture wounds of the bites are relatively shallow, so I'd say it's a pretty good bet. We'll know for sure with an enzyme immunoassay.'

Black mambas? Cobras? In Hove? She shudders. 'What's an enzyme immune-wassit, or do I not need to know?'

'We use enzyme labelled antibodies and antigens to detect the biological molecules distinct to a specific species. The enzymes remain active for a period after death, not indefinitely. Hence Dr Hall's rush with the blood sample.'

'Got it. So, we'll confirm the species. How soon?'

'A unit at Falmer in the university will do the test for us tonight.'

'Quick thinking, gents. Clive, is there anything behavioural about elapids that might indicate where it might hide?'

'In the wild, they'd probably hide in burrows, under rocks and holes. So anywhere where there's cover. My guess is, it must have got out before we arrived.'

'What's the risk to the public?'

'The poor thing is probably scared.'

She likes that he thinks of the snake's welfare as much as the health of Joe Public.

'It takes a lot of energy to produce venom, so it'll be weak, it'll take days to produce more. The main thing to consider right now is the cold. Elapids are tropical and sub-tropical. It's barely three degrees tonight. If it's outside it'll go into brumation, a dormant state, and will die eventually unless it finds warmth and a food source.'

'Doesn't sound like it'll be slithering around George Street looking for a cappuccino, then. We need to keep this tight, no need to cause unnecessary panic. We'll get a message out to any patrols covering Hove tonight. We will notify you the second there's a sighting.'

'Okay.'

'Clive, would you do a sweep of the immediate vicinity too, please? Let me know on my mobile if you find anything.'

'You got it.'

Dr Hall is tapping on his phone. 'The photographer's done. I'm going to get the body moved to the mortuary. I'll conduct a post-mortem tomorrow. See you then, Detective?'

'Wouldn't miss it,' Astrid says, with what she hopes sounds like jokey bravado.

Astrid and Collins give their protective equipment to the forensics team, who will test it for trace samples, and return to the pool car.

'That it for us tonight then, guv?'

She climbs into the passenger seat, the window covered in rain splatter, and pulls her jacket a little tighter around her chest. 'Get that heater on, Collins.'

Maybe it's the dead body, maybe the cold, but getting back to her snug flat and lying under a thick duvet next to Jenna's warm body can't come quickly enough.

'Drop me home, would you?'

'You got it.'

The Ford Focus pulls out, taking the seafront road. The sea and her mysteries lie beyond in the blackness. She raps at the window softly with a knuckle.

'You're thinking.'

'That I am, Charlie,' she sighs. 'I'm wondering what worries me more. That we don't know where the venomous snake is, or the wife.

6
Melody

Melody wakes. The empty space in the bed next to her is formidable. She rises, brushes her hair straight, checks the clock. Late morning. Most unlike her, but then, there were extenuating circumstances. They hadn't gotten back from Bradshaw's farm until gone two am. And, of course, Martin was… gone.

Gone too, is Ally. A note in the kitchen reads:

Listen to music. Call me if you need. A x

Foggy headed, she picks up her phone. Her home screen is mobbed with notifications and missed calls. For now, she ignores them, and makes the only call she has to.

Hugh picks up immediately. 'Melody? I've been trying to call all morning, what on earth has happened? There's police tape blocking entrance to the practice.'

'I know,' she says, 'I've got some difficult news to share.'

'Please, God no. Not Martin, don't say it's Martin.'

'He's gone, Hugh.'

Hugh's breath catches, 'But no. He can't… How?'

She tells Hugh how she'd found Martin the night before. 'I know it is a lot to ask Hugh, but could you tell Kathy and Lydia for me?' She imagines they've all encountered the same scene on arriving at work. Perhaps she should have told them the night before. 'We'll be shut, of course, until… you know, I have no idea. There's just a lot to process, and practicalities to attend to.'

'Leave it with me. The appointments, your call-out duties, I'll get it all covered, just forget the practice for now, Melody. Just…I can't believe it.' His voice wobbles a little and cuts off with a sob.

Word spreads fast. Her phone rings and peeps with message notifications. She ignores them all, she doesn't want to speak to anybody.

She makes a simple brunch; staring at the eggs jostling and bobbing in the boiling pan until the timer goes.

Dining room table. The lonely clink of cutlery on crockery. Cleopatra hops up on the chair next to her, curls into a ball. Melody chews, runs her hand over her warm, soft fur. It is too quiet.

She twists the radio on. Vintage U2, before the decade turned and all music curdled. After, she rinses the plate and starts to stack it in the dishwasher, then opts to wash it up in the sink instead. No need now. It's just her.

Time to face the music. She listens to her voicemails, four are from a detective with Sussex CID, increasing in urgency and exasperation. Better call this one back.

'DI Van Doren.'

'Hello, this is Melody Kitteridge, responding to your voicemail.'

'Mrs Kitteridge.' There is a high level of surprise in her voice. Between a seven and an eight. 'Thanks for finally getting back to me.'

'Finally?'

'Mrs Kitteridge, I have a rather urgent question that couldn't wait, and yet I struggled to get hold of you last night and this morning.'

'It's been a strange time. I'm ready to talk to you now.'

'At the practice, do you keep any snakes on the premises?'

She takes a beat to process the question. 'Snakes? No. We don't. Occasionally someone brings in a milk or corn snake but we tend to recommend Crawley or Kemptown for anything really exotic. Why do you ask?'

'And no snake at home?'

'No. Never.'

'And when you discovered your husband's body, you didn't notice anything moving in the room?'

'Why would– I think you'd better explain what's happening here, Detective.'

A pause in which she senses the shape of a mouthed swear word on the other end. 'Your husband had some unusual bites on his leg.'

'Snake bites?'

'Probably. Post-mortem is scheduled to take place in the next hour or two; but the official report could take a while.'

'Venomous, if you think it killed him.'

'I'm sorry, Mrs Kitteridge, but we don't yet have the full picture. Suffice it to say, we're extremely focused on trying to find it. We have a team sweeping the local area.'

'It'd be too cold for it to survive long outside.'

'I'd like to meet and follow up on your initial statement,' Astrid says, ignoring her helpful observation. 'We may know more then.'

They arrange a time to meet at the house, and the detective ends the call.

Melody raps her fingers on the table. Thinking. Cleopatra stares, then closes her eyes, indifferent to this revelatory news.

With the practice closed, home reminds her of Martin. So, she runs.

Melody plants a trainer on the beach wall, stretches into her calf muscle. "Africa" by Toto plays through her headphones. She hasn't been to any classes with Ally for a couple of weeks now. This will test her fitness.

She takes off, jogging past wrapped-up dog walkers, being

passed by electric scooters and cyclists. Frost lurks in the shadows, hiding from the weak sun. A Martin-less world. The very fact of him, gone. Impossible.

Her, a widow at thirty-eight.

Alone. Free. Terrified. Excited.

The sea is a deep Cook's Blue by Farrow & Ball. On the mudflats two men in wax jackets are out with spades digging for lugworms. At Hove lagoon a windsurfing lesson is underway; a girl in a wetsuit wobbles, falls and the sail timbers into the water after her. The world still carrying on, like nothing had happened.

Sea air to drink by the lungful. "Africa" ends, and the shuffle serves up "There Is a Light That Never Goes Out" by The Smiths. Death anthem. Was there nothing algorithms wouldn't leave their pawprints on?

Breathing harder now. Her arm throbs in time to her blood pumping, off beat to the drums.

Just keep running.

It's supposed to clear her mind but instead practicalities flood in. Her in-laws Harold, and bitchface Susan. The staff: Hugh, Kathy, and Lydia. And Kitteridge's? It would be entirely hers now. Should she bring in a new vet to replace Martin? Sacrilege to think something so soon. There was a funeral to arrange. If she could just fast-forward a few months, or even a year, she'd do it in a heartbeat.

She spins suddenly, taken off balance and it takes a moment to realise: someone has grabbed her.

'Excuse me!'

He's tall, in a thick black coat with the hood pulled up. A crescent scar on his chin, a sleeper earring. Pug-like.

Melody removes her earphones, and repeats, voice sharp to cut, 'Excuse me!'

'Mrs Kitteridge?' he has a low gravelly voice.

This checks her. 'Yes?'

'Sorry to grab you like that. I didn't think you'd hear me with your music on.'

'And you are?'

'An acquaintance of your husband. Your late husband, as I understand. We were sad to hear about it.'

'We?' She looks around. It's just him.

'Have you heard the name Richie Sheridan?'

'By reputation...' Her eyes narrow. 'You work for him? What do you want?'

'To talk about the Napoleonic code.'

'You've lost me.'

'In marriage a woman and a man share their assets, what's his is hers and hers is his. Nice and simple, like. We'd like to offer our condolences while reminding you of your husband's obligations.'

'Obli–' Martin's gambling. 'How much does he owe?'

Pug hands her a piece of folded paper, she opens it and gapes at the number.

'But...'

Pug holds up his hands. 'It's already overdue, but Mr Sheridan is not... shall we say *insensitive* to your predicament. He can be a reasonable man.'

Oh Martin... what did you get yourself into?

'The first five grand as a show of good faith, within forty-eight hours.'

She holds up the paper; the total, an astronomical sum.

'If you don't believe the number, just ask his mate. He'll tell you. Two days. I'll text you the address.' And Pug is gone.

You don't have my number.

And his mate? Which mate?

Then it hits her who he means.

7
Melody
Hastings 1990

Winter gives way to a chilly Spring, but Melody cannot forget. Those poor kittens. She wakes, desperate to cry but it's like the tears are blocked by some machinery.

It was all the boy's fault. He got away with it.

Above. The underside of the top bunk. She imagines a spike skewering up straight through the middle. She plots, finds a small box of tacks. Considers hiding them in his bed. Tests it by pushing two of them into her arm. The pain is sharp, but not unbearable. It isn't enough.

When the mother cat appears in the yard, it overwhelms her. The guilt is an over-stretched balloon.

It was all the boy's fault.

The idea comes while staring at the hearth.

One night, she stays awake, listens out for the sign that the lady has gone to bed. The boy has a cold. His wheezy breathing is rhythmical.

Downstairs. Orange smiles under the grey coals, their tops dusted with ash. Dusted. Snow. Like Christmas. She removes the fire guard, stands it to the side, thrusts the poker into the centre. Embers crackle and spit. She waits, then tests the heat with hovering hands. She carries the poker, creeping up the stairs. The shadow on the wall is a hero with a sword. The tip glows red, leads her. Like Rudolph's nose.

It still glows in the bedroom. Gently, so gently, on tiptoes, she peels back the duvet. Hard to reach. The boy's arm flops, dangles down. The perfect height. A sign. This is just. Not willing to let it cool any longer, Melody grips his wrist then holds the tip of the poker to the forearm. Presses it in.

Flesh singes, hisses. Then comes the scream.

They try and punish her. She is sent to bed straight after supper for a week. Her skipping rope is confiscated. The lady asks and asks, but she is silent. The boy's arm is wrapped in a bandage and he is watchful of her, wary.

When the lady dozes one afternoon, glass smashes. The boy has a cricket bat and jars. He lays out a carpet of jagged shards in the spots where mother cat usually drops down from the fence.

The woman with the frizzy hair appears. There is some problem with the lady; she can't look after them anymore.

Melody packs her belongings and waits at the appointed hour in the sitting room. The boy sits too, his own bag at his feet. He is going somewhere different.

'Can I see it?' She knows this will be her only chance.

He raises an eyebrow, roughly yanks up a sleeve.

The scar is shaped like a rocket. Red. Underwhelming.

He pulls his sleeve back down and stares daggers at her.

The lady comes in, and hands Melody her skipping rope, bunched up together. She takes it, stuffs it into the top of her bag.

The lady cries. 'I'm sorry. Just so sorry.'

But why? She has nothing to be sorry for, *she* didn't kill the kittens. The lady hugs her, she accepts it, dislikes the sensation, the smells, the closeness.

Frizzy Hair takes her away.

'They're a very nice couple, they've got three other foster kids. All boys. I think they were desperate to have a girl in the house, truth be told.'

Off the main road, streets corkscrew away. They take one. Terraced houses with plastic cladding and neat gardens. She gets out and hoists her bag on her shoulder, nearly topples over.

'Let me,' Frizzy Hair says.

She sniffs. Briny air. The sea must still be close.

A man and a woman wave from a doorway. They look tired. The man is slightly balding with big hands. The woman has a crooked nose, but pretty eyes. They give her a tour and a long list of rules. The boys aren't in, so as not to overwhelm her. They're all much older. She is shown a framed photograph. The oldest one is scary-looking. The sort of face that might appear on the evening news.

'Aren't you going to say anything, young lady?' the woman says.

She shakes her head; hands back the photo.

'She'll talk when she's ready,' Frizzy Hair says.

Her room is shared with the youngest of the boys. She won't bother with names. Not yet.

Posters of aggressive-looking rock bands cover the wall around his bed. Hers is bare. Stained wallpaper, spent Blu-Tack and pins. Must all the walls in her life be ugly? She must be replacing someone. One out, one in.

'Oh!' A cat appears. She bends to stroke it.

The adults all exchange a look.

'You like cats, don't you?' Frizzy Hair says.

She gathers it in her lap, strokes its grey fur.

'That's our cat, Ashy,' the woman says.

'Perhaps Melody could help feed it, help take care of it?' Frizzy Hair suggests.

'Is she, you know, capable?' the man asks.

Melody hugs it. The purrs are perhaps the most soothing of sounds. She loves it. Instantly and unconditionally.

Their cat? Not anymore. It's hers. And she will protect it. Nobody will harm this one. Nobody.

8
Astrid

Astrid steps out onto the balcony. Jenna's messily tied hair whips in the breeze. She taps her cigarette into an ashtray. She's in a black T-shirt, denim dungarees. She is so beautiful, Astrid's heart aches.

Astrid steals the cigarette and takes a drag.

'Morning to you too.'

Below, Brighton Marina is chock full of moored boats. Rigging whips and clangs.

'Christ, it's cold out here.'

'That's it. Last one ever. I've just quit,' Jenna says.

She might respond with a *Yeah right,* but if Jenna said this was her last one, then that's what it would be.

'And there was me cadging the last couple of drags off you.' Astrid scrunches it against the brickwork. 'You want to frame the stub?'

'Just bin it. I'll make breakfast.'

BBC Radio 6 Music is playing prog rock. Jenna cracks eggs into a bowl, whisks, dunks in some bread.

Astrid fills up their mugs with coffee, gets the milk from the fridge. Duck fillets? A whole coconut, half a pineapple, ginger, lemongrass, and chillies. Her heart sinks.

'Is it tonight that Caz and Sam are coming round?'

'It's been in the diary forever.'

Astrid pinches the bridge of her nose. Caz and Sam – though lovely – were in the slightly nauseating honeymoon glow of their recent marriage. Jenna had been inviting them over more and more often as if signalling, without consultation, a shift in their own relationship; fewer wild nights out and more dinner parties. For her, it was an uneasy metamorphosis not helped by the expectations of her work. Acting up to DI was a live audition. Her commitment, work ethic and intelligence were constantly under the spotlight. It was work with little respect for diaries.

'Christ. Sorry, not enough sleep. I knew that.' She thinks. If she busted her arse all day, barring anything unforeseen, she could probably be back in time.

Jenna flips the toast in the pan. Jaw set. Astrid knows Jenna. Every corner of the labyrinth. Jenna will want to say, *Make sure you get home on time,* but won't, hating the idea of being some domesticated "other" to the busy cop.

'Sugar, cinnamon, yeah?'

'Cover it until I can't see any yellow.'

'So, you got in late?'

'Suspicious death.'

Jenna slides the French toast onto her plate and one onto her own. It's good, way too sweet.

Astrid checks the time.

'I better get moving. Sooner I leave…' She winks, tips the rest of her coffee down her throat and puts the toast into a napkin.

'Yeah right.'

She gives Jenna a peck. 'See you tonight. Can't wait.'

Astrid slugs her way through traffic in her bright red Scirocco. Liquid drum and bass eases from the speakers. Fluid. Snaking. At odds with the logjams at the lights. Jenna's music, and it's inoffensive enough. She just digs guitars more.

Sussex House, Hollingbury, home of the Sussex CID. She grabs a coffee from the machine and gets a prime spot in the meeting room. At ten, Acting Detective Chief Inspector Smithes sits at the head of the meeting room table, fingers steepled together.

It is here where she gets a sense of her city's darker moods from her fellow detectives. Brighton had always been her home, but it has never stayed still. As the closest sea-side city to London, a lot of the capital's wealth and workers live here, and for good reason. It is a vibrant mix of urban bohemia, faded Victorian grandeur, flashy tourist attractions, and the gay capital of the UK, all wrapped up in one. A fun destination has its side effects too, attracting stag and hen dos from all over the UK and even Europe, but thankfully her days of being a weekend beat copper on West Street are long behind her. Outside London, Brighton has one of the busiest police stations in the country and the constantly shifting population of tourists adds an additional dimension to police work.

Smithes absorbs the latest briefing from DS Tomlinson. She knows how he works. He wants the barest facts, the escalations, and decision points. She's learning. Watching. Assessing. Not just the others, but Smithes too; this blueprint for a leader.

As a Detective Constable she'd been a known favourite of the former Chief Super, Ian Goodworth, but as he'd neared retirement, or as some said, fallen out of favour, she'd had to find others who rated her. Though not particularly senior, Smithes was highly regarded and getting into the slipstream of his favour now felt like a bold strategic move. She was a rising star. One to watch. A seat at the table.

'Acting DI Van Doren. Go.'

She gives a brief overview of the cases her four constables are working; a burglary from a jewellers' in the The Lanes, a bank vandalised by Extinction Rebellion protestors, three assaults: two domestic and one racially motivated. 'As for me, I've got court on Tuesday; the marijuana drug bust. Last night Collins and I picked up a suspicious death in Hove, of a vet. Venomous snake bites, snake whereabouts unknown, immediate risk to public very low due to outside temperatures and the spent venom. I'm expecting lab results to determine species today, though John Hall and the RSPCA believe it to be an elapid; that means a nasty one; a black mamba, cobra or taipan. The post-mortem is scheduled for one-thirty. For now, just a decision on whether to inform public of the potential danger the snake poses, sir.'

Smithes leans back. 'Recommendation?'

'We've informed local patrols, so we could just keep it tight for now, sir. The immediate risk is very low, we could hold it for at least another day.'

'If the grunts know, it'll be leaked. I'm surprised it hasn't already. Draft me a press statement for me to run by comms please, low risk, remain vigilant, call this number, et cetera.'

She slides a sheet of paper across the table. 'Already done, sir.'

He nods, turns to DI Maxwell. 'Next. Maxwell. Go.'

Collins fiddles with the radio while he drives.

'Suicide. Accident. Murder,' she says.

'What?'

'The vet. Those are the three possibilities.'

'You don't really think it could be a suicide? I mean, what a way to go.' He changes the frequency again.

'Just settle on a station, would you?'

Collins turns it off. 'We're basically here now, anyway. Suicide doesn't make much sense, guv. Alcohol and a snake would be a first, though.' He parks next to a patrol car.

'I doubt it too.' Astrid unclips her belt. 'Best to keep an open mind though.'

She flashes her warrant card to the scene guard. There is no activity in the house, but the scene still hasn't been officially released, so they don new forensic suits and return to the room where they'd found the body. Dark smudges and dust cover the room. It's like a grubby chimney sweep has pawed everything. The body would be in the city mortuary by now, in the chiller, hours away from the scalpel.

Astrid circles the desk. 'I've been thinking about those bites, Charlie. They didn't puncture fabric. They went straight to the flesh. Then the spots bled into the trousers.'

'Right… exposed skin.' Collins sits in the office chair. Astrid ducks her head under the desk. The lining of Collin's protective suit rides up exposing two bands of flesh above the ankle. 'So, he must have been sitting when he got bitten.'

'The snake bites above the right ankle.'

Collins rubs his chin.

'And three times, Charlie! In the same localised area. What does that tell you?'

'He's slow. You'd whip your leg away after the first bite, not sit around and offer seconds and thirds.'

This is Charlie Collins all over. Smart. Connects the dots but needs someone to put them in front of him. 'What else?'

Charlie stands. 'He does move, because his body is discovered on the floor, the other side of the desk. Could have been drunk or asleep when the bite happened? The whisky bottle suggests he'd been drinking.'

'I'm very interested to see what the tox screen says. So, he's bitten here, gets up slow, makes it around to the other side of the desk. Passes out.'

'Maybe he tries to make a call.' Collins takes out a pad. Not notes, but his growing to-do list.

'And if he doesn't call for help? It tells us he's incapacitated… or someone prevented it. She picks up the phone on his desk, gets a dial tone. 'Working. Check it out.'

Astrid looks at the clock. Lots of legwork to do. Statements of the staff to take. Collins is at the door, staring at the handle and the lock.

'What is it?

'Guv? I don't think this was a suicide.'

'Explain.'

'In Mrs Kitteridge's initial statement, she said the door was locked, and besides the set found on the body, she had the only spare key, right?'

'Correct.'

'Say you wanted to lock yourself inside, where would you put the key?'

'I'd leave it in the door.' She's stunned, realising what he's getting at. 'Which would block someone from putting in a key on the other side.'

'He was locked in here with the snake.'

He's jumping too far, assuming too much, but she can't shake the feeling that Charlie Collins might be onto something.

Christ, Charlie. I do believe you are starting to see the dots for yourself.

On the way to the mortuary, Astrid finally gets a call back from the wife, though she sheds no light on the snake.

'There's something strange about the wife, Collins.'

'Elusive. And if I'm right about the lock, and she has the only spare key…'

Theories were worth squat without evidence. She thumbs through her emails; one is marked urgent.

'The first lab report's in.'

'What's it say?' Collins glances over.

She opens the file, enlarges the text and scrolls to the summary.

'Holy shit!'

Collins doesn't take his eyes from the road. 'Guv?'

'The whisky bottle. Significant traces of Midazolam, an analgesic sedative typically used in veterinary medicine. It was found *inside* the bottle.'

There's a pause as he processes it. 'Someone spiked it?'

'Forensics got samples from the sink plughole and the trap in the plumbing, and it matches what's in the bottle too. That's consistent with the wife's statement about pouring the rest down the sink.'

'So, he was drugged? I bet Mrs Kitteridge was trying to destroy the evidence.'

'The problem with fixating on a suspect, Collins, is you blinker yourself to other possibilities.'

'Guv, the only way my mind could be more open would be on John Hall's post-mortem table. Any prints?'

'Yuk.' She winces. 'Multiple sets, only Martin Kitteridge and the wife confirmed so far.'

'The wife again? Hardly surprising, given her statement. Think it'll be enough?'

He means for it to be classified as an official murder investigation, for the machinery of the system to click into place. 'This is starting to reek of murder to me too, Collins. And with our current caseload…'

Collins is smiling. 'God, I hope we get Smithes. Is he duty SIO? He does technically hold the rank now, doesn't he? Can you imagine, the guru heading it up?'

Smithes as SIO was an appealing prospect. She knows how he likes to work, and would grab any autonomy given.

Collins sticks on his hazards, outside the Co-op. Astrid jumps out and grabs some sandwiches for them both. They eat on the way.

'Is this a good idea, eating before a post-mortem?'

'Better than after. No better test of your constitution, Collins.'

For all her tough talk, post-mortems always disturb her. How many would she have to attend in her career? Thirty? Eighty? More?

The organs, wobbling and slick on a tray, she could just about handle; but it was the getting to them that she hated. The slicing. The change in pitch of the surgical saw when it bit into bone and met that increased resistance. The smell of warm bone, like soil.

They pull into the car park. The single storey pebbledash building was unassuming enough, with a covered drive-in deep enough to take an ambulance.

Collins points. 'Wait. Isn't that Smithes' car?'

Unmistakably. Unlike Burrows and the upper echelons of CID, Smithes' drove the small, neat, electric Nissan Leaf.

'That can only mean one thing, Charlie boy.'

'The guru has landed.'

They park up, and sure enough, Smithes emerges from the Leaf, phone glued to his ear. He covers the mouthpiece, calls, 'Van Doren! Collins!' and ends the call by the time they're at his side.

'Sir.'

'Pending any surprises at the post-mortem, this is going official.'

'And the Senior Investigating Officer, sir?'

'Come on, Detective. Don't pretend you haven't worked that one out already.'

9
Melody

Melody sits in the Good Stock Deli in Withdean. The lunchtime rush is over, a staff member brushes breadcrumbs off tables and wipes them down. Tristan arrives, lanyard round his neck, a little out of breath from his walk from the BT building up the road where he's working Saturday overtime, dispatching broadband engineers to their jobs around the south coast.

'Melody, I was so sorry to hear the news.' He takes a seat, thanks her for the coffee she has ready in front of him. 'I've not got long. Ally said it was important?'

'What were you and Martin up to?'

'Huh?'

'The gambling,' she hisses. 'I know you and Martin used to go out for a flutter now and again, but this?' She slides over the piece of paper with the number written on it.

'Keep your voice down.' He gives a shifty look. 'What's this?'

'I need to know. Is the amount on there possible? Could Martin be into them for that much?'

Tristan pales. 'The exact amount? I couldn't say, but it's in that ballpark.'

Her arm throbs its dull ache, as if triggered by this confirmation. 'You complete knuckleheads. Does Ally know?'

He leans forward, hands cradling his coffee cup. 'Mel, come on. You know Ally has my balls in a vice! I'd drop no more than fifty quid in a night. We can't afford more and that's that. But

Martin…'

She wants to throw a shaker at him.

'Look, Martin was his own man.'

'You brought him into it.' A fresh horror takes over her. With so huge a debt, how much had he siphoned off from their savings already? And from the business accounts?

Tristan stares into his cup, shaking his head. 'Martin must have been at his wits' end, but he never asked me for any money. I assumed with your house, the practice, that he was good for it! He should have known we would have helped, done whatever we could – he just had to ask. I never for a minute thought he'd take his own life.'

'I don't believe he did.'

Tristan's eyes go wild. 'What?'

'One of Richie Sheridan's thugs visited me, shaking me down for the rest of this debt. Where do you think I got this figure from?' She stabs a finger at the paper.

He lowers his voice. 'Murder? I can't believe that… surely they'd just… you know, give him more time?' He shunts the paper back as if it's cursed. 'You need to go to the police.'

'Tristan, just when I thought you couldn't be any more stupid, you surpass my expectations again.' She stands. 'I'm still not sure what Ally ever saw in you.'

Like a wound, she has to examine it immediately.

The practice had been Martin's vision. A luxury vet for the Hove yuppy: kitted out to conduct small animal surgeries to give their pets the finest medical care; a salon to pamper their cats and dogs; a jug of iced lemon water in the waiting room to quench their thirsts.

Melody sits in the driver's seat, speaking to the accountant over the phone. The vision shatters, shard by shard.

Here was a business that last broke even three years ago. A marketing budget trebled by her husband had somehow yielded a dip in income. The numbers did not match the appearance of a runaway success.

Appear successful. Be successful.

'What if we strip and sell the theatre equipment? Or the salon equipment?' Even as she says it, she knows it's a bad idea, the surgery and the salon being their biggest earners. 'We could steady the boat, build it up again.'

The accountant is apologetic. 'Mrs Kitteridge, all the equipment you have; the computers, the medical equipment, the salon equipment, it's all on lease and most of it has a three-month notice period on return.'

She slumps as if punched. *Oh Martin…*

'The biggest issue is the rent. It's astronomical, and with you being shut right now you're haemorrhaging cash. And will your clientele want to come back?'

'Shut it down?' She whispers it into the phone. Really? The place she had decorated herself, where she had treated, saved, and said goodbye, to so many animals.

'Let me put it this way. What would you do if say, a dog comes in with a nasty flesh wound on its leg, it's infected, gangrenous?'

She rolls her eyes at his pathetic attempt to be relatable. 'You amputate.'

'Right. So that's what you need to do. Amputate. I'd suggest you give notice on the building, the equipment, your staff. Wind it up, move on, get out before the infection spreads.'

Melody hangs up the phone, a sick feeling burrowing into the pit of her stomach. No. Not just sick. Angry. Consequence leads to consequence.

She is going to have to fire the staff.

Tomorrow she has to pay Richie Sheridan. She's checked the joint account; there's enough.

Barely. But after that?

She stares into space, massaging her aching arm. No time to

think, the detective will be waiting for her. She takes a half a diazepam, turns the key in the ignition.

For a mad moment she considers just driving north, away from all this.

Instead she turns on her music, takes a deep breath and heads towards Hove.

10
Astrid

Outside the post-mortem room the air is heady with disinfectant, metal, and grim expectation. In the background, the constant sound of trolleys being wheeled and fridge doors clipping open and whoomphing shut; mortuary music.

Dressed alongside her, in blue surgical gowns is the Crime Scene Manager, the Coroners Officer, Collins, Smithes, and a new face. Smithes introduces him.

'This is Dr Jonathan Uzoma.'

'The criminal profiler?' Astrid shakes his hand.

'Don't know whether to be alarmed or flattered that you know who I am.'

'Flattered.'

'Let's hope I can be of help. Bill's asked me to provide an initial assessment. Not here to step on any toes.'

She raises an eyebrow. Being territorial was the last thing on her mind.

John Hall appears, white wellingtons, green apron and drains the last of his mug. 'Right. I'm all set. Let's get cracking.'

Astrid winces at the turn of phrase, imagining a rib cage being squeezed with giant nutcrackers.

White tiles gleam. Under fluorescent strip-lighting, the body lies plastic-sheathed on a heavy-duty metal table in the centre An assistant wheels the hoist bed to the side of the room. Lighting and refrigeration units hum in a dial tone duet.

Astrid positions herself so Uzoma's large frame blocks her

view of the drain gulley. The body she can handle, but there's something truly nauseating about the liquid and… matter draining away that really twists her insides.

She checks the line. Sets of watchful eyes sat above medical masks. They stand a spatter-free distance away; protective coveralls or not, nobody wants an arc of sauce.

Hall removes the plastic sheeting. Smithes lets out a muffled gasp. Uzoma leans as if drawn in by gravity. She feels it too; the need to look closer. What *was* that? A horrible spidering blackness starting to creep out from the bite wounds.

'Early necrosis.' Hall says. 'Localised cell death around the area of the bite.'

The assistant takes notes even though Hall's observations are being recorded.

'The size and shape of the bruising on the upper arm and hip suggest a fall onto that side, from standing height. No external evidence of trauma to the head or body to suggest a sudden loss of consciousness.' Hall continues the external examination, moving down the cadaver, past the nest of pubic hair and his penis, like a pale beak. Perhaps everybody looked ugly laid bare on Hall's indifferent table.

Hall is on the snake bites now. Comparing his measurements of the wounds to those he'd taken in situ. An assistant takes close-ups of the area with a digital camera.

'The fabric of the trousers wasn't compromised, which suggests the victim was sitting down when bitten, exposing the ankle. That the three bites are so localised would also suggest the victim was slow to react.'

'I believe you also made that observation,' Smithes says to her, and it is the first time anybody other than Hall has spoken. She is proud and embarrassed all at once.

'Sharp eye, Detective,' Uzoma says.

'Medal's in the post,' Hall says wearily, and motions for his assistant to pass him the surgical saw.

It's time for the internal examination.

She steels herself, but doesn't look away.

Hall saws the cap off the skull, like scalping the top of an egg. With the assistant's help he removes the brain, weighs it and cuts it into slices, like a suet pudding. Christ, she has to stop it with the food comparisons. Her stomach turns over.

Collins is white as bone.

She's actually glad she ate beforehand. There's little chance of an appetite later.

When the grisly business is done, Hall addresses them.

'With the usual caveats, the cause of death is sudden cardiac arrest probably brought about by the neurotoxic venom. I noted there was Midazolam in the whisky bottle, we should get toxicology back from Cellmark labs on Monday to verify it was in his system too. All signs so far would suggest so.'

'It all feels like design rather than an accident.'

'I'll send across the full report early next week. Good luck figuring this one out, Bill. Interesting to have something that isn't an RTA or an addict for a change.'

'Thanks, John. How's the wife?'

'Taking her out for a steak dinner tonight.'

Astrid can just imagine Hall slicing through bloody steak with implacable calm, his day job perfectly compartmentalised. How did he do it?

'Thanks, John,' she says, aware she's been too quiet.

Hall nods, turns to his assistant. 'Right, pack him back up.' He means wrapping any extracted organs that haven't been sent for analysis back into the body and sewing Martin Kitteridge back up. Coffin-ready. 'Couple more to go and we can get out of here. Chop-chop.'

In the changing room, the post-mortem attendees mutter to each other. It is discombobulating. Like stepping away from an all-engrossing film at the cinema into bright sunshine. Astrid pulls off one of her white wellingtons. There's a single spot of blood on the toecap.

'Van Doren,' Smithes says, catching her daydream. He pulls on his suit jacket. 'Could you come and see me back at HQ just before six, please?'

She checks the time. She has an appointment to see Melody Kitteridge at four-thirty, just enough time to get there for six, and then be back at home for dinner at eight with Caz and Sam. 'Sir.' This must mean she's on the team. But as what?

She stares at the blood on her boot. This little bit of Martin Kitteridge clinging to her, like an overboard sailor gripping to flotsam in vain hope.

Justice is all she can give him now.

11
Melody

She's like an old computer, being asked to process too many transactions at once, and if she's not careful things will start to jam up and crash.

When Melody pulls the Defender into her drive, two women emerge from a parked car on the street. One youngish in a suit, hair styled over a shaved undercut. The other is a uniformed policewoman.

'Mrs Kitteridge?' The suit shows her a warrant card. 'I'm Detective Inspector Van Doren and this is PC Baqri, a Family Liaison Officer, or FLO.'

The policewoman says hello, smiles at her, just the right measure of compassion and friendliness. What an art to be able to arrange your face like that.

'I expect you'll be wanting to come in. Follow me.'

The FLO offers to make the drinks but Melody doesn't want her rummaging around her kitchen. Herbal tea for the FLO, a coffee for the detective. As the water boils, the diazepam is rubbing the sharp edges of the world into something more rounded, smoother.

Melody takes a strong coffee for herself, and sits upright in the armchair. Cleopatra enters. The detective reaches down for a stroke, but Cleopatra ignores the advance, and leaps up onto Melody's lap. Good girl.

'You have a lovely home,' PC Baqri says.

For now. 'It's good of you to notice.'

'PC Baqri will be your point of contact, Mrs Kitteridge, to keep you and Martin's parents in the loop of any developments with your husband's case. She'll have a direct line into our investigation. She's here to support you.'

'That's right.' The FLO hands her a card. 'Here's my number.'

Melody doesn't take it. 'I'd like to opt out.'

'I'm sorry?' PC Baqri says.

'I don't need this sugar-coating and hand-holding. If there's anything I need to know I trust the detective here can just pick up the phone and tell me.'

PC Baqri gives the detective a look of bewilderment.

'It helps us too, Mrs Kitteridge. We can focus our resources on the investigation.'

'I don't intend tying your hands, detective, nor badgering you every day for updates. You'll need no human buffer, we're all professional women, are we not?'

'Right… well, let's see how we go.' The detective nods. 'I do have a few questions I need to ask you, Mrs Kitteridge. Could I just start by going over your movements again on Friday the tenth of January?'

Melody runs through her day, the call-out to Dapper's farm, the time of her return.

'And I understand after you gave your statement, you came back here to get cleaned up?'

'That's right. I had a bath.'

The detective purses her lips, 'And you stayed in all evening here with your friend, Ally Campbell?'

Why does she want to know about what she did after?

'No. I had another call-out. Bradshaw's farm, two more calves to deliver. Ally drove me. We returned after two in the morning.'

Something clouds the detective's expression. That wasn't the right answer to give. 'You went straight back to work after finding your husband dead?'

'If I hadn't gone, two more calves and quite possibly one of the mother's would have died. It might not seem much to someone who investigates death, but my job is to prevent it, which strikes me as a far more valuable service.'

The FLO jumps in here, struggling for relevance. 'Sometimes it can be best to keep busy. Take your mind off things.'

Melody doesn't answer. Mugs are sipped, and an uneasy atmosphere settles round the room.

'Let's talk about your husband.'

'How old are you, Detective?'

'What does that have to do with anything?' the detective's cheeks flush red.

'You just seem a little young.'

Van Doren looks at the FLO, smiles. 'I'm fully trained and experienced. Thanks for noticing my youthful complexion though, it must be my moisturiser. Let's return to your husband, shall we?'

Melody notes the recovery. To be a Detective Inspector so young, and as a woman, can't have been an easy ascent. It is something she can respect. 'Please.'

'How would you describe your marriage?'

Melody turns the ring on her finger. 'I don't really have a lot to compare it to, but we got on well. I'd say we complemented one another.'

'How did you complement one another?'

'I'm organised, he was a bit sloppy. He was the life and soul of the party, while I'm more reserved. He had the social skills, I had the work ethic. It worked well at the practice. A good division of labour.'

'Would you say he was happy?'

'Generally. We had a successful practice, he recently won Vet of the Year. We had this place, though Martin was drinking a little more than usual.'

'Why do you think that was, Mrs Kitteridge?'

'I really couldn't say.'

Detective Van Doren writes something down. 'And when you found his body, what did you think?'

Melody takes a deep breath, strokes Cleopatra on the belly. 'Initially, that he'd passed out drunk. I was annoyed.'

'You said he was drinking a little more than usual? Passed out drunk sounds more serious.'

'Quite.' She presses the back of her hand into Cleopatra's skull. She purrs. 'Perhaps it was like the frog in the slowly boiling water. So gradual it's hard to pin down when he started drinking to such excess. When I saw him on the floor, I thought it was pathetic, truth be told. I tipped the rest of the whisky down the sink.'

'How much was left, roughly?'

'Fifty per cent was left in the bottle, approximately.'

The detective makes a note. 'Was it open already, or did he drink that much in one session?'

'I have no idea.'

'When did you realise that he hadn't passed out drunk?'

'I prodded him with my toe, tried to made him stir. Then I checked his pulse. Maybe I thought he'd killed himself. Whisky and pills. That I'd grossly underestimated how unhappy he was. Disbelief. Questions, so many questions that I wanted to ask him. And then when you told me all about the snake bites… I didn't know what to think.'

'Think back for me. Did your husband have any connection to snakes, snake handlers?'

She shakes her head. 'Martin didn't really have anything to do with snakes, didn't even like them as far as I'm aware.' She stares straight into the detective's eyes. 'Any news about what type of snake it was?'

'We're still looking into it,' Van Doren says evenly, and

Melody wonders if she's lying. 'Anyone have a grudge against him?'

'I can't think of anybody. Everybody loved Martin.'

The policewomen wrap up their questions, the detective informing her that CSIs will be round to do a routine sweep as soon as a warrant is approved. People going through their home, their things. Traipsing through the rooms indifferent to her beautiful kitchen with its warm wooden worktops, the Mudejar tiling and tasteful lighting, the Calke Green paintwork by Farrow & Ball. Indifferent to the life they had here.

The house is hers again. The world darkens.

And for how much longer will all this be hers? She makes a painfully elaborate Martini with Honjozo Sake; dewed glass, spiralled lemon. Sips.

Dry as a gasp and sharp enough to cut. She allows herself two more sips, then pours the rest of it down the sink. She has to keep it together.

She tops up Cleopatra's water bowl with fresh Evian from the fridge. Unpeels the foil of the cat food. Cleopatra miaows, then eats.

An errant drip of the tap. New ice jostles for space in her Samsung dual-sided, ice-making fridge. The wet nibbling of Cleopatra eating her premium salmon-based food.

Was this the quiet sound of her life imploding?

12
Melody
Brighton 2000

Melody is up a minute before her alarm. Body clock. A marvel. How did it know? Such skill locked up in the subconscious.

She showers, dresses. Boot cut jeans, an old INXS T-shirt, a cable knit sweater on top, black boots. It is a strange thing. A camouflage. Like a chameleon. The more she dresses like her college classmates, the less fire she draws. She knows. She's been keeping a record.

Melody takes the batteries from the charging dock, loads them into her mini-disc player. Of all technological innovations in her lifetime, this one feels the most profound and impactful. The CD, miniaturised into an unscratchable cartridge. Customisable, to make her own beautiful playlists. Longer play time. No jogging. No skipping. It is her biggest indulgence.

Modern music is decidedly depressing; the Spice Girls, The Corrs, boybands galore, tired Britpop. She delves deep to find authenticity. INXS is loaded already but she packs a few of the small cartridges into her bag, a mix with Simple Minds, another of vintage Madonna. One unmixed: Prince's masterpiece *Sign o' the Times*.

Someone is in the shower. Paul, her guardian. She can tell by the humming. Carl, the last remaining of her foster brothers, is probably still asleep, his door closed. He is doing a plumbing apprenticeship. Goes out to the pub most evenings. She barely sees him. She is less a family member, more a lodger.

The kitchen is a mess. Dried rice on the work surface, the sink full. Slobs. She cannot wait to be out of here.

She washes up, wipes down the surfaces. It's part of the deal. Ashy purrs from under the table and she tops up his kibble. He lumbers over, and while he crouches over his food, she administers a jab into the muscle of the hind leg. The vet showed her how. It's easy. Routine now.

Melody takes a bus out to Whitehawk. It struggles up the incline. She switches disc to Madonna and the bright cords of "Into the Groove" nestle into her ears. She gets out and makes her way to one of the drab concrete council flats. It at least has the virtue of a sea-view. She should like a view of the Channel one day, contemplate it like it's hers. Not in Whitehawk though.

She takes the stairs to the fourth floor, and knocks.

'Coming!'

Ally opens up, she's loading an A4 pad into a record bag. 'Shit, come in.'

Melody walks through into the lounge where Mr Campbell sits, his belly stretching the seagull on his Brighton & Hove Albion T-shirt.

'Morning, Melody.'

'Yes, it is, Mr Campbell.'

'Shoo, you bugger.' He waves at the seagull perched on the window sill.

'Over there,' Ally says.

Melody takes the syringe pen from the dining room table and crouches next to Mr Campbell. She senses Ally behind her.

'Ally, you might want to look away.'

'No… I need…' She grips her father's shoulder. 'Just do it.'

'I really do appreciate this, love.' Mr Campbell has rubber bands over the joints of his fingers, and struggles to pull the T-shirt over his round belly.

Melody pinches his ample belly fat, and administers the injection. She glances up. Ally's pale but she's still standing.

'There. Nothing to it,' Melody says.

Ally rests pats her father's back. 'There's a sandwich made up for you in the fridge and your drink's just there.'

'Thanks, love, you run along now.'

'I'll be back about half three.'

They sit next to each other on the bus back into town.

'Here.' Ally holds out a fiver.

'What's that for?'

'Your time… your help.'

'Keep it,' Melody says. It was a paltry thing to be paid for, too unskilled.

Ally doesn't argue. Money is tight for them both, Melody suspects. 'I'll get there, just a few more times. Are you okay to come after college?'

Melody nods. 'Where else would I need to be?'

Ally snorts. 'Fair enough.'

They continue on in silence, until Ally asks, 'Are you going to apply to uni?'

Melody nods. 'Cambridge. Veterinary Medicine.'

'A vet? Good for you.'

Melody remembers to reciprocate. 'And you?'

Ally shakes her head. 'Don't think so.'

Ah, yes. Of course.

When the college is in sight, Melody slows.

'Go ahead if you don't want to be seen with me.'

Ally narrows her eyes, and pulls her forward by the arm. 'What are you talking about? This is sixth form college, we're all mature.'

'Oi, Ally. What you doing with that mong? Taking her out for her morning excursion?'

Giggles. Melody freezes, traces the voice to a girl. A popular one, for some reason, with a gaggle of friends around her.

Melody walks on. 'I'll see you later, Ally.'

'No,' Ally says, a sneer turning her ugly. She stabs a finger at Melody and shouts back 'She's worth ten of you. Fuck off!' She gives a double middle finger.

Melody absorbs the look of shock on their faces, and is pulled again, forward, through the college doors.

'Holy shit, that felt good,' Ally says.

Melody tucks her hair behind an ear, unsure what to say. 'I'll see you here at three, then?'

'Bugger that,' Ally says, linking an arm through hers. Melody eases into the contact instead of fighting it. It is strong. A chain. Bound to one another by bones.

'So,' Ally says, 'what do you normally do at lunch?'

13
Astrid

Sussex House. Smithes' office door is open. Her heart hammers. 'Sir?'

'Good, you're here.' Smithes is barefoot, and his lower half is in what she thinks is Tree Pose, while he reads messages on his phone.

Bemused, she sits in the offered chair.

'We're up and running. Operation Windbourne.'

'Neat and discrete, sir.' The operation names are generated randomly by computer, though vetted to make sure the name doesn't hint at the operation's contents. While Operation Snakebite would have sounded fierce if generated, the blandness of Windbourne would always triumph with the technocrats.

Smithes sits on his chair, crosses a leg over and threads a black sock over his foot. 'Van Doren. You're ambitious, bit of fire in your belly.'

'I like to think so, sir.'

He jams on a shiny black lace-up and ties it with quick fingers, keeping eye contact with her. 'If you'll allow some advice from someone who's been round the block a few times?'

'I'd value anything you have to say, sir.'

Other sock. 'Ultimately, you help solve this murder, solve ten, a hundred.' He puts on his second shoe, throttles the strings up tight. 'It won't bring Sandy back.'

'I know that.'

'Do you? Do you really? Ask yourself. Are you doing this to even up the check and balance? Or to bring comfort to bereaved families looking for justice? You need to know your own *why*.'

'I–'

He holds up a hand. 'I don't want an answer. It's not for me.' He does a soft chopping motion with his hand in the air, as if bestowing a blessing. 'Know yourself. Bring your motivation, your method and your desired outcome into alignment. It helps you to keep it together up here.' He stabs a finger at his temple.

She notices for the first time, the buddha paperweight on Smithes' desk. It's no wonder the grunts nickname for Bill Smithes is "Guru", though she likes to think it's more reverent than disparaging.

'You want to be SIO one day, correct?'

'I do, yes, sir.'

'So, let's go down to the Major Incident Suite. The team's waiting. I'm going to introduce you as deputy SIO. If you want it of course?'

'Sir.' She doesn't know what to say. It's a fudge to put someone of her rank as deputy, it'll put some noses out of joint, but to hell with that. She wants this. 'Thank you,' she manages.

'You're in the weeds with this, I want you to take a lead role in the operation. You know how I like to work.'

Smithes has a reputation. The watchful captain on the bridge, rarely seen laying a hand on the tiller, even in a storm.

Smithes grabs his jacket, shrugs it on. 'You're going to brief the team on the case so far. Uzoma will give us his initial thoughts from a profiling perspective. Got it?'

'Sir.'

'This is it Van Doren, the next step. Ready?'

The Major Incident Suite is split in two, with interview rooms, a room for press conferences, meeting rooms and adjoining offices to house the temporary teams. A bigger operation, Phalanx, occupies MI Room 1, so Windbourne is stationed in MI Room 2. It is carpeted, smart, climate-controlled. Its glass fronted walls have vertical blinds permanently pulled down.

Someone has made a good start on the murder board; a blown-up image of Martin Kitteridge at its heart. There is a stack of photographs of the wife and the rest of the staff. Crime scene photos, printed on photo quality paper. A zoomed-in map of the Hove area with a couple of pins; the Kitteridge house and the veterinary practice, an annotated timeline template. A canvas with just the background layer of paint applied.

Of course, there is investigative planning software that does all this digitally, and it'll all be there too. For Van Doren nothing quite beats standing shoulder to shoulder with a colleague and letting your mind wander the board on this scale. To move and arrange things about by hand, to stretch red string between victim and a suspect brought a special, tangible, satisfaction. Most important however, is seeing the victim's face each time you enter the room.

A reminder: here is a victim.

It triggers a thought. Every time she steps into her mother's hallway, she sees a photo of her father there on the wall. Like a private murder board. Stuck in time.

She shakes it away. Writes Operation Windbourne in green marker on a whiteboard.

Then the team bustle in.

They settle noisily in their seats and she feels like a supply teacher. Unprepared. Ready to bluff. A cocktail of adrenaline and nerves does the rounds. She stares out at them, all familiar faces. Charlie Collins is in as Reader/Receiver filtering the lines of enquiry, logging it on the HOLMES system, an unglamorous but important rite of passage for almost every detective constable working in major crimes. She'd steal him away when time allowed for field work, but he'd be made up to be in the tent.

Smithes is last in, followed by Dr Uzoma. Smithes claps his

hands twice to silence them, and then the guru gives a brief introductory welcome, and introduces her as Deputy SIO.

The room doesn't erupt in surprised murmurs. They watch her, pens poised.

'Thank you,' she says. *This is too quick.* 'Afternoon, everyone. Let's get you up to speed.' *You've got this. You know it better than anyone.* She begins fluently with the dates, times, the victim's particulars and the circumstances of the death, including the fresh summary from John Hall's unofficial verbal forensic pathology report. She expects to hand over, but Smithes waves her on. 'Good. Carry on, Detective Inspector. What should we do next? I'll just jump in when something occurs.'

Christ. Was he going to put any stamp on this investigation?

'The CSI team are out now conducting a routine sweep of the Kitteridge household. Our main task at hand is to build our list of potential suspects. We'll need to tooth comb the tech, the business, check the CCTV in the area, financial records, mobile records, flag absolutely anything that relates to snakes. Interview the suspects and check alibis.'

'Who do we have so far as potential suspects?' the question comes from Sarah Gardner, an Intelligence Analyst with a good reputation.

Van Doren indicates the photos on the murder board and flashes Collins a knowing grin. 'The wife, Melody Kitteridge.' She slides her finger down to the staff photos. 'And by default, all the staff. This gentleman is Hugh Forrester, the receptionist. Next is Kathy Spellerman, the veterinary nurse and Lydia Gregorivic who runs the Pet Salon. I expect we'll add some faces to this in the coming days.'

She looks over to Smithes. *Anything else?*

Thankfully he stands, hands in pockets. He takes a position by her side, massaging his neatly clipped beard.

'Thank you, Detective. A couple of things before I hand over to Dr Uzoma.'

Smithes radiates calm as he turns to face the team. 'I've just had confirmation that the snake venom detected in the victim came from a cobra. Highly unusual.' He turns to her. 'You talked about the importance of finding and checking alibis. Our murder weapon didn't need a human hand to wield or strike it. What real value is an alibi? It wouldn't eliminate a suspect, because no human needed to be present during the death window.'

You arsehole. In front of everybody? Is this some sort of test? She opens her mouth, closes it like a goldfish. Every eyeball beaming shame for her to absorb. She imagines them at the coffee station, in the corridors. *See, I told you, she isn't ready. Did you see her face?*

The silence stretches.

'Detective?'

Her mind clears with an answer. 'I respectfully disagree, sir. A human hand very likely was needed during the death window.'

He narrows his eyes. 'Explain.'

'We haven't found the snake. Up until now we assumed it escaped. But there's a much more likely possibility. That the perpetrator was there, released the snake into the room, then caught it and took it with them.'

'Actually, Sir, Ma'am.' A hand goes up. Pete Wade from forensics.

Smithes motions for him to speak.

'I'm still writing up the forensics report on the crime scene, but we did find traces of substrate bark on the floor of the office, but not outside it in the corridor… or anywhere else in the practice.'

'Substrate bark?' someone asks.

'It's what you'd typically find in a snake tank, like the wood chippings.' Van Doren says, excitement gathering. 'Which strongly suggests the snake didn't slither out of the room. Somebody had to have been there to release it into the room and then gather it in.'

'May I?' Doctor Uzoma practically leaps up and she steps aside, buzzing at this breakthrough.

He connects his laptop to the projector. 'This feels like the moment to talk about a possible profile.' Dr Jonathan Uzoma, with his thick glasses, short greying hair and erudite air is an absorbing presence in front of the projector screen. A rare breed, a former detective turned psychologist, plying his trade as one of the most respected criminal profilers in the UK.

He talks in a baritone with faint traces of cockney, testament to his years with the Met.

'Disclaimer. Profiles are a guide, never an absolute. Use it to prioritise the suspects, never to discount them.' He turns to the murder board and taps a long finger on the blown-up photo of Martin Kitteridge. 'I always begin with the victim. Who was he? Why him?' He glances down briefly at some notes.

'The victim, who I'll refer to as MK, was a popular man. Thirty-seven years old, had been married for eight years. Cambridge-educated, where he met his wife. No children. Started the Kitteridge veterinary practice with his wife and lives in an expensive, statement home.' An image of the house on Medina Villas comes up on screen.

'MK was a success, and he wanted you to know it.' Uzoma shows a crime scene image of the certificates and plaques on the wall of MK's office. 'He was someone who wanted respect.'

'Plenty of doctors put their qualifications on their walls, isn't adoration a bit of a leap?' Collins asks.

Uzoma inclines his head, considering. 'Maybe. Come to think of it, I have a few framed certificates on my own office wall, Constable. Saying all this makes me feel self-conscious.' He gets a small chuckle. He indicates to Van Doren for the board pen, and she only realises that she's been gripping it the whole time, like a stress stick. She chucks it and he catches it, pops the lid.

'Now let's talk about the killer.'

Van Doren listens intently, eager to hear Uzoma's thoughts.

'How MK was murdered tells us an awful lot about his killer.' He writes in caps: DEEPLY PERSONAL. 'There are a million ways to kill someone, the methodology used here was, let's be frank, complex. To me this is classic message as method. The way MK died was a message, most likely to MK himself.'

Van Doren stuffs her hands in her pockets, intrigued.

Uzoma clicks onto the slide showing the leg bites. 'The pathology report will likely confirm what we suspect: MK was lightly sedated with Midazolam. What if the killer wanted MK to see the snake, to have some comprehension of what was happening? I believe it is a symbol of something that is significant to him, to them. The snake, the murder weapon, was probably removed by the killer. Why?'

He waits.

'Because the snake mattered to the killer too?' Pete Wade offers.

'Yes! Otherwise the attending officers would have found it with the body. The snake symbolised something private between killer and victim.'

Uzoma writes SNAKE = SYMBOL, returns the lid and pushes his glasses higher up his nose.

'The killer dosed MK just the right amount. Stop for a moment and just think about how hard that is. What's his exact weight? How much has he eaten? How much of the whisky would he probably drink? The variables at play here are dizzying, nigh on impossible *unless* you knew MK and his habits intimately *and* had the pharmaceutical knowledge to pull it off.'

He writes: PHARMA KNOWLEDGE. 'This was meticulous and thoroughly planned.' He writes up the words as he talks: 'You're looking for a planner, someone intelligent who was close to the victim *and* has pharmaceutical knowledge.'

'All the staff at the practice would fit the bill.' This from Critchlow, one of the uniforms.

Uzoma lifts a finger, 'Motives are statistically likely to be revenge or jealousy.'

Van Doren finds her voice, 'Do you think this is the first time for the killer? Or could he or she have killed before?'

'I'm glad you didn't just assume it was a man. Poison –which is what this is, technically speaking– is statistically the method preferred by women. As for your very excellent question...' Uzoma pushes his glasses up again. 'None of your main suspects so far have any previous, correct?'

'Not according to HOLMES,' Collins says.

'Then if you put a gun to my head – don't!' He holds up a finger and gets a polite chuckle from uniform. 'I'd say due to its personal nature, that this is a debut. Now,' he holds up a long finger, 'a question for you all. Out of your initial suspects, does anyone leap out at you given the initial profile? Someone to investigate deep, question further. After all, that's my role here, to help you narrow down to high probability targets. You get to streamline resources, go for the jugular, get a result. Detective Van Doren? You've a keen eye from what I've seen so far. Thoughts?'

'I like to be led by the evidence,' she says.

'Me too. But where will you look for that evidence first?'

'Gun to head time?'

'Gun to head time.'

'The wife,' she says. Collins nods vigorously. 'Everything in your profile fits. Intelligent. She's a veterinary surgeon, has pharmaceutical knowledge. Nothing is more personal than a spouse. On top of that she had access, her prints are there, she poured the spiked whisky down the sink. She would probably know how to handle a snake.'

'Sounds like a high-probability place to start.' He turns to Smithes. 'Any reason she's not in here for questioning already?'

'She does have an alibi for the whole window. She claims to have been on call at a farm in the Downs.'

'Is it cast iron? You can always give it a kick, see if it's solid or if it'll wobble and topple over. That's the ex-detective in me talking.'

Smithes nods to himself. 'Let's keep an open mind, but I like the fit too. Let's bring her in for further questioning first thing tomorrow, see how she responds to a bit more pressure.' He nods to her, to let her know she is to arrange for this to happen.

The temptation is there, a quick, clean result with Smithes' crack team. Perhaps the Acting could be dropped from her job title.

But first. Her intuition is being put on trial.

It's gone nine by the time she leaves Sussex House.

She's buzzing, and calls Mum from her handsfree.

'Mum! Great news, I just got Deputy SIO on a big case.'

'That's wonderful news, poppet. That was what you wanted wasn't it?'

'I just needed to tell someone; I feel like I'm going to explode!'

She hears Adam, her step-father ask something, and her mother relay the news.

'Well done Astrid!' Adam shouts.

'He says well done.'

'Yes, I heard him. Thanks.'

'Have you not told Jenna yet?'

'I'm nearly home now. I'll come and see you soon, okay?'

'I'll see you on Thursday, won't I?'

She smacks her forehead. 'Yes, of course, Thursday. See you there bright and early.'

The clock on the digital display reads 9:32 p.m.

Up in the flat, Jenna, Caz and Sam sit around the dining room table, empty dessert bowls in front of them, wine glasses still charged.

'I'm so sorry, it's been a mad, mad day,' Astrid says,

greeting and hugging Caz and Sam, giving an apologetic squeeze of Jenna's shoulder.

'There's a plate for you in the microwave.'

'Great, thanks.' Astrid pops the door, suddenly ravenous, and on seeing the plate of curry, her stomach turns. It's like John Hall had taken a bowl and scooped out someone's insides and added some rice. Instead she finds a bottle of prosecco in the fridge.

'Is there a celebration?' Caz asks.

There's an icy silence, which she, Astrid, destroys with the pop of the cork. 'Maybe a little. I just got made Deputy SIO for the first time on a murder investigation.'

Jenna accepts the glass and raises it. Her jaw set hard. 'To you, then Astrid. Congratulations.'

'Cheers!' Caz and Sammy say in unison, missing the coldness in which Jenna had delivered it. The borderline irony.

But she hadn't. She'd worked so damn hard for this… yes, she was a little late for dinner but she could make it up to them.

Astrid leans forward, smiles with all the energy she can muster. 'So, tell me everything. How's married life treating you, ladies?'

14
Melody

Sunday morning. Melody removes her scarf and gloves, scans the cafe. Full tables. A line at the counter. The milk frother roars over the robotic hum of the coffee machine, the clink of saucers roughly stacked, a room of conversations scrambling over the din to be heard.

I can't think, can't breathe here, there's no space.

Turn. Leave! But they've spotted her, waving from a table at the back of the cafe. She covers her ears, hunches as she sidesteps past the line.

Hugh and Kathy stand to greet her, then Lydia more slowly. Melody slides into the vacant seat.

'Good morning,' Hugh says. He's the only one still in his winter garb; a smart herringbone coat with a mustard scarf.

'Just sit, would you?'

They exchange looks, sit. In front of her is a latte and a croissant dusted in icing sugar. Why would they do that? Wasn't it unhealthy enough already?

'How are you holding up?' Hugh says.

She pushes the plate away, and drags the coffee nearer.

'Melody… we are just so sorry,' Kathy says, voice catching.

Lydia draws her into a hug and mutters, 'Come on now, hold it together.'

Melody stirs the coffee, the milk swirls into a galaxy, dissipates. 'Have the police spoken with you yet?'

'Kathy's had a call from the detective who's handling the case. I expect we'll be next.'

'I trust you'll all help them to the best of your abilities.' She takes a sip of coffee. There is probably a right thing to say now, but she doesn't know what it is.

'I have bad news. More bad news, I mean.'

Kathy is holding a tissue under her eye. Melody can almost see the tear ducts. What a curious thing that words can trigger that anatomical response.

'What is it?' Lydia asks.

'The practice is going to have to close.'

Lydia rolls her eyes, shakes her head, but Kathy and Hugh stare at her.

Hugh recovers first. 'You mean until the police let us back in?'

Melody tips the rest of her coffee down her throat. She cannot stand this, this place, this situation.

'She's firing us, Hugh,' Lydia says.

'Yes. Clearly. I'd rather not, but I have little choice. I'll pay your notice period and you can all rely on me for a good reference. Even you, Lydia.'

'I can't believe this!' Lydia says. 'You're not going to even talk about Martin?'

She stands. 'Martin? He should be the one telling you all this, not me.'

'I don't…' Kathy shakes her head through new tears.

'There is no alternative.' Melody wraps her scarf around her neck, pulls on her gloves. 'Good luck.'

She escapes outside, gulping at the frosty air. She'd gotten through it. Unpleasant, but it was done. That was the main thing. Through the condensation in the glass, Hugh and Lydia each have a consoling arm on Kathy's back, who is crying in juddering sobs.

15
Astrid

Kathy Spellerman's apartment block is set back from the pricier blocks closer to the seafront. The rail line is close enough to hear, but it's a well painted, clean enough looking place. This is all procedural legwork, quite literally, as Spellerman's apartment is on the fourth floor and there is no lift. The stairwell reminds her of school for some reason. Echoey and glass-fronted. She's worked enough cases by now to have a handle of how important this step is. Get the key people down on the record and as time progresses, new evidence emerges. Stories change, people entangle themselves, contradicting their initial statements. It's simple. Elegant. Part bureaucratic record, part trap.

Spellerman greets them, barely looking at their warrant cards. Above average height, young, a little plain. Brunette with matching brown eyes that contain a mixture of shock and grief.

'Thanks for seeing us on a Sunday.'

Kathy shrugs. 'Of course.'

'Nice place. View of the cricket ground and everything,' Collins says, completely misjudging the mood.

Spellerman gives a weak smile. 'You can hear the Elton John concerts from the balcony when he plays, no need to buy a ticket.'

Astrid takes in the place. Clean, spacious, cheap furniture, and a hard-wearing carpet that suggests it's a rental. Two bedrooms, probably got a housemate.

They refuse a drink, and get right to it. Collins leads with the factual questions, establishing timings and movements up to the time she finished work.

'I finished at six thirty with Hugh and Lydia. The last time I saw Martin was at the door to his office, waving us off and wishing us all a good weekend.'

'And then?'

'I went with Lydia for dinner at hers. Must have got back here at about eleven.'

Van Doren takes over. 'What was your relationship like with Martin?'

'Great. Both he and Melody have been amazing to me. I started there on work experience when I left school, then they part-sponsored me through my studies to become a qualified vet nurse.' Spellerman has tissues rolled up in balls in her sleeves, bulging there like little tumours.

'So, it's a good place to work then, everybody gets on well?'

She shakes her head, letting out a snort. '*Was,* you mean. Melody had to let us go this morning. She's shutting Kitteridge's for good.'

'I'm sorry to hear that,' Collins says, and she wonders if he's thinking the same as her; that it feels off. It's too soon, wouldn't she let the dust settle a bit? Or is this all about the money, stripping the business, selling the house? She'll have Gardner look into it.

Kathy plays with a necklace, shaking her head. 'I always loved working there. We were a team. I know Lydia finds Melody a bit much sometimes, but she's just very exacting.'

'And how about Martin and Melody? Must have been hard living and working together all the time.'

She shakes her head. 'I wouldn't know.'

'Do you know anyone who might have held a grudge against Martin?'

Again, she shakes her head, stares at her feet. 'No. Martin was such a lovely–' She flaps a hand to fan herself. Tears burst out. 'I just can't believe he's gone.'

Tissues, tissues… she fishes in her pockets but Kathy has plucked one of the sleeve tumours out and dabs at her eyes.

'I know this is hard, Ms Spellerman. You're doing very well. Only a few more questions and we can leave you in peace.'

She runs a wrist under her eye, nods.

'There was a whisky bottle found in Martin's room. Was he a big drinker?'

'He liked his whisky.'

'Do you know where it came from? Did he buy it?'

'A client brought it in. One of Martin's friend's, actually. Austin Pemberton, had a golden Lab called Lucky who's been coming in for years.'

'When was this?'

'It must have been close to Christmas. I remember I was in reception when Mr Pemberton brought it in. He was in a rush, dropped it at the reception desk wished us a merry Christmas.'

'Did you ever handle the bottle at all?'

'I looked at the label, just to see which one Martin liked. Not that it means much to me.'

Astrid notes this, knowing that Spellerman's prints will probably now match those found on the bottle.

'Who took it to Martin's office?' Collins asks.

I presume Martin did. Or Hugh. Melody even. I have no idea.'

Astrid picks at a loose thread. 'You said that this Mr Pemberton *had* a Labrador…'

'Yes. It died, unfortunately, just after new year. Terrible thing.'

'Go on…'

'There was some misunderstanding I think, Martin couldn't save it. I don't really know. I was out with Melody at the time.'

A possible line of inquiry? She looks at Charlie, who is making a note.

'Mr Pemberton and Martin were good friends.'

'Just trying to build a picture,' Astrid says. 'Last one. Did Martin have anything to do with snakes at all? Any interest you're aware of?'

'So, it's true? What the papers are saying?'

'I'm afraid so,' Collins says.

'What sort of snake was it?'

Collins gives Astrid a look; it'll be common knowledge soon enough. She gives the go ahead.

'Cobra.'

Spellerman sits back in her chair, as if pushed. 'A cobra?'

Shock? Or something else? Later, in the car, Collins acknowledges it too.

'That set my spider-senses tingling. Or my snake senses. Whatever. Tell you something else. I bet you don't like that two of the staff alibi each other.'

'Fine if it's true.'

'Let's check her story against Lydia Gregorivic's account.'

16
Melody

Ten a.m. One hour to go.

Melody takes the Defender through light morning traffic, stomach still tight from having to fire the staff. She focuses on the music.

Absolute Eighties pulsates with beautifully dramatic synth, "Fade to Grey" by Visage. Insistent. While her foster brothers rolled from grunge to Britpop and then nu-metal, she was there, steadfast to the point of obsessiveness, reaching backwards into the eighties. Making mixtapes according to mood; The Cure, The Smiths, Duran Duran, Joy Division, The Stranglers for the darker times. The antidote: the joyful pop of Madonna.

Moulsecoomb. She beeps twice. Ally's place has seen better days. Rusted swing in the front, and grass up to your knees.

'Strimmer's broken,' Ally explains. 'Awaiting repair in the shed, by me I expect, don't think Tristan's set foot in there since I had it put up.' She clips her belt in. 'I said to Tristan, we should tie a sheep up to the swing set, future mutton pie plus we get the grass cut in the meantime.'

'Better to send Tristan out with his nose hair scissors.'

Ally raises a brow. 'How did you know he cuts his nose hair?'

'Obvious. I always knew there must be some secret quality to him you loved.'

'Gross. You be nice. He's taken the girls out for the day so I could come.'

Least he could do. She takes them back into Brighton, past the domed meringues of the Royal Pavilion, down to the sea front, past the Palace Pier and onto Madeira Drive, the mood changing as they near their destination.

'So, what do you want me to do, exactly?'

'Read the situation. I've never had to do something like this before.'

'And I have? If you've got the full amount then there shouldn't be any issues.'

'This instalment, yes, but even this much was pretty close. I won't be able to pay the next one. Not without selling the house.'

'Holy shit, you're going to have to sell it?'

'Or not pay them… and tell the police and hope they can protect me somehow.'

'I don't like the sound of that.'

'Me neither.'

'We'll work it out, Mel.' Ally might have rested a hand on her shoulder perhaps, but doesn't. Her presence is enough.

The beach volleyball nets on the sand lie empty. Up ahead, the music venue where she's to meet Pug.

'Mel.' Ally's voice is steel.

In the rear-view is a police patrol car, lights on, no siren. She indicates, and pulls over, hoping it will pass. It doesn't.

'They've stopped behind us. Stay calm,' Melody says.

'Where's the money?'

'They're watching us.' She winds down the window.

'Good morning, Mrs Kitteridge?' the uniformed officer says.

'Yes, is there a problem?'

'I wonder if you could accompany us to the station to answer a few questions?'

She stares ahead. There past rows of metal arches is the entrance to the Concorde 2. It's so close. 'Which station, officer? I can meet you there in, say, an hour?'

'I'm afraid we need you to come in now, please.'

'Hold on.' Ally cranes her neck. 'Is she under arrest?'

The officer sighs, 'This really would be a lot easier if you voluntarily accompanied us, madam.'

'Voluntarily?' The implication hits her.

'Don't go,' Ally says and mutters, 'They'll probably back off.'

'And if they don't?'

'It makes the clock tick; they have to release you after like twenty-four hours or something. But if you go in, talk for a bit, and *then* they arrest you, they have even longer. Trust me.'

'Madam, we are investigating a murder and require your assistance.'

'No!' Ally yells at them. 'She'll come later, we're busy.'

Melody feels warmth flush into her cheeks. 'You do realise how that makes it look, Ally?'

'Trust me, Melody. I watch a lot of cop shows, I know what I'm talking about.'

The officer clears his throat, annoyed. 'Please remove the keys from the ignition, madam.'

'I'm not about to drive off! What's wrong with you? Can everyone just calm down!'

'*I'm* perfectly calm, madam. Please step out of the vehicle.'

The money. Ally gives her a desperate look.

Pass it to me.

I can't.

She gets out. Handcuffs dangle by the officer's side. Dull, scuffed metal. How many wrists had those two circles enclosed?

'Last chance to come in voluntarily. Mrs Kitteridge?'

She looks to Ally. In all things, in Ally she trusts.

'Make them do it. It'll start the clock.'

Melody presents her wrists by way of answer, and the officer arrests her for the murder of her husband, and reads her rights.

17
Astrid

Collins pulls down the busy residential street, leans to the window with half an eye on the road, lip-syncing the house numbers. Two breakfast croissants lie in the drink's holder, the grease leaching through the paper packaging.

There's no parking on the street, but a car pulls away from the curb just in front of them, gifting Collins a space.

'Jammy bastard,' Astrid says.

'Make your own luck.' He pulls the handbrake and takes a bite of croissant.

'Tell that to Martin Kitteridge.'

It's a neat, flint-stone townhouse. Seagulls caw at them, and Collins gives a potted history on the way to the house, dusting his hands of pastry flakes. 'Lydia Gregorivic started at Kitteridge's as a kennel assistant, then went on to help set up and run the pet salon. Been with the practice four and a half years. Divorced, two kids grown up now and moved away.'

Lydia Gregorivic is above average height, hair thick with highlights outgrown by a few centimetres at the roots. Straightened hair, certainly pretty once, though not her type at all. A bit of a show-pony. Too much of everything; lipstick, fragrance and long shiny, fake nails. Early fifties, but trying to pull off late thirties.

A team of yappy chihuahuas blur and hop around her ankles. 'Don't mind them, they just love their mummy don't you my little squidgy-biddy…' and she gathers two up under her arms, baby talking and giving one a kiss on the lips.

She and Collins exchange a disgusted look. And "Mummy"? She'd never understood the need to humanise pets. She scuffs her feet on the mat, takes in the spray of photos in the hallway. Aha. A boy and a younger girl in various stages of growing up, testament to the now empty nest. Laughter, conversation, arguments, that richness of existence swapped involuntarily for the yips and barks of a tribe of ratty dogs.

'Nice place you have here,' Collins says, just to wind her, Astrid, up. They could walk into an abattoir and he'd say the same thing.

Gregorivic sits. The legion of chihuahuas scramble up a well-situated stool, and burrow into her sides, scamper over cushions, so many cushions everywhere; zebra print, tiger print, and printed word cushions saying *Home sweet Home* and *Love*. This place would be Jenna's idea of hell, decoratively speaking.

Collins starts the questioning and Gregorivic corroborates what Kathy Spellerman told them about spending the evening with Kathy. Timings align. Neat. Maybe too neat. It's hard to imagine Lydia and Kathy as friends, the age difference, the styles, but work brings all types together, Christ, she knows that.

There's a small desk in the corner with an old PC, a job site open. She can't resist. 'I heard that Mrs Kitteridge had to let you go.'

Gregorivic glances at the computer. 'Oh yes. Can you believe it? Not even had a bloody funeral and Melody's firing us all like she's Alan Sugar in *The Apprentice!* Real piece of work that one.' Gregorivic strokes one of the little dogs. 'Kathy will be alright, but me and Hugh, we're a bit more… experienced.'

'You have a strained relationship with Melody Kitteridge?'

'Strained? Let's call it as it is, shall we? I don't like her. Never have.'

'Why?'

'She's a robot. Barely laughs or cracks a smile. I'm just glad I rarely had to deal with her. I swear when she looks you straight in the eye, it's like she's trying to vaporise you. You know what I mean?'

Van Doren narrows her eyes, 'Any specific incidents you can recall?'

'She's just rude. You know when people say, oh So-and-so is the life and soul of a party? She's the opposite of that.'

'And her relationship with her husband?'

'What he saw in her I'll never understand.'

Van Doren balls her fists up. What is wrong with this woman? Did she just live in the world of opinions and moral judgements? She changes tack.

'Do you think it's possible she could have had anything to do with Martin's death?'

Lydia Gregorivic stares at her. 'The papers are saying it was a snake?'

'You can't try snakes for murder,' Collins says, 'but their handlers…'

Lydia frowns. 'I suppose something was up between them. He was drinking more recently, whether it was to do with her, I don't know, but being married to her all these years must have taken its toll. Would be enough to drive anyone to the bottle I should think, but hand on heart, I can't see it. I just can't imagine Melody Kitteridge feeling enough emotion about anything, let alone be moved to do something like that.'

'You'd be surprised what people can hide inside,' Collins says.

'If you're asking me, I think you should look at Austin Pemberton.'

'Martin's friend?' Astrid says, remembering that he had given Mr Kitteridge the Balvenie Whisky as a Christmas present. 'Tell us why?'

'There was a falling out between them, right before Martin

died.'

'When, exactly, Mrs Gregorivic?' Collins asks, pen poised.

'It would have had to have been last Monday.'

'Can you describe what happened to us, please?'

'Austin first came in with Lucky in the morning. He's a beautiful Lab retriever, former prize winner, the whole deal. Austin thought he might have ingested a plastic bag, but isn't sure. Martin couldn't see anything on the X-ray, and asked Austin to bring Lucky in the next day if he hadn't improved.

'Then of course, Martin's back in his treatment room, thinking his afternoon's largely clear…' Mrs Gregorivic mimes drinking.

'He'd drink during the workday?'

'That day he did.' She strokes the underbelly of one of the dogs, like an unlikely Bond villain.

'And then?'

'Lucky got worse. Austin came back at six, Lucky was unconscious and at death's door. Austin demanded that Martin operate. And I mean *demanded.*'

'But Martin was impaired?'

'Yes.'

'And where was Mrs Kitteridge while all this was happening?'

'On a call-out, took Kathy with her. You know lambing and calving season is my favourite time of the year. Melody's barely in.'

'So, Martin operates?' Collins says, getting her back on track.

'Yeah, he gets me, *me,* to assist. I can shampoo and wash a dog, cut the hair off a cockapoo, trim claws, and all that. But be in an operating theatre and be useful?'

'What happened?'

'It was a disaster. I don't know at what point he killed it, but even I could see he was being sloppy. His hands weren't steady.

He did make it to the intestines at least, and found the plastic bag. Martin took the plastic bag out and showed it to Austin.'

'Then what happened?'

'Martin was slurring, apologetic. Austin cuffed him, not particularly hard, but he was angry, shouting about smelling the booze on Martin's breath.'

'Did anyone else witness this?'

'Hugh saw it all from reception. He'll tell you same as me.'

'Then what?'

'Then Austin brushed past me, went into the theatre. Saw Lucky there all in a mess, dropped to his knees and bawled his eyes out.'

'Extremely upset, it sounds like?'

'I'll say. Then he said, "Martin Kitteridge, you will pay for this".'

On the way back to the car, Van Doren is quiet, thinking.

'What do you make of that?' Collins asks.

'We'll have to follow up… but maybe it's just me. Do you think someone could commit murder because of losing their pet to negligence?'

'Stranger things have happened,' Collins says. 'And you shouldn't underestimate how much people care for their pets. He did supply the whisky bottle according to both Kathy Spellerman and Lydia Gregorivic.'

True enough. Her phone rings. It's Critchlow.

'Ma'am, we tracked down the wife. She refused to come in for questioning voluntarily.'

'Really? Where is she now?'

'We arrested her. She's currently at the custody centre at Sussex House being checked in.'

Astrid raises her face to the sky and pinches the bridge of her nose. She should have told them to back off if she didn't come in voluntarily. She tries to keep calm. 'Can you get over to Dapper's farm, check out her alibi as soon as you can?'

She hangs up. Tells Collins, 'The clock is ticking, and we aren't as ready as we ought to be.'

'But she refused to come in. She basically asked to be arrested! Tenner says she'll confess by the end of the day.'

'God, I'd better tell Smithes.' She puts the phone to her ear. 'I hope for our sake you're right, Collins.'

18
Melody

Melody presses her index finger onto the glass of the scanner. They already took her prints the night Martin died, why they need them again now is beyond her. Were she not experiencing arrest for the first time, she might have said something cutting about taxpayer inefficiency.

The custody officer, a pudding of a woman, scans her for metals and conducts a thorough search. For a moment it's almost like she's just going through airport security en route to St Lucia, to relive her honeymoon with Martin. Her belongings are even in a little black tray – including the envelope containing five thousand pounds in cash – and here the daydream ends. These things won't be returned to her – at least not for a while – and are being bagged and labelled.

Would she like to inform anybody of her arrest?

Who would she tell? Ally already knows, Martin's dead, who on earth would she call? Her indifferent foster mother, Jean, who she'd not spoken to in five years? Hugh or Kathy? God, the burning shame of it.

Would she like to contact legal counsel or have access to the duty solicitor?

Why? She'd not done anything wrong.

She is taken to a holding cell. St Lucia it is most decidedly not. A cream metal letterbox flap in what is probably Fencepost by Dulux. The bright blue easy wipe mattress that looks more like a crash mat is rather firm. There's an echo of someone humming, a guard or another detainee.

The lidless stainless-steel toilet is bright in the caged strip lighting. It'd be just her luck to take a pee and for that letterbox flap to open or the door unbolt.

What was she doing here? Not only had she failed to pay Pug on time but she'd contrived to get herself arrested. She'd trust Ally with her life… but now, in a cell, with only a wall to stare at, doubt gives a little flutter of its wings.

An hour passes. A uniform comes in – thankfully not when she's peeing – and leads her into a boxy room with a table and a camera in the corner. Detective Van Doren is there with another suit, older.

'Mrs Kitteridge, take a seat. I'm Detective Chief Inspector Smithes, and I believe you've met Detective Inspector Van Doren already?' His eyes are close to a Parma Gray by Farrow & Ball.

'I have.' So, this Smithes is Van Doren's superior.

There's a coffee in a paper cup on the table with a stirrer and a packet of sugar. She undoes the lid and the pent-up steam billows out.

DI Smithes reads out the time and date for the camera, and formally cautions her. He then offers her the chance to talk to a solicitor.

'I don't need one, I've nothing to hide.'

He asks her to go over her movements the day of Martin's death. There must be some method to it, to compare her accounts, to get her to slip up but it seems an infantile approach. Outside the Kitteridge Practice to the police officer, in her own house to detective Van Doren and now here: her story is the same. Why would it suddenly change?

Van Doren, quiet until now, leans forward, wets her lips.

There's something intense about her. 'Why did you refuse to come in voluntarily?'

'I'm busy. A dead husband, a dead business, there are things to take care of.'

'You do realise that in a court of law, a negative inference could be drawn from your refusal?'

'Just tell me what you think you know and I'll tell you why you're wrong.'

DCI Smithes crosses his arms with an amused look, but Van Doren's cheek bulges where she's pressing out her tongue. 'Have you ever handled a snake, Mrs Kitteridge?'

'Yes, I have.'

'Care to elaborate?'

'A couple of corn snakes, a milk snake I think once. As I told you before, we don't handle exotics at Kitteridge's. I'm a domestic and a large animal vet. I mean, honestly! What a waste of time.'

'Excuse me?' Smithes says.

'These facile questions. What is it you think I'm going to say? Oh yes, detective I once saw a python and an anaconda at a zoo and then I decided to get my own venomous snake to play with. I shudder to think that my taxpayer money is wasted on these kinds of investigations.'

Van Doren is clearly annoyed. 'Mrs Kitteridge, this is a murder investigation.'

'No, it isn't, Detective. It's a Melody Kitteridge investigation when the murderer is out there somewhere!' She points at the door for effect.

'Mrs Kitteridge,' DCI Smithes says. 'Let's keep calm, you can help us here. Let's just recap the key facts, make sure we have it all straight.'

'Whatever gets me out of here soonest.'

'In your earlier statement, you stated that you had the only other key to Martin's office, correct?'

'Correct.'

'Good. Now, who has access to the pharmaceuticals kept in your husband's treatment room?'

'Any of the staff with access to Martin's room. They're kept in a lockable cabinet but the key's usually left in. Martin locks his door when he's not in there. Though whether he always did, I couldn't say.'

'Good. See, we're learning something. Now. The whisky bottle. Traces of the drug Midazolam were found within it, which is one of the sedatives you keep in stock. Your prints were on the bottle, correct?'

'I picked up the bottle and tipped the contents down the sink.'

'You can understand how that might look?' Van Doren says.

She rolls her eyes. 'Unfortunately, there wasn't a big red label on the bottle saying it was tampered with. How was I to know it was significant at the time? I didn't even know he was dead! I can't believe I have to listen to this nonsense.'

'Mrs Kitteridge, by your own admission you were the only person with a spare key to the room. You had access to the Midazolam. Your prints were on the drugged bottle of whisky which you, yourself, said you tipped away. You are also a vet who could presumably handle a snake. All that. Then you refuse to come in voluntarily for questioning? What did you think would happen?'

Melody closes her eyes, takes a deep breath. *These people.*

Van Doren leans forward again. 'We're searching your house. If there is anything to find there, trust me, we will find it. This moment, right now, is your best chance to co-operate with the investigation. Tell us what really happened, for your own good.'

'God. You really are a bunch of idiots, aren't you? I wasn't even there! I was on a call-out at Dapper's farm! I called you in! Where does that fit into your theory?'

Back to Van Doren. 'We're asking the questions here Mrs Kitteridge.'

'How much longer are you legally allowed to keep me here?'

'We found five thousand pounds on your person,' Van Doren says. 'Care to explain?'

She tries not to, but feels herself stiffen. 'Spending money.'

'Or paying someone off? Someone who had done you a favour perhaps?'

There's a knock on the door. Van Doren's features contort in annoyance. One of the uniformed men who'd picked her up bends and whispers. Van Doren locks eyes with her, and Melody knows that whatever is being whispered is about her. Van Doren signals to DCI Smithes.

'Mrs Kitteridge. Excuse us a moment.'

As if she had any choice.

She waits, staring into the barrel of the camera mounted in the top corner of the room. The coffee is lukewarm, but she swallows it down anyway. There was the proof, freshly ground beans just taste better, but she'll take it. The clock on the wall says it's coming up to midday. They'll have to let her out soon, surely? So much to do.

The detectives return. Brisk. All business now.

'You haven't been entirely honest with us, have you, Mrs Kitteridge?'

'I have no idea what you mean.'

'One of our constables has just been over to Dapper's farm. George Dapper says you were never there on Friday night.'

Stunned, she cannot compute this error. 'George Dapper is lying! I categorically *was* there.'

'Oh, categorically? That's fine then,' Smithes says. 'Why don't you cut the bullshit, Mrs Kitteridge? You killed Martin, didn't you?'

'I loved Martin.' She shakes her head. Why was George Dapper saying she hadn't been there? 'You're just plain wrong.'

Detective Van Doren pins her with a stare. 'Tell us about your relationship with him, why are we wrong? Help us out here, Mrs Kitteridge, because right now, things are looking pretty bad for you.'

19
Melody
Cambridge 2001

Pre-clinical. Betsy, her lab partner lowers the scalpel, hesitates.

'Actually, you do it.' She hands it to Melody. 'I can't. It's just too much like Babe. I can't get it out of my mind.'

'No place for sentimentality.' The foetal pig is about the size of an A4 page, legs splayed out and tied down to the tray, as if it were about to be cooked. The barrier is not mental, only physical; flesh, bone, connective tissue, organs all which yield under the correct instrument.

Melody's gloved hand grips firmly, slicing straight and true. Two diagonal incisions towards the sternum, then a mid-line incision around the umbilicus. The flesh parts with a little pressure.

'That's good.' Betsy says. 'Now... pin the flap to the lower jaw.'

'I know what I'm doing.'

Her scalpel cuts away easily at the fibrous jelly of connective tissue.

'I think I'm alright now; I'll do the next bit.'

Melody gives Betsy some space. With the surgical scissors, Betsy makes awkward transverse cuts to the bottom of the rib cage and to the groin. 'And... what's the next bit?'

Melody rolls her eyes. Trust her to get stuck with the only

dunce in Cambridge.

'Cut low on both sides of the thoracic cavity, and remove the chest plate.'

Betsy does a reasonable job of this, handing her the chest plate. 'Are you going to the dinner and Dr Hutchence talk?'

She thinks of INXS. 'Should I?'

'You know, Melody, part of being a good vet is to be personable, and social, you have to deal with people too, not just animals. We have a module on our *petside manner* for a reason.'

She sighs, irritated, and saws through the trachea and oesophagus. As if she needed a lecture from Betsy on what made a good vet. All the more irritating because she probably has a point.

'Fine. I'll come.' She peels up the trachea and cuts away at the connective tissue holding the organ block in place, makes an incision on the last intestine. 'There.'

'Nicely done.' Betsy lifts up the organ block, places it on a new tray. The glistening organs wobble a moment.

They both stare at it.

'And what's on the menu at this dinner?' Melody asks.

Prioress's Room. Jesus College. The ceiling is wood beamed, the floor a rich oak. Oil paintings hang on the wall. The tables are arranged in a horseshoe. Cutlery gleams. Vases burst with constellations of pink Egyptian star clusters.

Cambridge. So in love with its own pomp, though she does appreciate the beauty. The course is first rate, the facilities first class and it had, in Queens, a superb teaching hospital. And if the reputational halo shed a little magic dust onto her shoulders too, well that could hardly hurt.

She hitches her dress a little higher on her shoulder. It itches. She'd searched the charity and thrift stores of Cambridge, and this grey knee-length was the best she could come up with on her budget. No time to wash it. It looked well enough in the mirror but the fabric was thick and cheap.

There's a seat next to Betsy and she's about to sit, but Betsy holds up a hand.

'Melody, it's boy, girl, boy, girl.'

She checks. Yes. That appears to be the pattern. 'Why?'

Betsy shrugs, 'Tradition, I suppose.'

She sits next to Betsy anyway, disrupting the pattern. Not because she particularly likes her, but she's at least tolerable. Why risk the unknown?

There are only twenty-five, maybe thirty people at the dinner, but they're all faces from her course. Hutchence sits at the head of one of the tables and to her surprise, is a woman. The INXS namesake perhaps had wrong-footed her into expecting a long haired, handsome Australian chock-full of inventive lyrics.

'Lots of handsome boys here,' Betsy mutters into her wine glass.

The black ties, slicked hair. Guffawing. She'd barely noticed any of them.

The waiter hovers the bottle of red over her glass. She darts a hand over.

'Would you prefer something else, Madam?'

Madam? That's what her foster mother, Jean, called her when she was supposedly being rude. *Oh, you little madam.* 'What gins do you have?'

The waiter looks at the ceiling, as if the drink menu is printed there. 'Tanqueray, Gordon's, Plymouth, Bombay….'

'Two ice cubes, Plymouth, tonic, squeeze of lime, slice of lemon and a few pomegranate seeds if you have them. Oh and a dash of Angostura bitters.'

She turns back to the table, the boy sitting opposite her – the man, she supposes – has an amused grin on his face.

'What?'

'Good for you.' he raises his glass. 'To knowing what you like.'

'I don't know what you expect me to toast with, they're mixing my drink now.'

'You're right,' he says easily. 'We'll wait.'

Someone tongs a little roll of warm bread onto her plate. What will everyone do with it? Make their own sandwiches?

A salad arrives with something lettuce-like on it smothered in a white sauce and nuts. She takes a bite. The foul taste covered by the sweet sauce.

'What is this?' she whispers to Betsy.

'Endive salad.'

'It's horrible.'

Someone snorts a laugh. At her?

'I'm looking forward to going back into Queen's to see some live animals next week.' Betsy says between mouthfuls.

'Perhaps you'll see a live Babe,' Melody tries.

'Yes! That'd be nice.' A smile. Melody had put it there. How interesting. She dips her bread in the sauce thoughtfully.

The main is pork belly, which causes much hilarity amongst the students. Yes, they'd dissected a pig earlier that day. But it wasn't *this* pig. It wasn't *that* ironic.

'What's really funny is that here we have a table of so-called animal lovers, and there's just two, no, three, vegetarians,' she says, emboldened by her little success with Betsy.

Cutlery chinks. Throats are cleared.

Once the plates are collected, and her second G & T sits in front of her – sans pomegranate seeds – Dr Hutchence gives her talk. It is fairly interesting, though essentially a précis of her article that had appeared in the Journal of Veterinary Science; a meta-study on the time lag of transferrable *Homo sapiens* treatments to the animal world.

They clap, the brown nosers simper, flatter.

What will dessert be?

A nudge.

'He's looking at you an awful lot,' Betsy whispers in her ear, breath sweet with white wine.

'Who?'

'Opposite.'

Sure enough, as she looks up, their eyes meet.

The dessert arrives, white and wobbling. Splotches of red sauce dot the rim like blood spatter.

'Did you enjoy the talk?' he asks, spooning the desert into his mouth.

She prods it, doesn't like the way the material responds. Pushes the plate away. 'Her article was interesting. The talk was just the soundbites, I certainly didn't learn anything new, except Dr Hutchence's gender.'

'Nice dinner though.'

'Is it?' she says, half an eye still on her desert, that somehow still seems to be oscillating.

'You know, I think you might just be the most interesting thing in Cambridge.'

She sips her poorly mixed drink. 'A thing, am I?'

He laughs at that, and a little jolt of pleasure surges through her.

'You're Melody, aren't you?'

She gives the barest of nods, knows she is expected to ask his name in return, and as such, doesn't.

'It's a pleasure, Melody.' He threads a hand between the glasses and candles.

She stares at it, not intending to shake it. But it's like her hand has its own brain, moving towards his.

And they touch. Actually touch.

It is warm.

Firm.

Safe.

'I'm Martin. Martin Kitteridge.'

20
Astrid

In the incident room reserved for Windbourne, half the team are hard at work but Smithes sends them all out.

'Clear the room. Take five.'

As soon as the door is closed, Smithes begins.

'So much for an easy confession, Van Doren. With me and you running this, we can't fuck up. A hasty arrest before we had the evidence in place? We haven't established a motive or a connection to the snake!'

'But we broke her alibi. And, in fairness, sir, you did ask for her to be brought in for questioning.'

'I didn't say arrest her though, did I?'

He hadn't given clear instructions either way, but saying so won't get her anywhere. 'Nobody expected her to not co-operate voluntarily. I know it isn't ideal, but we can always release Melody under caution and re-arrest later.'

'Optics, Van Doren. From the outside it looks like procedural disorder. All the right notes, but in the wrong order. That's not how I want to run things. We should count ourselves lucky she didn't get a lawyer. I know you want a quick result here, we all do, but let's do it the right way.'

She bites down her annoyance. 'On the same page sir.'

'We've got,' he checks his watch, 'a smidge over nineteen hours before we have to apply for an extension, release or charge her. Nothing like a bit of motivation, I suppose.'

Jenna is in the car park outside Sussex House. There's a

sandwich waiting for her on the passenger seat.

'You know you can come inside.' Astrid says.

'Fuck that.' Jenna leans over, they kiss. 'It smells in there.'

'Of what?'

'Bureaucracy.'

'Bitch,' she says playfully, and takes a bite of her sandwich. 'I'm so hungry.'

'How's the case going, big shot?'

'It feels like we're pinging from one screw-up to the next. Errors at the crime scene and now we've brought our prime suspect in for questioning when none of the legwork's been done. The worst thing is I can't tell if this is down to my inexperience, or if it's just Bill giving me enough rope to hang myself with.'

'Or plain bad luck?'

She tilts her head. 'Could be. Whatever it is, it reflects badly on us.'

Jenna squeezes her shoulder. 'Try not to sweat it, you've got great instincts. Always a few potholes in the road, people only remember if you get to the destination or not.'

'Christ, you sound like Bill.' She checks the digital clock on the dash, wondering how long she can take. 'I'm just recalling that I'm not the only person in the universe. Are you up to London now? When will you be back?'

'Shooting starts tonight. Maybe a week. Radical thought, but you could come up if you get free? Walk the set, even place that lovely arse of yours on one of those director's chairs.'

'They have them for real?' What was the name of the damn programme? Some drama for BBC3, called back for a second season. If she goes up, she'll have to watch an episode, refresh her memory and not look like some unsupportive ingrate. 'You know I might just do that. Especially if we can get back on track.'

'This is really bothering you, isn't it?'

'I hate feeling like I'm not doing a good job.'

'Why don't you go and see Ian?'

Astrid looks at the clock again. *Now that isn't a bad idea. Not a bad idea at all.*

Ian is repairing the pane on a greenhouse when she arrives.

'Astrid! I wasn't expecting to see you until Thursday.'

Thursday? Her mind races, locks onto the date. Of course. 'You will, this one's not a social call I'm afraid.'

'No time for a tea then?' His cheeks are red, capillaries attesting to the stress and hard living of his career.

'Afraid not. After some advice actually.'

'From me?' Ian slots the pane in place with gloved hands, squints at the joins.

She plays up to it. 'Yes, Ian, believe it or not there are plenty of us in the force who really value your opinion.'

'You wouldn't know it. I know what they think of me over there. All the talk of a fresh perspective, new leadership. The other side of the coin to that is a stale, used up has-been.'

'Not how I see you.' In the greenhouse, lines of pots brim with dark earth, though there is no sign of life. Is this how he fills his time since Laura died? Her heart aches suddenly for him. Career. Marriage. From everything to nothing at light speed.

Ian picks up a plastic bucket filled with the shards of the broken pane. 'Bloody kid next door. Into cricket. So, out with it then. You mean to tell me it's not a bloody perfect wonderland since Burrows elbowed his way in?'

She cocks a head to one side. 'I mean it's different.'

'Different how?'

'Speed is prized. Quick results.'

'At the cost of quality.'

'That's kind of why I'm here. Bill Smithes is heading up a murder investigation with me as his deputy. Did you read about it? The vet that got bitten by the cobra?'

'Big case, media-wise. I can't believe Burrows trusted Smithes with it.' He shakes his head dismissively. 'Don't get me wrong, I always said *you* had potential, Astrid. It's no less than what you deserve, but Bill? That man's made a career out of other people doing his work for him.'

'He's always been very generous with me.'

Ian snorts. 'Simple enough. You make him look good.'

Had he always been so cynical? And didn't any boss want good people under them?

'I'm not doing a great job of that so far.'

'Oh?'

'It's early days but there's been some procedural mistakes. Uniform let a potential suspect leave the crime scene to go home for a wash before forensics took any samples. Then we arrested this same suspect without enough evidence, which was just miscommunication. Smithes is worried it's starting to look like we don't know what we're doing. Bill gave me a bit of a dressing-down for it.'

'I see.' He nods. 'You're Acting DI, and with Bill's famous hands-off approach, I bet he's gently manoeuvring you into the spotlight for any mistakes, am I right?'

'I know you don't like him, Ian, but I don't think Bill would screw me over to protect himself... or am I being naive?'

'Politics. You're still learning.'

'So, does the former Chief Super have any advice for a fledgling Acting DI? How do I avoid becoming a scapegoat?'

He gives her a wry smile. 'Would a hard truth do?'

'Go.'

'Sounds like a few procedural bumps so far, nothing major. But it shows us one thing: you make any real mistakes on this and Bill will pin them on you. Why? Because you're an Acting DI. Easy for him to say he put you in too early, that you weren't ready. I'm afraid in offering you a lane to promotion, Bill corralled you into a trap. You do well, he takes the credit. You screw it up and you'll get the blame.'

'So... the wisdom I'm taking away from this is, don't fuck it up?'

He winks at her. 'Sharp as a glass shard, you.'

No more fuck-ups. The same pearl of wisdom patrolman Tom Weston had given her at the Kitteridge Practice on Friday night.

Her phone rings. Collins.

'Sorry. I have to–'

'Go ahead.' Ian watches her, hands on hips. He must miss this, the cut and thrust of an operation.

'What is it, Collins?'

'Guv, sorry, I know you're grabbing lunch, but it's the wife.'

'What about her?'

'She's demanding to speak to you, says she's remembered something.'

Collins waits at the door of the interview room nearest Major Incident Room 2.

'Smithes will want to interview too. Where is he?'

He points across the corridor. 'In there, doing a press conference.'

Should she be jealous or glad that Smithes was handling all the press himself? She'd half-thought she might be sat at his elbow, but then again, the point of having a Deputy was to have an extra pair of hands to drive the investigation when the SIO was waylaid.

'Bloody hell.' She chews at her lip. After her chat with Ian, she's second-guessing herself. *Be decisive.*

'With me, Collins.'

They enter. Melody Kitteridge glances up. 'Thanks for seeing me, Detective.'

'For the record, you requested to see us with some fresh information, is that correct?'

'Yes.' Melody nods. 'Correct.'

'Then please, go ahead.'

'George Dapper is lying to you.'

Hardly fresh. 'Yes, you said that before we terminated the last interview, Mrs Kitteridge. Also, that he was a…' she consults her notes, '…a cantankerous old bastard who is trying to make a point.'

'Yes, yes I know what I said.'

'OK.'

'I stand by those words. He just hates being told what to do, especially by a woman. I think I can prove that he's lying.'

'Oh?'

'It's my car, the Defender. When we bought it, Martin insisted on getting a security tracker installed.'

Astrid straightens in her chair. Now this is interesting. 'A GPS tracker?'

'Yes, an anti-theft device. It was his idea, said that if we're spending all that money on a car, we should at least protect it. I'm sure he has an app on his tablet or his phone that tracks it.'

'Does it show historic data, Mrs Kitteridge?'

'I don't know for sure; I've never actually seen the app. Barely remembered he did it.'

'These trackers all tend to record historic journeys, all stored on the cloud.' Collins says.

Astrid taps her pen onto the table, once, twice. The vet's confidence is interesting. If it's proven to be true, they may have to admit to making an error in bringing her in; though she'd maintain the reasoning had been sound. After all, would such a clearly intelligent woman incriminate herself with her own statement? To leave her prints over the bottle? To carelessly dispose of evidence? It didn't fit.

'We'll look into it right away.'

She hot foots it to the Windbourne Major Incident Room, Collins in tow. She assigns Horley the task of checking the GPS tracker and getting the data, ideally from Martin Kitteridge's requisitioned tablet if possible.

'And Gardner, prioritise the traffic cameras, run Mrs Kitteridge's plates through the ANPR system on all possible routes between the vet practice and Dapper's farm at these times.' Another thing they should have done already. She's got to get back on the front foot, that's where she's at her best, not playing catch-up.

'On it.' Gardner says.

'Get a visual of the driver if you can.'

'Always do.'

'How long?'

'Tight time parameters, the AI to do the heavy lifting, I'd expect to have something in the next hour, two tops.'

She turns to Collins, 'Get Simmonds or Critchlow back over to Dapper's. I want them to press him on the statement.'

'I could go if you want?'

'No. I need you here to help me go through the things we got from the house. We need to start again, do this properly.' She drums her fingers on the whiteboard.

'You really think her tip's good?'

'You saw how confident she was, Collins. Why make something like that up? She'd know that it wouldn't take us long to check it. Either way, there's no harm getting a jump on the investigation while we confirm it, have something to show Smithes.'

'I'll tell them now.'

'Collins?'

'Yeah.'

'If it turns out George Dapper gave a false statement, then let's throw the book at the bastard. Maximum fine. I won't have this investigation interfered with.'

21
Melody

Melody walks around the cell. What's taking them so long? She imagines a rectangle of Martin appearing through the hatch. His brown eyes, or his bright smile.

'Oh. Moody,' he'd chuckle. 'Looks like you've gotten yourself into a right old pickle. Come on, let's get you out of here.'

She sits on the bed, puts her head in her hands. Footsteps. The clanging of metal and the door swings open.

A uniform makes way for detective Van Doren.

She stands. 'Am I free to go?'

'The tracker corresponds to the timings you gave us, and we have it corroborated by CCTV. On behalf of Sussex po-'

'Idiots. Come on then, move.'

'Follow me, please, Mrs Kitteridge.'

The detective leads her to the desk of the corpulent custody officer. Melody signs various papers and her effects are returned in plastic ziplock bags.

Van Doren signs in loopy cursive. 'I'll drop you home.'

'It's fine. I'll take a cab.'

'I get it. You're pissed off. I would be too. But you weren't brought in for nothing.'

'I'm a doctor, detective. I went to Cambridge. I won't spell it out for you.'

'Point taken, Mrs Kitteridge. But rest assured I'm no fool

either. Top of my class in criminology, youngest female to be made a detective sergeant in the history of Sussex Police.'

'A man would say we're comparing our reproductive organs right now, Detective.'

'We could really do with a saying for that, couldn't we? Comparing vaginas, well… it just doesn't work. I mean who wants the biggest one of the those?'

She thinks. 'Measuring legs.'

'Excuse me?'

'It's what dominant female Portiid spiders do, they measure the length of one another's front legs to determine size and therefore primacy. Nature has an answer to most things.'

'Measuring legs, classy, I like that. Well done the spiders. So?' Car keys dangle from her fingers. 'Why don't I spare you from breaking into that five grand?'

The detective switches from Kiss FM to the local Radio Reverb. It's on low. Just the staccato rhythm of the DJ's voice, something next to silence. Free she might be, but the passenger seat is a new kind of interview chair. They are barely past the Hollingbury Asda when Van Doren begins.

'We interviewed Lydia Gregorivic yesterday. She said you're closing the practice?'

'That's right.' Melody reads a message from Ally saying she'd dropped the car at home, fed the cat. Apologising too that she had to get to work, then get the kids but she'd be up to the station later to see if she could be of any help.

Did she not realise that her phone would be confiscated at the station?

I'm out. Talk later.

'It must be hard, closing down something you've spent all those years building up,' Van Doren tries again. Persistent at least, she'll give her that.

'It's good that you support local radio. I like Absolute

Eighties. It's just about all I listen to.'

Van Doren smiles. 'You really don't want to talk about the business, do you?'

'Martin ran the finances, Detective, but not as well as anybody thought.'

Van Doren hums, interested, and indicates, waits for a break in the traffic and bursts through the gap. 'And you know, that five grand… I'm just naturally curious. What *was* that for?'

It's like she's having her thoughts sniffed out of her. By answer she turns the volume up on the radio. 'If it's on we should at least be able to hear it.'

At one point the detective's phone goes, cutting the radio and bluetoothing automatically onto speaker.

'Van Doren.'

'It's me,' a man's voice she recognises as DCI Smithes who had interviewed her. 'Listen–'

'Sir, I have Melody Kitteridge in the car with me on speaker,' she says quickly, darting a quick apologetic look at her. 'I'm dropping her back after release.'

There's a pause. 'OK. Please pass on my apologies for inconveniencing her. Come and see me when you get back to Sussex House.' The line goes dead.

'Not in trouble, I hope?'

'Don't you worry about me.' Van Doren's jaw is set into a bite.

Medina Villas. Van Doren gets out the car.

'There's really no need to chaperone me to my door, Detective, I won't be inviting you in for a nightcap.'

But the detective stares at the house and puts her phone to her ear.

'Hussain, when you left the property on Medina Villas, did you lock it? Yeah. You're positive?'

Melody sees it now: the front door is ajar, wood splintered around the frame. A sickening feeling lodges in her gut.

'There's been a break-in, I need a patrol unit here, right away.'

Van Doren hangs up. 'Stay back.'

But she follows. The detective tries again to usher her back, but Melody refuses. Van Doren places a finger over her lips. Quiet.

The door swings back silently on well-oiled hinges. Her beautiful oak door. She runs her hands over the black rivets and passes into the hallway.

Van Doren holds up a hand, stop. She listens. A seagull cawing. The distant sound of traffic. The house is silent. The detective moves well, like a panther, quiet and purposeful, but at the threshold to the lounge she freezes, her hand darting to her mouth.

'What is it?' Melody says.

The colour on the detective's face drains to the colour of weak tea. 'Please go outside, Mrs Kitteridge.'

'What is it?'

'Please.'

But she pushes the detective out of the way. The whitewashed walls are zigzagged in bright blood. Sick calligraphy.

'Wha–?'

She steps in.

'Don't touch anything,' Van Doren says.

Red stains on the rug, and a ball of fur, matted with blood.

Melody drops to her knees. 'Cleopatra…'

22
Astrid

The whole team is assembled for the p.m situation-report. Smithes is rolling off from a meeting of his own with Burrows and catches her for a quiet word beforehand. 'I heard about the cat. Covering it in sit-rep?'

'Yes, sir.'

'Good. About this business with the wife. I'm telling you this for your awareness, Astrid, not as a reprimand, understand?'

She nods, but can already feel her muscles tensing up, her defensive walls being mounted again.

'For Burrows, arresting and releasing the wife so quickly isn't the sort of start that they were expecting.'

She thinks back to what Ian said, and listens with a new scrutiny.

'There are a few grumblings out there that I put you in because you're a woman, to even up the percentages a bit ahead of the gender equality review.'

The thought hadn't even occurred to her. Who the fuck was saying that? 'Tell me that's not true, sir? Did Burrows say that?'

He waves it away. 'You're in because of your potential. But errors, even little ones, reflect badly on my judgement as well as your own. Let's put it behind us, and move ahead thoroughly, carefully, and diligently. The next time we make an arrest, I want it to be for the killer.'

Maybe Ian was right. 'As do I, *sir.*'

'Good. Then let's see where we are.'

The room goes quiet when they walk in, Astrid still biting

down her annoyance. All these middle-aged white men, drunk on the smell of their own farts, passing judgement on her, based on what? She always knew there was a game to play to move up, but when she got up, oh boy, things were going to change.

To business.

Astrid updates the team about Mrs Kitteridge's release, and the discovery of the cat.

'Mrs Kitteridge doesn't want us involved, and claims she has no idea who did this or why it happened. Clearly, she's still hiding something.' She gives Smithes a sideways look, 'Our slightly ill-advised arrest may yet have borne fruit. When we picked her up what did she have on her?'

'The five grand,' Hussain, the Exhibit's Officer, says.

'Cash. Next fact. We brought her in, let her out some four hours later and someone's broken into her house and done a paint job with her cat.'

'A missed deadline, a warning?' Collins says.

'Money trouble?' says Gardner.

Astrid shrugs. 'It's a flag, and could well be connected with the murder. Mrs Kitteridge is closing down the vet practice for good not two days since her husband's death, and intimated at some financial mismanagement by her husband. Nothing specific.'

Heads are bowed, notes being taken.

'Multiple lines of enquiry.' She lists them off on her finger. 'The money trail to follow – Gardner, Horley – on the e-mails and phone records, Austin Pemberton and the snake trail – me and Collins. What else?'

'Ma'am?' Hussain raises a hand.

'Go ahead.'

'I've been going through some of the business expense receipts this afternoon and found something that might be interesting.'

'Go.'

'It's a receipt from Timpson, the key cutters, six months before the murder. Maybe it's nothing, but what if someone was getting spare keys cut to Martin Kitteridge's office?'

'This is what I mean,' Smithes says as if to himself, 'just good fundamental police work.'

'Gardner, Collins. That receipt will be timed to the minute and Timpson's is a big chain, pretty sure they'll have CCTV. Let's see if it's anyone we recognise.'

23
Melody

She hates her eyes. The weak pinkish hue. Crybaby. Can't help it. Cleopatra… the mangled mess, like that time with the kittens. Worse maybe.

It had happened again. On her watch.

The back yard is overly decked. Martin, unable to exercise any influence on the interior of the house, had overcompensated here, decking over the little square of lawn they'd had. A patch that would have been an ideal spot to bury Cleopatra.

She looks around. Potted plants, raised beds; she couldn't bury her beloved cat in those. By the little fountain, the outdoor seating surrounds a clay chiminea. Yes.

Melody takes kindling from the fire box, some firelighters and old newspaper and starts a fire. She feeds it dry imported olive wood until the fire crackles and rages. There's a new problem. By sight, it's clear that Cleopatra won't fit in the chiminea's mouth.

In the house, she retrieves her call-out bag and her emergency surgical tools, the last time she'd used this was to give a cow a Caesarean Both the cow and the calf lived. Now though, a different assignment.

With Cleopatra, her unshakable surgeon's hands fail her, their dispassion gone.

It takes longer than it should. Cleopatra divides into three parcels, not as neat as she deserved. Melody adds more olive wood to the chiminea until the heat is a being that seethes and coils.

It is time.

Melody feeds her beautiful cat to the flames. A piece at a time. Cremation, seen through swimming eyes.

Enough. She goes inside, and makes herself a dry vodka Martini. A lemon spiral bobs, then sits, suspended in the clear liquid. Helical. Like DNA.

No. Like a snake.

She drags her chair closer to the radiant heat of the chiminea, a pad and pen resting on her lap. On the left side she writes the name of everyone she can think of connected to Martin. Then draws three straight columns and writes: Motive, Alibi, Snake; the logical things that would convince the police that a suspect was worth investigating.

It is like a scientific experiment. Hypotheses on the left, the test criteria on the right. Against the name of Pug/Sheridan she gives a tick for motive. Rests the tip of her pen on the barren columns to the side.

Takes a sip of her Martini.

Barren. Acute. Antarctically cold.

A second sip, then she pours the rest onto the decking. *Drip, drip, drip* through the gaps. The lemon helix looks springy and vibrant. She stands, crushes it under her boot and goes inside for her car keys.

The Defender growls along the sea front and ghosts past the burnt-out west pier. Outside, normal people walk to their hotels and step into restaurants. A couple on a bench point out at the lights of the fishing and dredging boats.

She has no appetite.

Martin is beside her, an understanding expression on his face.

'You've had better weeks, Moody, old girl. Chin up.'

'This is all your fault.' She keeps her eyes on the road. When she next looks over, he is gone.

The Palace Pier. A dog walker, a few tourists. A couple share chips from a paper bag. Her stomach rumbles. She hasn't eaten since… when?

The lights change to green and she goes on, back down onto Marine Parade for the second time that day. Was it really this morning that she'd been arrested? It feels like ten days lived in one.

This time she passes unheeded and parks up by the Concorde 2. It's open. Young people hang around outside, smoking.

There's marihuana in the air and music, but it's tinny and incomprehensible.

Pug is at the bar, a pint fizzing, his enormous back hunched over a phone. He's sitting on a folded leather jacket.

Melody slaps the envelope down on the counter next to his glass.

'There.'

'Mrs Kitteridge.' Pug glances left, then right and conveys the envelope into a pocket. He narrows his eyes. 'Tell me, something's been bugging me.' He takes a sip, and twirls his finger. 'Were you one of those TV vets? You've got a familiar face.'

'No small talk. I'm a bit upset, you see. On account of my cat dying.'

'Mr Sheridan doesn't like to be inconvenienced. To business, then. Half the outstanding amount this time next week.'

'Impossible. I'd have to sell the house. There's the will, probate, putting the house on the market–'

'I don't care how you get it. Only when.' He turns back to his drink.

'But–'

He holds a hand up. 'Not my problem.'

She takes out detective Van Doren's card and her phone. 'You leave me no choice but to go to the police.'

He turns to her now, wraps his massive hands around her phone. 'Now, now, Mrs Kitteridge. We didn't have anything to do with your husband's death.'

She yanks the phone away from his grasp, having the sense that she can, only because he permits it. 'The authorities can be the judge of that.'

'Sit.'

The word pins her, like she's a conditioned dog. He is one of those men whose every breath you can hear, struggling through undersized nostrils. He is thinking.

'There is another way.'

'How?'

'Are you aware of some of the work your husband did for us, Mrs Kitteridge?'

'By work do you mean gambling away our savings?'

He shakes his head. 'Husbands, eh? No, Martin was our vet. The dark vet we called him. Black market work and that.'

She is totally bewildered. What veterinary work could Martin possibly have been doing for these thugs?

'Say you were to fill his shoes, we could maybe knock a few points off that debt, give you time to sell the house and clear the rest of what you owe. Walk away from all this, clean break, like.'

'Veterinary work. But what type?' Illegal dog breeds? Perhaps a private racehorse?

'Mostly events. The address is sent out last minute. Best you see for yourself.'

'I'll do it.'

'Keep Saturday evening free. Bring everything you normally would.' He levels a sausage finger at her, his arm raised in warning. 'You mention talking to the pigs again, it'll be the last conversation you ever have.'

On his forearm. A scar, shaped like a rocket.

24
Astrid

Astrid wakes. The bed, the flat, has never felt so empty, so Jenna-less. She's been gone one night, so why does she feel the absence so acutely now?

It's early.

Lycra.

High-vis.

Cleats.

Helmet.

The sea breeze slices her cheeks. Keep moving. The lights on her bike reveal the next few metres ahead of her, as if with each turn of the pedal she discovers a few feet of new world. Astrid powers up and freewheels down the undulations of the coastal road, through the port of Newhaven. A huge ferry is docked, one of the regular services to Dieppe in France. A copshop joke pops into her head: this part of the coast was great because you had Newhaven for the continent, and the nearby retirement town of Eastbourne for the incontinent.

She cuts back to the seafront at Seaford. Briny air. The invisible sea sucks and splashes at the stones.

Maybe she should propose to Jenna. She wouldn't drop to her knee but she could buy a ring, something colourful and vintage from the South Lanes perhaps. Top of the i360? On the Pier. Under the pier?

She stops, plants a foot. Cuckmere Haven, at dawn. A rich green carpet snaked through by the ethereal gold of the Cuckmere river and her tributaries, the pastel blue of the sea. Yes, here, at dawn. She would do it here.

With her phone she takes a couple of pictures, a mark of memory, and carries on two more miles to Beachy Head, one hundred and sixty plus metres high. Beautiful and one of the most notorious suicide spots in the UK, if not the world.

How convenient, she thinks with a smile, she could always come here if Jenna said no.

Not that she would.

By nine, she's showered, breakfasted and in Kemptown.

Collins is already waiting for her on the street.

'Hard to miss this place.'

'Must have walked past it a hundred times and never been inside.' Astrid appraises the bright chameleon and various reptiles graffitied on the facade. They go in, the air heavy and unusual, damp and woody. The side walls are dominated by tanks. It's clean and neat, with wood finished frames. Upmarket, ordered, a little at odds with the chaotic graffiti on the storefront.

'Hello, there. Can I help?' The man, presumably Mr Lawrence, the owner, holds a blue-flecked chameleon in front of an open tank. A dead insect is balanced on his forearm.

'Feeding time at the zoo,' Collins says and sure enough the tongue flicks out, the insect retracts at hyper speed into the jaws of the reptile. It chews awkwardly.

It takes her a moment to recover from the display, and fish for her warrant card. 'DI Van Doren and DC Collins with Sussex Police, major crimes. Nothing to worry about sir, we're actually hoping you might be able help us.'

'Sure thing.' He has a soft American accent and tattoos on his arms. Gently, he puts the chameleon back in the tank. 'I'd hate to presume, but is this about the death of that vet?'

The tanks all look like mini rainforests. There are small frogs in one, lizards in another, some sort of tortoise in another and there, finally a snake coiled in one at the bottom.

'We'd like to ask you about snakes.'

'In general, or cobras?'

'Somebody reads the news then.' Collins grins.

'A hypothetical. Say I'm someone who wants a venomous snake. How would I go about getting it?'

The owner puffs out his cheeks, 'You can't just walk into a pet shop and buy one, you need a license to own a venomous snake.'

Collins has already checked this, and outside of zoos, there are a baker's dozen of privately kept cobras in the UK, all accounted for.

'How about, without a licence?'

The owner laughs, 'Are there unscrupulous people is this world, detective? Of course, big black market for it. There are breeders out there who don't care a hot damn about snakes or reptiles, just want to make a quick buck. Big problem, and the authorities are asleep at the wheel. Then what happens? Someone gets bitten, someone dies, and suddenly people start to take notice.'

She wants to say it's not her department, but it would hardly matter, "they" were the establishment all lumped together in public consciousness. The number of times she'd had people refuse to co-operate with the police because they'd got one too many parking tickets was a personal gripe. 'Do you know any of these breeders, Mr Lawrence?'

'Hell, no. Not personally anyways. But I'd welcome any investigation into their practices. When there's no accountability, reptiles, any animals really, are liable to be kept in poor conditions.'

'So, you've never kept venomous snakes yourself?'

'No, never. I held a venomoid mamba once at an event, beautiful thing.' He sees their incomprehension. 'A venomoid's where the snake has its venom-producing glands removed. Me, I'm more of a lizard guy. Snakes are fine, I stock a couple of corn snakes.' He rubs his beard.

'How would someone access this black market?'

'There's this Icelandic, or Norwegian, guy known in snake circles. I've never met him though.'

'Name?'

'Olaf Gudmundson.'

Collins scribbles it down. 'And you know about him how?'

'Originally, just rumours. But then I had some teenage girl come in with a viper a couple of years ago. Didn't want it anymore. Said she'd bought it off this Olaf guy but then was scared of getting bitten, didn't know how to look after it, take your pick. Folks just don't think!'

'Did you get this person's name?'

'No, she couldn't wait to get out of here. If we'd been closed, I bet she'd have left the transport tank right outside the store on the street. It happens. We took it in, called the RSPCA.' He shrugs. 'I reported it at the time, but who knows if anything was done about it. Probably lost in the machine.' He twirls his fingers round in their general direction, implying that they were *the machine.*

Astrid shakes his hand, 'Mr Lawrence, you've been very helpful. We'll be looking into it, I assure you.' She hands him her card. 'You hear anything about a cobra, or a way to contact Mr Gudmundson, then you give me a call, any time day or night.'

He looks at the card, give it a little shake. 'You can count on it, Detective.'

Astrid makes a call to Sarah Gardner while Collins does the coffee run.

'Where are we with Timpson's?'

'Visited the outlet, they have CCTV but it's stored centrally. I've been dealing with their head office, been bounced around to the IT security department.' She sighs, weary. 'I'm expecting a call back within the hour.'

'Keep me posted. Meantime, I need a background check for

one Olaf Gudmundson. That's Oscar, Lima, Alpha, Foxtrot…' She spells out the rest of his name for Gardner and ends the call. Unprofessional to think it, but there's something about Gardner she quite fancies. Jenna, aesthetically, is more beautiful, but Gardner... What was it? The intellect maybe – not that Jenna was stupid – far from it, but there was an incisiveness that she was drawn to, easier to grasp than Jenna's nebulous talent.

She shakes the thought away, guilty that it had even crossed her mind, annoyed at herself even, given that her ride to Cuckmere Haven had brought some clarity.

'You look troubled.'

She turns. Collins. A coffee in a reusable take-out cup in each fist. He takes them home and washes them up every evening – or so he claims.

'I'm fine.'

'How's Jenna?'

She narrows her eyes, grudgingly impressed at his intuition. 'Great. Filming in London, that BBC3 thing's back for another season.'

'That show is the shiznet.' He hands her the cup. 'Latte with full fat milk.'

'You star. And the *shiznet*? And you wonder why you're single?' She climbs in.

'Ouch,' he says buckling up, but with good humour.

'Sorry. I'll turn off bitch mode now.'

'No problemo. What's next?'

'I think a visit to see this Austin Pemberton is overdue.'

25
Melody

Melody starts the day at the practice; now officially released from crime scene status. The "For Lease" sign is already out front. They didn't waste any time.

Hugh sits on the steps, wrapped up in a coat, scarf, hat and gloves.

'What are you doing here?'

'I thought you could use some help. I am still technically in your employ.'

'You're right.' She rips a bin liner from the roll. 'I could have got Kathy and Lydia in too, but you'll have to do.'

He smiles. 'I missed you too.'

'Right. Let's get to it.' She opens up and pauses in the lobby. This space, jammed with so much life, of bustling people, clients and their pets, is now bereft. It died with Martin.

She tugs down the police tape, stuffs the coil into the bottom of the rubbish bag.

In Martin's room, the filing cabinet is empty and his computer gone. Even the sink plumbing has been removed by the police forensic teams. Powder covers every surface. A wall of certificates, framed newspaper clippings, and plaques. She hasn't brought nearly enough boxes.

Hugh, a presence behind her.

'I really am so dreadfully sorry, Melody.'

'Perhaps you could find out about the equipment leases, Hugh. Find out what our obligations are. Then we'll have to sort out what's left.'

'And what will we do with that?'

'Sell it, I imagine. Feed it into the chomping maw of the debt collectors.'

Hugh removes his boxy glasses, rubs his nose. 'I still can't quite reconcile all this, Melody. Kitteridge's was a roaring success.'

'To all appearances. That, above all else, was Martin's talent.'

'I'll get the kettle on.' Hugh busies himself. The welcome note of his computer starting up, the clink of china in the kitchenette. For a moment it's like old times, on the odd occasion they'd both been first in.

In the pharmaceutical cupboard, unsurprisingly, the police have taken the Midazolam, but there's still a fair bit of stock: anaesthetics, antibiotics, worming tablets, syrups, syringes. She loads a selection into the carry bag, having no idea what she is in for with Richie Sheridan. Go broad. Cover the bases.

From the reception, the radio is tuned to Absolute Eighties. Hugh appears with a mug of steaming tea.

'No milk, I'm afraid.'

She takes the mug off him.

Melody works efficiently and ruthlessly. There is little room for sentimentality. She learns, even now, new things about her husband. That he has an entire drawer stuffed to jam with thank you cards, some so old the colour is faded. She flicks through a few, names of pets and owners long forgotten. She bins the lot. Were there no depths to his vanity?

In another drawer a bunch of A4 photo frames and a Manila envelope of newspaper and magazine cut-outs from previous waiting room displays. Vet of the Year. Another about the time two cockatoos had escaped and were flying around Hove. Where "Local vet Martin Kitteridge was on hand to coax them down and return them safely to their owner." She'd forgotten about that.

Back in time she goes, glancing quickly at the headlines and moving on. Funny that there are no images of her. It was always Martin, like a one man show. Like history had omitted her existence. She didn't particularly mind; she wasn't one for the spotlight.

As she turns to the next frame in the stack, her heart almost stops.

It's a newspaper article from the *Argus* dated seven years ago, but it's the picture that gets her.

Martin with a snake draped over his shoulders and curled up his arm, its head resting in his hand. A teenage Kathy, standing next to him holding up a smaller snake, a delighted smile on her face.

She grasps it between her hands. Reads the whole thing once, then a second time. A visit to sixth form college for Animal Awareness Day. The snakes were a royal python and a corn snake. She looks at the date. Kathy had been doing work experience for a good year by then. Was this some favour she'd asked Martin, to come into the college?

Melody crosses the lobby and enters her own room, more or less identical to Martin's, except smaller and not as well lit. Her computer blinks into life and within a few moments she's searching through her digital calendar, back-arrowing, but even as she reaches five years back the days are blank. She's fairly sure she'd chucked her old paper diaries when she went digital. E-mail?

She constructs a search for the dates in question and yes, there, she has a confirmation for her attendance at a two-day conference in Birmingham.

She leans back on her office chair, taps out a beat with her fingers on the rest. Her first thought is that perhaps it was too an insignificant for Martin to mention… but if it meant nothing, why keep the newspaper cutting?

Bizarre. Yet for the police, this would prove nothing, some vague yesteryear connection between Martin and snakes, perhaps. Back when they were still the new vets on the block and were doing lots of community outreach and marketing.

Still, she folds it up and adds it to her swelling folder of research.

26
Melody
2010

She should have said something. Put up more of a fight. Conferences were decidedly not her thing. Yes, she's a vet. But not this sort of vet.

But it's Paris! The head vet had said, as if it weren't a city with buildings and sewers like any other. *Besides, you need to network. It takes practice.*

This was a common theme in her appraisals with the head vet at the Ely practice. Her work with animals was extremely good, by all accounts. Networking was shorthand for something else. Her manner with humans, apparently. The soft skills.

Yes, she could be abrupt and direct, but it shouldn't really matter if her veterinary skill was excellent. But matter it did. Melody needs his signature to attest to her competence, his name as a referee.

So here she stands.

To observe the smarmy smiles, handshakes and faux friendliness all masking the desperate hope of personal gain. And this was the template she should aspire to? How on earth does someone even begin a conversation with these people?

Her lanyard clunks against the coffee urn as she leans to fill her cup.

Naturally there are a lot of French. A few pockets of British. A small group of Saudis, white robed and head-dressed. A

Hungarian contingent.

A woman in a business suit approaches.

Smile. Melody forces her face muscles to obey.

'Are you okay?' The woman asks, filling her cup. French accent.

Melody gives a quick nod. Tries to think. Offers her mug in a sort of a cheers.

'We all need our coffee. You, are English, *non*?'

'English. That's correct.' What would be appropriate? Light-heartedness? 'Caffeine can help. In case the keynote is soporific.'

Thin smile. 'Let's hope not.'

Kindred spirit? 'Do you think anyone actually enjoys these events?'

'Excuse me?'

Melody glances down at the woman's lanyard. Matches the name to the program of events. This is the keynote speaker.

'If you'll excuse me.'

Melody drains her coffee. Terrible and bitter. Why was this all so complicated?

She wanders over to the poster for various workshop sessions after the keynote. Varied. It's as if someone wrote random ideas on paper and put them in a hat, then picked them out at random. Perhaps that is how these things are organised.

Veterinary Epidemiology
Camel Science
Veterinary Toxicology
Veterinary Surgery & Radiology
Aquaculture
Animal Cloning & Transgenic animals

Camel Science? Intriguing. If she'd done more equine work since qualifying, she might have been tempted. Surgery and Radiology is the obvious choice, but Toxicology, there could be a thing or two to learn there.

'Moody? That's not you, is it?'

It's like someone has tipped a bucket of ice on her. Martin fills up his cup with coffee. Smiles. He's in a checked shirt, brown corduroys, and loafers. Unruly coal black hair. Handsome.

'What are you doing here?'

He shakes his lanyard. 'Got in a little late.' He nears, stands at arm's length, knowing better than to kiss her or offer a hug.

'Are you still working for that old codger in Ely?'

'For now.'

'How was the morning session?' He takes a sip, winces.

'As good as the coffee you're drinking.'

'I bet you hate this, don't you?'

She doesn't contradict him.

'Mr Bloody Self-Development sent you, didn't he?'

'Nothing wrong with your powers of deduction, Martin.' She stuffs her hands in her pockets, to stop herself wringing them raw.

He places his cup and saucer down on a nearby table. 'You see, the thing is, Moody, I've read some research that suggests we shouldn't work on rounding out our weaknesses. Instead, we should stretch our strengths. Accelerate them, become exceptional at a few things rather than being an average all-rounder.'

'Interesting.'

'In short, it's a waste of time you being here, Moody.'

An announcement comes for them to return to the lecture hall. But Martin doesn't move.

'Do you want to get out of here? Sack this thing off? I know a great place for lunch.'

It's scandalous. They couldn't… surely?

'We could call it… networking?' Martin offers.

Martin dabs his lips with the napkin, then empties the last of the

Beaujolais equally between their two glasses.

'This is fate, Moody, me finding you here.'

She holds the glass to her chest.

'Do you ever miss me?' he asks.

She closes her eyes. *Don't admit it.* 'I have thought about you, occasionally.' *Damn.*

'We met too young,' he says. 'I was too immature and, for what it's worth, I regret the way it all panned out.'

'Good to hear.'

'Time clarifies things. You're not seeing anybody, are you?'

She shakes her head, takes a sip. It's like her blood is electrified.

'Good. That's good. So, here's what needs to happen. You leave Ely, and come with me to Brighton.'

'Brighton?'

'Your old stomping ground. I'm going to set up in Hove. Got the money from the bank of Mum and Dad.'

'You want me to work for you?'

He moves his wine glass by the stem, as if moving a chess piece. 'Not precisely. We'll live together, run the practice together. If all is well in say, six months, we'll get married, have children.' He twizzles a finger in the air. 'You know, the whole kit and caboodle. You could be Melody Kitteridge.'

It sounds so funny. So radical and impossible, yet... 'And you decided this, when, exactly?'

'Now. It just makes too much sense, Moody. I've never met anyone like you, you're one of a kind and we dovetail just perfectly, wouldn't you say? I mean, who else understands you like I do?'

'Ally.'

'OK, except Ally.'

'Nobody.'

He drains his wine. Triumphant. 'See? Tell me that doesn't sound like the best fucking plan you've heard in your life?'

He holds up a hand to a passing waiter, asks for the bill in what sounds like perfectly accented French. Then he turns to her with a grin, cocks his head to the side.

'Take your hair down.'

She reaches back, pulls away the hairband and lets her hair fall down onto her shoulders.

'Still as straight as uncooked spaghetti.'

She touches it, smooths it.

'My hotel is nearby,' he whispers. 'No kissing, I promise.'

27
Astrid

'Pretty,' Astrid says, winding around the country lanes, a smidge over the limit. They're in Fulking, five miles north-west of Brighton in one of the grooves of the grassy Downs. They pass a picturesque pub.

'Good ale in there,' Collins says. 'Nice beer garden.'

'Is there an eatery or pub you've *not* been to?' Astrid rounds a bend, then slows the car, squints. 'Here we are.'

It's a lush, green entrance overhung with ferns and a pulled back wooden gate. She swings the car in, crunching to a stop on pea gravel. Before them, a detached cottage straight out of a postcard.

'Make a note of the reg. Get Gardner to run it through the ANPR for the night of the murder.' Astrid nods to the red Volvo hatchback parked in front of them.

She steps out, brushes the creases from her suit. It's freezing. The air bevel-edged The flower beds are neat, thoroughly weeded. Hanging baskets on the porch, tasteful touches.

'Is he married?

'Widowed.'

She knocks on the door, waits. Collins hangs back, covering the windows.

'Anything?'

'Nope. No smoke from the chimney.'

'But his car's here. What time is it?'

'Eleven and change.'

'Hmm.'

'No. You don't think?'

'Well, it is next door. Country rules. Why don't you run down there and ask while I have a little snoop around?'

While Collins walks to the pub, Astrid follows a path around the house. There's a wooden side door, but a twist of the wrought iron handle lifts the latch. Lax security. These people forget how close they are to the city. The rear garden backs onto the Downs with a knee-high gate. Patches of frost claim the shadows, protected by the low sun fighting its way up in the sky. The path beyond meanders around scrubby bushes and up, presumably to the Devil's Dyke.

Astrid presses her face to the window. A lounge; piano, hearth, comfy looking sofas and coffee table buried in magazines. Kitchen, study. On the far side of the house is a picketed area of fake grass, and it takes her a moment to realise what it is.

There's a balance beam, miniature hurdles, slalom sticks and a foldable tunnel. In the corner is a large wooden kennel, exquisitely painted, with fleece blankets and a bed inside. A hand-painted sign hangs over the entrance: a horseshoe and the name Lucky.

'You're inviting fate with a name like that,' she mutters, not quite believing the set-up.

A hard, cold part of her thinks, how sad, how pathetic. Another invents a narrative of a childless couple who find an outlet for love in a dog named Lucky. In that light, what was the harm?

She's back at the front by the time Collins returns, accompanied by a man in an oilskin jacket, wellington boots and a flat cap. The farmer without a farm.

'Mr Pemberton, thanks for seeing us. I'm DI Van Doren.'

'Detective.' His handshake is firm, his cheeks flushed. 'You caught me.'

'Excuse me?'

'Your man here, caught me having a glass of rosé with the morning paper and a bacon sandwich.'

Collins raises an eyebrow, amused.

'Sounds like an interesting combo, I must try it sometime. Did DC Collins explain the purpose of our visit?'

'Indeed, please, come in, come in.'

A few minutes later, they find themselves in the lounge. The sofa is comfy as it had looked from outside. On the mantelpiece is a row of tacky-looking dog trophies and colourful rosettes whose ribbons droop down like sad tails. Austin Pemberton puts the tray down: a teapot, some carefully arranged biscuits, and a jug of milk, a sugar bowl.

Astrid feels like Miss Marple.

'Nice place you have here,' Collins says.

'Thank you, yes. Chrissie, my wife, discovered it. Late wife, I should say.' He pours tea with careful concentration. A melancholy air settles around him. 'It feels like everyone's dying around me. First Chrissie, then Lucky, and now Martin. All in eighteen months.'

'It must be a very hard time for you,' Collins says, convincingly.

Astrid doesn't want to waste time wandering down memory lane. 'Mr Pemberton, we'll need to ask you some difficult questions today.'

'Help yourselves to milk and sugar, Detectives.' He eases back with his cup. 'Fire away.'

'Thank you. Mr Pemberton, how would you describe your relationship with Martin Kitteridge?'

'He was one of my closest friends. Met at Fitz in Cambridge. Shared a house with him until graduation.'

'Forgive me for asking this, but you're a little older than Martin?'

'I was a mature student. I'm only, what, eight years older

than him? Age didn't figure. We just got on famously.'

'Always?'

He takes a sip, thinks. 'Friends have their spats, but I suspect you're referring to something more recent.'

Astrid inclines her head. 'We'll get to that. First, could you walk us through your movements on Friday, the tenth of January?'

'The day he died?' He looks up at the ceiling, 'I can't really remember anything precise. I would have worked in my study – wealth management –' he adds before she can ask. 'I went for the usual walk up on the Downs around lunchtime. Funny, I've kept the routine I used to do with Lucky. Take the ghost dog for a walk, as it were. I stop, look around, expecting him to burst out of the bushes. The other day I was calling him, and a kind walker stopped and asked if I needed help searching for him. I didn't have the heart to admit Lucky is dead.'

Astrid tries, and fails, to close her heart to this sad man. 'Roughly what time do you return from these walks?'

'I would have been back by one. Spot of lunch. Then I was in for the rest of the day. In the evening I would have watched television.'

'What did you watch?' Collins asks.

'The news. *Newsnight*. Bit of *Bloomberg* in the gaps, I should imagine. The days tend to blend into each other.'

'And there's nobody who could confirm this? Any phone calls you remember, anything?'

He holds his hands up, 'No. If I'd have known I needed an alibi I would have gone to the pub, Detective. Sorry, bad joke.'

'I need to ask you about your argument with Martin Kitteridge the Monday before he died.'

His face darkens. 'What a way to leave things between us.' He sighs. 'A most unfortunate business. It began with Lucky on our normal walk. He was off in the bushes; I heard some rustling of what sounded like a plastic bag. You know what people are like leaving rubbish about. Thought nothing of it. But he didn't touch his dinner, and the next day it was like he'd lost his light. I took him into Martin, he took X-rays, but couldn't see anything. He gave me a watching brief. To cut a long story short, Martin had to operate on Lucky, emergency surgery. But the fool was soused and made a hash of it.'

'And how did you react?'

'I might have said some regrettable things.'

'Such as?'

'I believe I said that he would pay for it. Or words to that effect.'

'And what did you mean by that, Mr Pemberton?'

'I meant that he'd pay for it. Literally. I was going to sue him and get him, whatever it is, struck-off, lose his licence, whatever.'

'And did you start proceedings?'

'No… I said it in the heat of the moment. Losing Lucky was a terrible blow. I won't deny how deeply I felt betrayed by Martin. Drunk and irresponsible though he was, he was still trying to save Lucky. The litterbugs are as much to blame as Martin, and I couldn't face losing a friend on top of Lucky. I'd planned to patch things up.'

'We've had reports that Martin had started drinking more heavily. Do you know why?' Collins asks.

Astrid sips her coffee, reading his reaction.

'Unhappy sod. I couldn't fathom it, to be quite frank. Beautiful house, intelligent wife, a thriving business and me losing Chrissie and Lucky, you would have thought I'd be the unhappier of the two. Perhaps I am. Martin wouldn't talk about it, he had to project this image of success. If he admits his unhappiness, then the illusion wobbles.'

'And the whisky? The bottle of Balvenie, can you confirm that you gave him that as a Christmas gift?'

His brow furrows. 'I get him a single malt every year. It's

tradition. It was before all this business with Lucky. What of it?'

'Just trying to establish the provenance of the items found at the scene of Mr Kitteridge's death.'

They wrap up the interview and Mr Pemberton shows them to the door.

A question flies into her head. 'One last thing. As a wealth manager, did you ever manage anything of Martin's?'

'Confidential…' he begins, but then rubs his chin. 'Though he's no longer with us, I believe I am allowed to say that he was once a client of mine.'

'Until when?'

'Six months ago.'

'He withdrew funds? Did he give a reason?'

'He didn't need to. It was his. He could do what he liked with it.'

She hands him a card. 'Thanks for your assistance, Mr Pemberton, we may be in touch to follow up. If anything occurs to you…' She nods to the card.

'Best of luck, Detective. I pray for a speedy conclusion.'

28
Melody

After a quick lunch, Melody returns home to find a delivery man skipping down her steps with a box under his arm.

'Wait, I'm here, I'm here!' she calls from her window.

'Just in time! Sign here please, madam.'

In the lounge, the tape parts effortlessly beneath the blade of her box cutter.

Gleaming tins of paint. Little Greene this time. Two of a muted yellow Chamois, two of a faded blue Grey Stone, and the rest a simple Loft White. There is no question of "touching up" or painting a single wall in the lounge. The shades are never quite the same, the freshness of the paint won't match the rest of the walls. The current incarnation of the lounge is about ten months old, all Farrow & Ball. The switch back to Little Greene means she must do the ceiling again too, to keep the room paint-loyal. It is one of her rules.

She scrubbed the walls late into the night and the blood stain is now just a pinkish shadow. A whisper of violence. She readies her roller, letting the paint soak into its thirsty fibres. A roll on the tray to take off the excess and avoid drips. There's a light thud as it kisses the wall, then she pulls it across the wall in a stripe, the Chamois paint disappears the last molecules of Cleopatra, to the human eye at least.

Later, in coveralls, she sits on an old sheet by the window, and pull on her Marlboro Light. A rare treat. There's plenty left to do, no need to cram it all into a single day. She draws in deep and empties her lungs into the gap of the cracked window.

She sees them. Her in-laws. Coming up the road. Howard and bitch-face Susan, with someone in a suit.

'What the…?' She stubs the cigarette out on a saucer. Cleopatra's wall is now a clean block of summery yellow. No hint of blood to explain.

There's a clatter of keys in the lock, conversation, the scuffing of feet. She doesn't know what to do with herself so she stands in her coveralls waiting to be discovered.

'Beautiful flooring, is that solid oak or wood laminate?' A male voice says.

And then they are all face to face.

'Melody?' Susan says. 'I… didn't think you'd be in.'

Howard appears behind her, holds up a palm in greeting with an awkward grimace. It occurs to her how strange this is, that they haven't spoken since Martin's death.

'This is Mrs Kitteridge?' The suit says. 'Truly sorry for your loss.'

'You're redecorating *again*?' Susan says with a pinched expression. 'And that colour? Isn't that a cheery colour, doesn't that look like a cheery colour to you, Howard? What could you possibly be feeling so happy about, Melody?'

No. Not so strange that they hadn't spoken. She points at the suit. 'Who's this? And what are you all doing in my house?'

He lunges forward, offering a hand, 'Paul, from Cubitt's. The estate agency.'

Susan waves him off without meeting his eye. 'Go and have a look around, Paul, begin your appraisal.'

Bitch-face scowls, she's wearing so much make-up she looks like a gaudy, scrunched-up flyer.

'You're not smoking, are you? It stinks in here.'

'Only when I decorate. Not that it's any of your business. Now, why is there an estate agent here?'

Susan looks at Howard. 'Little dove doesn't know.'

'Susan.' A low, resigned warning from Howard.

'Doesn't know what?'

'He cut you from the will, dear. It must have been a month before he died. Told us all about it.'

'He what?'

'Whatever you think you're getting, you can forget it. He's kept it all in the family, left it all to us and Andrea.'

Them? And Martin's sister? Could that really be true? 'Didn't Andrea run away to the other side of the world to be rid of you? Good luck with that.' Inside she seethes. Martin had seen his sister… when? At the wedding. And that's been about it for the last decade. And he cut her in, and cut her, his wife, out? Complete bastard.

'I need a coffee.'

'A tea would be lovely if you're making, thanks,' Howard says. 'I might use the little boy's room.'

Melody escapes to the kitchen to buy some space, to compute what she's just heard but Bitch-face follows her, her perfume drifting in with her like a marsh gas. Melody flips on the kettle and the instant roar of it tells her there's no water in it. She tops it up with the Brita filter jug, then rests against the back of the full-stave oak worktop. Bitch-face is watching her, arms folded, using the island as a barrier. Kitchen knives gleam in a line on the magnet bar, just asking, begging, to be thrown.

They stare at one another. Susan, a smug expression on her face appraising the space, the wooden worktops, the Mudejar tiling and tasteful lighting, the Calke Green paintwork, as a hard-nosed valuer might.

'We'll get a lot for this place.'

Bitch! Someone yells at the back of her mind, but she smiles. 'You need my agreement to do anything. I still own half of it.'

'On that, Howard and I are easy. We could be your

landlords and you could pay us rent, or maybe you'd like to buy us out?'

The kettle comes to a crescendo, clicks off.

'But I think you need the money. Kathy told me you've shut Kitteridge's. Without Martin at the helm I knew it wouldn't be long, but to barely last a couple of days! That's impressive, even for you.'

She makes Howard's tea in a mug, knowing Susan only ever uses teapots, cups and saucers. 'I'll expect you'll want some of Martin's belongings while you're here. Most of it's only fit for the charity shop.'

'He must have really, really hated you. To leave you with *nothing?* I mean, incredible when you think of it.'

That's it. The gloves are off. 'Anything of his of value I've already pawned,' she lies.

'No doubt you'll need every penny.' Her face contorts. Darkens.

'Howard doesn't take sugar, does he? You were both watching your weight last time I saw you. I'd ask how that's going, but…' She shrugs. 'I can see that for myself.'

Susan smooths down her jumper, places her hands on her hips. 'You vindictive little…'

'Would you take this in for Howard? Could you manage that?' She doesn't hand it to her, but places it on the island, slides it across. Tea slops over the sides.

Susan leans in. The light creates angles on her face, sharp as origami. 'You always were a barren useless lump. You know what I wish?'

Melody leans in too, their foreheads inches apart. 'Grandchildren? No, wait, I know. That it was me who died and not him?'

'Exactly.'

'Trite and unoriginal.' Melody takes out another cigarette, lights it, and blows smoke in her face. 'You never understood

Martin and me.'

'You ruined him. My boy… my…' Susan looks away, but holds it together. Strength is a quality she appreciates, even in the enemy.

Melody lowers her gaze. 'We hate one another. That won't change. But we've both lost him and it hurts. Someone's going to pay for what happened to Martin, I promise you that.'

Susan gives her a look up and down, her expression unreadable and purses her lips. 'The Family Liaison Officer called, PC Baqri. His body won't be released for at least a week or two. We'd better discuss how we'll handle it.'

Why hadn't she received a call? Then she remembers, she'd opted out of that. 'Yes, the arrangements.'

'I think it best if *we* organise the funeral.'

The protestation dies in her throat, the last thing she wants to organise is a funeral. Something off her plate at last. 'If that's what you want.'

'It is. We'll do it down here, where his friends are.'

Out the window, the estate agent ambles around the decking with his hands in his pockets. He pauses in front of the chiminea. She hasn't checked, but it is quite possible he is looking at Cleopatra's charred rib cage.

'And Susan. If you want to sell the house, you have my permission. Let's have as clean a break from this horrible mess as we can get.'

Susan picks up the mug with Howard's tea. 'There is no clean break from something like this.'

29
Ten months prior to the death of Martin Kitteridge

Absurd, these lengths she must go to.

The bathroom door is locked. She unwraps the tampon, drops it in a cup. Fills the cup with joke shop blood. She waits, curating a playlist on her phone. After a few minutes she removes the tampon and wraps it in a tissue. Red blooms over the paper. A Velvetine No.442 by Crown. Then she deposits it carefully, obviously, at the top of the bin. She sets a reminder on her phone to do the same the next day.

Martin would give in. They could just be one of those unlucky childless couples. He would content himself with being a godfather or an uncle.

'Moody?' A yell from downstairs. 'Come on, or we'll be late!'

'Coming!'

It's a busy morning at Kitteridge's. There's a limping gerbil whose leg she splints. A chocolate Lab who is off its food. Kathy takes the bloods. There are e-mails. Ally wants to try a body pump class. The British Veterinary Association remind her that her annual membership fees will be renewed via direct debit at the end of the month. At a quarter to eleven Mrs Waterford brings in her cat, Maisie. A simple case of conjunctivitis. Melody administers some drops and writes out a prescription.

At eleven, she seeks out Hugh.

'Martin finished?'

'All done.' Hugh points to the room where Lydia is tending to two bitches, post-op, both spayed one after the other. Assembly line surgery, Martin called it.

She goes to the kitchenette and makes two coffees. Hugh winks as she walks by.

Melody knocks twice.

'Come.'

She enters. 'You sound like a headmaster.'

Martin has a letter opener in his hand, a small stack of mail in front of him. 'Moody. Lovely, you've bought my rocket fuel.'

She perches on the edge of his desk, takes out the digestives from the pocket of her pinafore, takes one out and breaks it in half.

'Have you washed your hands?

'Half? Are you rationing me?'

'You're not fat. Just, robust. Let's keep it that way.'

'So, Thursday. I'm thinking the Giggling Squid, or Moshimo.'

'Did the operations go smoothly?'

'Fine, fine. Thai or sushi? Or do you fancy something different? There's that new French place, you know, *Le* something. Oh, what's it called?'

'We had sushi last year.'

'Thai, then? Or that French place, I'll ask Hugh to find out what it's called.'

She dips her half-biscuit into her coffee, sucks it and lets it disintegrate in her mouth. 'You know, if you ever fancy a break from the operating theatre. I wouldn't mind...'

'Bloody NHS backlogs. Well… it's a start I suppose.' Martin has a letter in his hand. 'I got Hugh to get you an appointment. Check the plumbing and all that.'

'You need to stop treating Hugh like your PA.'

'I'll get the old mucker to carve some time out for you.'

'I thought we said we'd give it a few more months?'

'The appointment isn't until July. That is a few more months. If we get pregnant in the meantime we can just cancel. Glad I got the ball rolling now.' He has a mischievous smile, jiggling the letter opener into the next envelope.

She sighs. 'Let's go with sushi.'

Martin screws up the next letter, bins it, opens another. 'Good idea. Get that raw fish in, you know, just in case.'

'So, surgery. How about it?'

'A switcheroo? But why? You already assist on the complex stuff.'

I'm a better surgeon than you. 'It's not the same.' She lowers her voice, 'I prefer being away from consults.'

'You do all the large animal work, the call-outs, you're hardly one dimensional, Moody. You do surgery in the field. We all have to do our share of consults, it's the nature of our family practice.'

'But you're more peopley than I am.'

He puffs out his cheeks. 'Let me think about it, alright?' He checks his appointment book, smiles, 'Austin's bringing Lucky in for his jabs. What do you have next?'

She notes the subject changer. 'Check-up. The setter with leishmania.'

'Ah, leishmania. That's exotic, see?' He's not even looking at her, multi-tasking, reading his next letter.

'Taking blood and dishing out Alopurinol is hardly exotic.' She drains her mug and for a flash wants to throw it at Martin's head.

'Ho-ho!' a smile spreads across his face.

'What?'

'You won't believe it!'

'What?'

'Go and get everyone in here.'

She sighs, irritated, and rounds up Hugh, Kathy, and Lydia. The people in the waiting room look up, bemused.

When she re-enters with the rest of the staff, he's got one foot up on his chair, like a cowboy might rest a leg on a rock and survey the plains below.

'Sorry, everyone, this will just take a moment, but I've got some fabulous news.' He holds the letter up facing them. She leans forward, squinting, but it's too small to read.

'Well?' Kathy says.

He turns the sheet, snaps it taut and starts to read. 'Dear Mr Kitteridge, I'm delighted to inform you that you have been nominated for Vet of the Year…'

The next lines are drowned out by a clap from Hugh and a squeal from Lydia. One by one they go over, Hugh offering a handshake, the women a congratulatory hug.

'It's a public vote, so Hugh, perhaps you could manage this for us? Get this letter framed and put it in the waiting room, e-mail the voting link to the clients, that kind of thing.'

'Of course. Some flyers perhaps, with the voting details? I could get in touch with the *Argus.*'

'Good man.'

'Congratulations, darling,' Melody says.

She clears out with the rest of the staff with the two empty coffee cups and washes them up in the kitchenette. Two minutes until her next appointment.

She goes into the toilet, locks the door behind her.

With the palm of her hand she thumps the mirror. Her image wobbles a moment, like she might be about to vanish.

30
Astrid

At Collins' insistence, they stop for lunch at the pub though Astrid insists they sit at the bar and order something quick; the last thing she wants is for people to think the police are having leisurely country pub lunches while there's a murderer to catch.

'Thoughts, Collins?'

He dabs his mouth with a napkin, casts his eyes left and right. 'Here?'

'Nobody's within earshot.'

Collins leans in and whispers.

'Boiling it down, the man has no alibi and a possible motive.'

'Lucky's revenge. You should've seen the set-up out back. It was like a mini-Crufts.'

Collins gets up from his stool, brushes crumbs off his trousers. 'It takes all sorts.'

Astrid checks her phone, grabs his arm. 'Gardner's just sent through the CCTV from Timpson. Let's go to the car.'

They hurry out, Astrid starting the engine to get the heater going.

She taps the link on her mobile screen to the encrypted Windbourne folder, then opens the video file. Collins leans across. Sweet chorizo on his breath. It takes a few seconds to load, the network coverage not being great in Fulking. Then there it is, an image of the shop counter in clear black and white.

'You think we are about to see Mr Pemberton again?' Collins

says. 'That'd be convenient, we could pop straight back over.'

A man walks into the shop wearing a woolly hat.

'Now who is that?

The man puts two keys down on the counter, is saying something. There's no sound but it's easy to guess he is asking for copies. Then the man takes off his hat, and rubs his short hair.

It takes a moment but she recognises the face, his photo is on the board in the Windbourne incident room.

Astrid and Collins pull up behind an illegally parked white van outside the Kitteridge vet practice.

'Shall we give them a ticket?' Collins jokes.

Two workmen on ladders are taking down the brassy Kitteridge Practice sign. The man they've come to see, the receptionist, Hugh Forrester, appraises the men with folded arms from the pathway below.

'Be careful with that. It's very valuable.'

Mr Forrester appears to be more interested in the arse of one of the workers than the sign.

'Mr Forrester?'

He turns. 'Hello?'

Rumbled. 'DI Van Doren. This is DC Collins. Could we have a word in private?'

They duck under the workmen and enter the practice. Hugh leads them into the lobby and pulls the chairs into a circle. 'As good a place as any. Is this to follow up on my statement?'

Astrid has read it, Mr Forrester was without an alibi, and now they have something even more concerning. She decides to test him out first, see if he'll lie.

'We're just checking some inconsistencies between some of the staff statements.'

'Really?' His eyebrows rise. 'I'm happy to clear up any misunderstanding.'

'It's about access to Mr Kitteridge's office. There was a key on his body, and Mrs Kitteridge says she had the only other key, which she used to access the room.'

'That's not accurate, Detective. There were more copies of the key, in fact I made two copies myself a few months back. One to keep at the practice behind reception for emergencies and a spare for Martin.'

Well that opens up the field. 'Why was Mrs Kitteridge under the impression she had the only spare?'

He rolls his eyes. 'She misses a lot. She's often on call-outs, the odd conference. It didn't really warrant a big briefing to all hands, as it were.'

She senses Collins shifting his weight on the seat beside her, his signal. 'Were you asked to make the copies by someone, Mr Forrester? Or was it on your own initiative?'

'Martin asked me to do it. In fact, the office spare…' Hugh pops up and rummages around the drawers in reception, '…is here, but also…' He returns and holds out two keys. 'He got me to cut him a couple of spares of this one too.'

Astrid nods, remembering that there were two different keys in the CCTV video. 'And what does this second key open?'

'No idea,' Hugh says. 'I was Martin's errand boy. I did as I was bid.'

'May I?' Collins takes both keys and tries them in every door. 'Yep, this one's for Martin's office. But the other one, it's not a cruciform key like the others.' He tries it anyway, and confirms it fits no door in the practice.

Astrid sighs inwardly. A mystery key.

'And the drawer those were kept in, Mr Forrester, who has access to that?'

'Just me. It's locked.'

'I see.'

It's like he realises the implications of what he's just said: he shifts uncomfortably on the spot.

'Could you remind us of your movements the day of Martin's

death please, Mr Forrester?'

'Now look.'

There's a rap at the door. The workmen.

'All done.'

'You'll have to excuse me a moment.' Mr Forrester springs up.

'We can wait.'

She huddles with Collins at the back of reception.

'Is it me or are you picking up some shady vibes?' Collins starts. 'The guy has no alibi, we've got him on camera getting keys cut to the office which he *says* he was asked to do. He had private access to the room.'

She can tell by his excitement he wants to bring him in, but the Melody Kitteridge debacle is still fresh in her mind. Plus, she has her reservations. 'There's a big hairy *but*.'

'Which is?'

'MK's office key. We now know there are at least four sets. One found on the victim, the wife's set, this one that Mr Forrester has in the reception, and a fourth copy which is unaccounted for. Can you imagine in court? We'd get ripped to shreds.'

'We're a long way from court.'

She sighs. 'Collins, you think the roles are neatly defined; the police gather the evidence and make the arrest, the baton passes over and the Crown prosecutes.'

'And that isn't how it is?'

'On paper. But if you start to think like a prosecuting barrister *and* the defence during the investigation, testing out and disproving the counter arguments, you stifle the possibilities for the defence. It leads to better conviction rates. Less like partitioned roles, and more of a symbiosis.'

'Interesting,' Collins admits. 'That receptionist, he's setting off my alarm bells.'

She respects his instincts, but evidence must be their overriding guide. 'Let's gently apply a bit more pressure, see how he reacts.'

'Okay.'

Mr Forrester returns, hands clasped together. 'Sorry about that, lot to sort out as you can imagine. Are we just about done for today, Detectives?'

'We do have a couple more questions,' Collins says.

'Happy to. But I think as a precaution, I'd like my lawyer present for any further questions.'

'I see,' Astrid says. 'No need to trouble your lawyer for today. We've got all we need for now, Mr Forrester. We'll be in touch.'

As soon as they're in the car, Collins slaps the dash, more jubilant than annoyed. 'We rattled him. Wanting to lawyer-up like that, he's got to be hiding something.'

Astrid twists the key in the ignition. The car hums to life. A glance back. A stony-faced Hugh Forrester, watches, framed by the dark doorway.

31
Melody

Tuesday. Pug has sent her an hour and GPS co-ordinates. Nothing more.

Fog hangs low over the shadowy Downs. The GPS directs Melody to turn, though she can barely make out the road. The Defender dips into a puddled pothole and squeezes between hedgerows down a single track. She's barely doing fifteen miles per hour, her nose practically pressed to the windscreen. It's like trying to see through milk. The hedgerows guide, pawing at her paintwork when she strays too far to one side.

A shape darts in front of her.

She stabs the brake. The Defender lurches to a stop. She hasn't hit it, has she?

Melody opens the car door into the hedge and squeezes out.

The engine hums, fog swirls in the headlamps.

Nothing on the bumper or the ground. She steps forward. Can smell them. Shit. Mud. Earthy smell of matted wool. One bleats. Finally, her eyes grip onto something. Outlines. Two. No, three. No, four of them.

'How did you get out?' She traces a hand along the hedgerow until she finds a gap. The field gate is open, the twine snapped. Melody ushers them back into the field, then gets some wire from her car and makes a new loop to hook over the post.

A low rumble. It's the engine of another car, a Jeep or Discovery maybe. It's followed by another. The faint orbs of light grow larger, and settle to a stop behind her Defender.

A parp on the horn.

This must be the right road then. No going back now.

She drives the Defender another mile or so up the road, followed, like a military convoy.

The navigation app speaks, telling her to turn. The wooden sign reads: Plum Tree Farm.

You have reached your destination.

Bright security lights battle the fog. She parks in front of a flint stone farmhouse. There's scaffolding erected by what looks to be old stables. She can guess the story; turning them into holiday lets or accommodation. Farmers used to farm. Now they diversify.

More cars arrive around her, parking up either side. Two men in long winter coats jump out, laughing about something. They could just as easily have been Martin and Tristan.

Outside, the air is thick and smoky, yet sharp as iced vodka.

The new arrivals seem to be heading to the hive of activity by the hay barn. Melody grabs her field bag and crunches over, looking for Pug. A man heaves a large log onto a fire. Embers crackle and snap, briefly illuminating a hog on the spit above it. The skin is blackened and hissing. From a van, a burly sort unloads a keg and barks an instruction to someone unseen.

A distinctive looking man, in circular John Lennon glasses, with long blonde hair and a beard, slides open the door of his Transporter. Their eyes meet as she passes.

Inside the barn, stacked hay bales make perimeter walls. Lighting is strung, trestle tables and bales for seating. A long bar is already dotted with punters drinking beer from plastic cups. Melody walks in further, seeing a circular arena made up of bales. Cockfighting, she supposes, with a sickening feeling in her belly. Diversification indeed.

This will not be an easy evening.

Pug waves her over. He's sitting at the bar talking to a skinny, swarthy looking man. Sheridan?

'Here I am.' She flashes a look at his companion, but Pug

sends him away with a look. Some underling then. 'What are the requirements?'

Pug chuckles. 'Your husband was a lot chattier; he'd be halfway into his first ale by now.'

'I was under the impression this was a job, not a jolly.'

'Too right, too right. Well, Mrs Kitteridge, the terms are these. While you help us out, the interest on your debt is frozen, and the payback time extended to six months. Like I said, Mr Sheridan *can* be an extremely reasonable man.'

'Where is he?' She looks around. 'I'd like to thank him.'

'Don't you mind about that. You go snooping for him, I'll break your nose. Got it?'

She doesn't doubt it for a second. 'Understood.'

'You are our new dark vet. That means any animal treatment you deem necessary.'

'What sort of animals?'

'You'll see. And second, we don't want the authorities to know about our little gatherings. Which means if anyone needs treatment here, they'll be put into your care.'

She narrows her eyebrows. 'I'm a vet. I treat animals.'

'Humans can be animals,' Pug says. 'Other than that, have a flutter if the mood takes you, be on standby.'

'So–'

'You can fuck off now,' Pug says with a shooing gesture.

The barn swells with people. There's chatter, ale, the roar of laughter over the distant hum of a generator. It is easy to imagine Martin here, laughing at the bar. She looks around for a would-be Richie Sheridan, but instead sees a familiar pinched face.

'George?'

He scowls. 'What are you doing here, you bitch?'

'Charming. I'm not sure what you have to be angry about. You were the one who lied to the police. Whatever got into you?'

'Bastards fined me,' Dapper says.

An uneasy silence stretches between them. 'It was hardly my

doing, George. They accused me of murdering Martin and locked me up in a cell because of your false statement. What were you thinking?'

He shuffles from foot to foot, scratches his head under his flat cap. 'You had me all hot under the collar. I didn't mean...'

What would someone kind say? Someone like Kathy? 'Let's put it behind us, George. Call it a moment of rashness.'

He nods. 'That'd be agreeable.'

Perhaps she should copy Kathy more often. 'Tell me. How are the calves?'

'We lost one in the end.'

She sighs. 'That's disappointing.'

'Not compared to losing your husband it ain't.' He folds his arms. 'But, you should know. I am getting the ventilation sorted next week.'

'It's the correct decision.'

He looks at his boots. 'Is it true, that Kitteridge's gone under?'

'Word gets around fast.'

'This lot here are a good bunch,' he indicates the group he was chatting to. 'Farmers all. I'll get them to send some work your way if you're setting up on your own.'

'It's too soon for me to say. I'm here, working, as it happens.' She leans in. 'Do you know which one Richie Sheridan is?'

He raises an eyebrow. 'If you're looking for a new husband, he's rich alright, but there are better places to look.'

'So it would seem.'

Dapper cranes his neck. 'Can't see him this minute, but he's about.'

Someone clears their throat behind her. It's the wizard with the circular glasses.

'You. Come and help me please.' He has a strange accent.

She excuses herself, and follows.

Feedback whines. A mic taps. 'Goooood evening all, the

first event of the evening is about to start in two minutes, two minutes, please make your way to....'

The voice fades as she exits the barn.

Pug waddles past. 'Olaf, you ready or what?'

'Yes, yes,' he says, and pulls back the sliding door of his Transporter.

Inside, stacked in rows, are tanks.

Melody takes a step closer, squints.

In each is a snake.

32
Nine months prior to the death of Martin Kitteridge

The oak kitchen worktop is protected with old sheets and easily supports her weight. Melody works the brush into the corner. There is a right angle of masking tape to protect the Wimbourne White No. 239 by Farrow & Ball on the ceiling, but she's so precise she doesn't really need it. She's gone with Green Calke, also by Farrow & Ball, for the walls above the kitchen tiles. It's a soft sagey green to replace the previous Slipper Satin, another Farrow & Ball whose off-white tones she'd thought would blend beautifully with the ceiling, to give a kind of classy, shadowed effect. The result is disappointing. A rare misjudgement.

The creamy ceiling, tiles and walls. The vanilla-enamelled Russell Hobbs toaster and kettle set. The clotted cream of the bread bin with companion tea and coffee tins. In concert, it is like being trapped inside a giant meringue. Even Martin – who didn't give two pips about interior design – had declared it: fifty shades of beige. Galling though it was to admit it, on this one occasion, he was right.

Melody finishes, hops down off the counter, hands on hips, and surveys her handiwork. Much better: the light greens bring out the darker shades of foliage outside the window and contrast nicely with the rest of the farmhouse-chic kitchen. Martin is plodding down the stairs and appears in his dressing gown, scratching his beard.

'Bloody hell, Moody, you were up early.' He is reading something and switches on the coffee machine to warm the pot already there, oblivious to the decorator's sheets and the state of the kitchen.

'What do you think?'

He doesn't look up from his paper.

'The new colour.'

He looks up, then frowns. 'Didn't you only just do this?'

'No.' Five months was hardy recent.

'A bit better, actually.' He notices the paint tins. 'More Farrow & Ball? Jesus, you'll bankrupt us.'

She isn't a snob exactly, but she will keep a room loyal; that is, not switch brands of paint for each discreet room. The bathroom for example, was all done with B&Q's own brand of Brilliant White for bathrooms. She points this out, and Martin just smiles, arms crossed, a strange expression on his face.

'What?'

'Just you.'

She assumes this is a positive.

He smiles, sips his coffee, then his expression changes. 'Your period started on the sixth, correct?'

'What?'

'The sixth? Your period.'

Where had that come from? Was he trying to catch her off guard? The dates of her fakery are etched into her mind. 'Correct. Yes.'

He nods to himself. 'Thought so. I made a note. Got one of these apps, it predicts when you'll be ovulating.'

Then why ask?

'We should hit the window, what do you say?'

'I say I'm all painty and that is a far too mathematical a

proposition.'

'Come on,' he grins, stepping nearer. 'Paint coveralls are surprisingly sexy.'

'You need a shower.'

He yanks at her collar and the popper buttons burst apart. 'See?'

She relents and lets him unpeel her, her coveralls fall and pool at her feet. He slides her hair band from the pony tail.

'Turn around.'

She does, and bends over the kitchen island. He pushes her stance a little wider and spits into his hand. He's a little awkward at guiding it in at first, she adjusts and then he's inside her. It's neither good nor bad. Just a thing that's present, like a stranger in the corner of a room. The sink needs cleaning, there's a little ring of mould around the outflow. He pumps, his breathing getting harder. The resting lid on the nearest paint tin wobbles, rattles, and threatens to topple. It is a soothing green, the Green Calke.

He comes in a juddering fashion, palm pressed firmly on her back. He draws out, reaches past her and grabs some kitchen roll, hands her a couple of sheets and keeps one for himself.

She snatches the sheets and holds it between her legs, walking awkwardly out of the kitchen.

'Where are you going?'

'Toilet.'

'Are you mad? Leave it. Go and put your legs up in the lounge.'

She does as instructed. The vessel.

Later that week. Melody is at her doctor's surgery. She runs her finger over the tiny little bump in her upper arm.

The practice nurse applies a local, she waits.

'Can you feel this?'

Melody looks over, sees her skin absorbing the prodding

of a pair of tweezers. 'No, I can't feel anything.'

The nurse wipes the skin again, takes a fifteen blade out of its sterile wrapping.

'Be still for me, love.' The nurse makes a small, neat incision.

'You've got a steady hand.' Melody says.

The nurse glances up, 'Most people like to look away.'

'I'm a veterinary surgeon.'

'Ah.'

Blood, her life juice, forms a beaded line. Somewhere between Salsa Red by Dulux, or Little Greene's Atomic Red No.190.

The nurse removes the implant with quick efficiency. A tiny, thin cylinder. Then she inserts the replacement. She really is rather good.

'Who'd have thought something so small… Amazing little things, aren't they?'

'Progestin is the real wonder, but yes.'

'Do you find you still get your period?'

'I think once in the last three years.'

'Very common with hormone implants.' The nurse places a little strip of adhesive gauze over the incision. The nurse turns, and as she's washing her hands, says something Melody can't quite catch about feedback.

'What? Yes, all very good.'

The nurse cuts the tap, dries her hands. 'That's you all done then, good for another three years. You can remove it at any time, of course.'

'Uh-huh.'

That evening, watching the *Blue Planet*, she feels eyes on her, Martin not paying attention. It's irritating. He cradles his bulbous glass of red wine, takes a sip. It looks good, a Ruby Starlet by Dulux. He smirks.

'What?'

Martin strokes her forehead with the back of his hand. 'Is it me or do I detect a little radiant glow about you?'

She fans herself. Perhaps the heating is up too high. 'Your imagination, no doubt. Go on, let's have a sip.'

He moves the glass out of her reach. 'Better not, Moody, you know. Just in case.'

33
Astrid

The Shard building looms, as if London, pierced, has since fallen and pooled around the hilt of a blade. Christ, what a day. A morning lost in court, watching the parents and uncle of the Vietnamese marihuana growers getting torn to shreds. It looked like the children would be put into care. The whole case was uncomfortable. The letter of the law should be followed. Then, why did it feel so wrong?

She walks fast, making up for her lateness. Bloody trains. She checks the name of the pub, and thumb scrolls up to the exchange with Jenna that preceded it. Something niggles at the detective in her.

A: I think I can make it up later x

The reply:

J: Only if you can. No pressure.

A: Pa—lease. Pressure? Me? See you on shoot. x

J: For reals? Can't wait! For you, I can ALWAYS make space in my busy schedule, xxx

She darkens the screen, pockets it. Keeps walking. On face value, it's all fine but she sifts. Analyses.

I can *always* make room for you, and what? You can't for me?

Completely unfair. She could probably sleep for twelve hours straight, but where was she? In London, making the effort. Astrid fixes a smile, not letting the negativity in.

You're here to have a good time.

The pub is warm, noisy. Jenna's crowd are easy to spot. A

few actors she vaguely recognises, the film and production crew. All young, edgy types and she self-consciously runs her hand over the bristles of her undercut, as if clinging onto her one little touch of rebelliousness.

Jenna, wearing an olive-green beret and a loose Argyle sweater, has her knees up to her chin, hugging them in as if on their own couch at home. She's deep in conversation with a pretty redhead; the female lead in the series. Astrid plants a smile on her face and banishes away any jealousy.

'Hey, you made it!' Jenna pops up, abandoning the redhead and plants a soft, lingering kiss on the lips. Ice cold. Breath strawberry-sweet.

'Hi, you. On the daiquiris already?'

'It's not *that* early. Come and meet everyone.'

Self-consciousness melts. Confidence manifests.

'Hey everyone,' she holds up a hand, 'my round, what's everyone want?'

By her third long-neck, she's enjoying herself.

Investigations were a drug, enthralling, but wore you down. She really needed to blow off a little steam.

A drunk scriptwriter mines her for real-life situations she's worked on to add *verisimilitude* into scenes of a crime thriller he's writing.

'Give it up, my Astrid's a total pro. Whenever I ask her about that cobra murder case she's working on, she won't tell me shit.'

She likes the possessive *my,* Jenna inserts before her name.

'Hooooly shit,' the redhead says. Irish, blue eyes and a constellation of freckles on her beautiful symmetrical face. Astrid hates her. 'I read about that in the paper, you're working on it?'

She nods, takes a swig, aware all eyes are on her suddenly.

A boy leans in. 'You can talk generics though, right? Like I'm auditioning for a part as a detective next week. What's it like for real?'

She frowns. 'Right now… like being a dog in a field full of rabbits and not knowing which one to chase after.' In her head it sounded funnier. Her audience is left flat. 'I'm just… It takes a lot of energy and focus and–'

'What she's too diplomatic to say, folks,' Jenna cuts in, 'is that this is her night off and she doesn't want to think about the bloody case, so someone buy her a drink!'

The one with the audition volunteers, and Astrid mouths a thank you to Jenna, though in truth she'd have loved to have talked about it. Could have chewed their ears off all night about it. But she can't. Keeping it bottled up, her thoughts to herself, *that's* what takes the energy.

Jenna squeezes her knee under the table.

Her phone vibrates in her pocket. An e-mail from Gardner. She skims it, gathers that the AI has picked up Austin Pemberton's Volvo within the vicinity of the Kitteridge Practice during the death window. Her heart pounds.

'So much for the night off?'

'Right.' Astrid closes her eyes, admonishing herself. 'Sorry. What were we talking about again?'

Out of her periphery, the redhead is playing with the straw, rolling it along the line of her lips while staring at Jenna.

34
Melody

Melody carries one end of a large tank. Inside, a twisted mess of snakes writhe and coil. Four? Five? She can't tell.

The crowd parts revealing a roped-off area. Behind it, is what Olaf refers to as "the track". The track is made up of a series of transparent tubes, each its own lane.

'Down,' Olaf grunts. The relief in her shoulder is bliss. 'Wait here,' Olaf says, and disappears to the end of the track.

She scans the crowd for a likely Sheridan. Men are dotted around, standing on strategically positioned crates next to whiteboards with odds written on, taking money, making a note for those with lines of credit. The crowd strains to look at the tank by her feet. She crouches down and counts them properly. Five. Patterned with identical near-diamond patterns on greyish-black skin. Betting on this must be beyond random. No form guides or physical tells in the paddock. The snakes were indistinguishable. And this was where Martin racked up his debt? *Their* massive debt.

Olaf is lowering something into the end of one of the tubes. 'Oh…' she says, realisation connecting like metal to a magnet. What were they? Iguanas? Chameleons? He places one at the end of each tube.

Olaf holds up his hand to someone, then the voice booms on the speaker, 'Place your final bets, please.'

When Olaf returns, she can't help herself. 'This is patently wrong! What are you doing to these poor animals?'

He shakes her off. 'Trust me. If I had a choice, I wouldn't be doing this.' His voice is hitched with worry. 'There'll be time for a morality lesson later, not now! Open the hatches on the lanes.'

With a pair of long snake tongs, Olaf fishes into the tank and secures one of the snakes while she opens the transparent box for lane one. He drops the snake in, she closes the top hatch and they repeat the process until all five snakes are loaded.

'What are they?'

'Racer snakes,' Olaf says, he doesn't look happy. He makes a sign to someone to hurry up. 'It's too cold in here, these lamps aren't generating enough heat.'

'One minute. Final bets paaalease,' the voice on the PA booms.

'When I say go, I need you to pull the release.' He shows her where.

All around the track, behind rope, men gather. Pre-race chatter and excitement echoes around the barn. At the far end of the tube, the little reptiles twitch and assess their final prison.

'Three should win,' Olaf says, almost to himself. 'It better.'

Melody doesn't know what to say, the sense that she is part of this spectacle, enabling it, disgusts her.

The countdown starts over the PA.

'On zero, release!' Olaf shouts.

'Three, two, one…'

A roar explodes from the crowd. For a moment nothing happens.

Olaf taps the back of the boxes, trying to frighten them into action, urging them on in some Viking tongue.

Then one goes, number three. Then another, then a third. They shoot at incredible speed down their tubes, draining from one end of the tube to the other like sand in a tipped rainmaker.

Braying shouts, the red-faced excitement, swearing, jostling of the crowd. The emotion spilling out of them all, it made no sense.

A bell sounds.

'Number three, the winner!'

Pockets of celebration. Moans from the rest. Olaf lets out huge sigh of relief, mutters something under his breath. The excitement recedes, winners and losers reconvene at the bar.

Olaf tongs the two that didn't leave the starter boxes and returns them to the tank.

'The humidity, the heat, it isn't right.'

Melody walks along the tube to the end. One of the snakes is in a ball, squeezing the life out of the baby iguana, like a twitching intestine. This might be prey and predator, but it is not natural, not on a January evening in a hay barn in Sussex.

Olaf returns each of the snakes back to the tank. Melody helps him carry it back to the van, thinking, *How many more hours of this do I have to endure?*

'I guess that sort of worked,' Olaf says, sliding open his van. 'Richie saw a nature documentary. Wanted to recreate it. It's not easy though, these reptiles aren't performance animals. He doesn't want to hear it though. It's all, just make it happen.' He snaps his fingers.

'Where is Sheridan?'

Olaf doesn't answer, but affixes clasps to hold the tank in place. There are other tanks in there, covered in cloth, the tank light spidering into a halo through the black fabric. There's the hum of a generator, Olaf checking the temperatures of each of the tanks, back turned to her.

She takes two quick pictures with her camera phone. 'What else do you have in here?"

'You should go, you'll be needed,' Olaf says, without turning.

There's a small queue at the hog roast, but she isn't the slightest bit hungry. Inside, the men gather around the central baled arena.

Vet bag slung over her shoulder, she pushes through to the front and sees two dog-handlers. their muzzled charges straining at their leashes. A Staffy and a Japanese tosa, the handlers barely able to keep hold. People hold out fistfuls of cash and yell out numbers.

The handlers remove the muzzles. The barking is razor sharp with intent. Foam gathers around the black lips of the tosa, it doesn't look as intimidating as the muscular Staffy, but it is no less dangerous.

The countdown begins and her mettle gives way.

She cannot watch, turning her back as the barking reaches a crescendo. The mauling, the yelping of one, the deafening yells of the crowd. Melody holds her hands over her ears, clamps her teeth together. She tries playing music in her head, but nothing comes.

The crowd's excitement pops like a balloon. It is over. She turns to see a limping tosa and the Staffy lying in a bloody heap on the floor. The handlers are in the ring.

Melody climbs up the bales and drops into the arena, snapping on latex gloves and drops next to the Staffy.

It's bulbous rib cage shakes and shudders. Still alive. Just.

The owner is lock-jawed, tears welling up in his eyes.

'I'm a vet.'

'Do it,' he says, with an edge to his voice.

Melody can't process it. The pain she is seeing. If he cared about his dog, why would he fight it? Let it get hurt? She gets out a syringe and a vial of Pentobarbital and for a moment considers jabbing it into the arm of the handler.

'How much does he weigh?

'Forty pounds.'

'About eighteen kilos?' She calculates aloud, drawing forty mil into the syringe and sinks it into the rear leg muscle. She pats the dog on the flank, stroking it. 'It'll all be over in a moment, shhh.'

The idiot handler rests a head on his fur, muttering something.

She excuses herself to check on the tosa, more wary, instructing the handler to muzzle it. There's a nasty bite mark near the neck.

'He'll be alright, fucking hard bastard this one,' the handler says.

'I'll need to clean the wound and I'd recommend antibiotics to be on the safe side.'

'Hear that?' He yells over. 'Mine's fine. Not a fucking pussy like your Staffy.'

Something shifts in the atmosphere, she back-pedals. The Staffy owner rises from his crouch slowly, fists trembling by his side. When he turns, there's a knife in his hand.

Her back bumps into something soft. The bale wall. She's retreated as far as she can. She could climb out… but doesn't, she stands transfixed.

'Fucking come on then.' At his side, the tosa growls.

In a moment the two men are a blur of tangled limbs. The dog, limp, jumping around them in excitement. A shout goes up, people appear around the arena, shouting, jeering.

They fight over the knife, rolling through the dirt and bloody hay. A chaos of limbs and grunting. Then Pug is there, two henchmen fall in behind, but Pug doesn't need them. He separates the men and without even a microsecond of hesitation thumps one in the face and then headbutts the other. They drop in turn, like felled trees, each unconscious before they even hit the floor.

Her hand clutches her chest.

Heart beating through it fit to burst.

He wipes his forehead with a handkerchief, motions to his helpers. They drag the unconscious and bleeding men into a sitting up position, against the hay.

'Kitteridge. Sort these two pricks out.' Pug thumbs to them, and climbs up out of the arena to cheers.

She unsticks her feet from the ground and moves forward, stepping through the smeared blood.

She stands over the men a moment, knocked out and lying in her shadow. Imagines having done it herself.

Oddly, it makes her feel a little stab of power.

35
Astrid

Astrid escapes from the duvet. She stretches. Stiff, uncomfortable. Bloody pull-out beds. Her head is fuzzy, mouth so dry, cotton wool would come out instead of words. Jenna still sleeps. There's a small patch of drool in the shape of a comet by her mouth. Adorable.

They're somewhere in Peckham. The flat belongs to some film school buddy of Jenna's, who lets her crash when she works in London. Astrid pads into the kitchen; full ashtrays, the sink crowded with dirty dishes, and barely an inch of countertop clear. Of course, there's no clean glasses. She holds her hair and hangs her head under the tap, plastering the other side of her face with ketchup and gravy from one of the stacked plates.

'Gross.' She turns on the tap, rinses the plates and lifts them onto the draining board, clearing the space. Then she washes her face, hangs her mouth under the tap and gulps the water down greedily.

Does Jenna like this chaos, this break from the order of their flat in Brighton?

Astrid washes up some mugs and makes two cups of tea, and sits in the lounge by her sleeping lover.

She sips at the tea, reads her messages. There's one from Smithes sent at seven thirty this morning.

Call me when you're up.

It's a quarter to nine.

She's heard whisperings that the guru is getting impatient.

Which can only mean the higher-ups are downright restless. Fucking infuriating really. One moment they were moving too fast by arresting the wife, now they were being too slow and methodical.

Astrid pulls a jumper over her head and takes her tea outside, leaving the front door ajar. It's an ex-council block, spruced up with lots of potted plants and flower trays. On the street people are out, delivery trucks, and cyclists.

Smithes picks up on the second ring.

'Morning.'

'Good morning, sir.' She hears birds. 'Are you outside?'

'Only in my garden. Meditating.'

'On the case?'

'Not exactly…' He says slowly. 'Emptying the mind rather than filling it. Are you in Brighton?'

She leans on the railings, the invisible hands of her hangover squeeze and compress her skull. 'London. Why?' He's forgotten she was supposed to have the day off.

'I have a favour to ask.'

'Ask away.'

'I've been invited to a retirement luncheon today with Burrows, and a lot of present and former top brass. Someone dropped out, and Burrows is nudging me to do a bit more schmoozing to raise my profile. I've told the control room and the team that you're in the chair for the rest of the day. I hope that's okay?'

She could hardly say no. Perhaps Smithes could casually drop her name into conversation too. 'I could be back by lunchtime.'

'That'll be fine. I appreciate it, Astrid. I'm keen to follow up on this Austin Pemberton, I saw Gardner had a hit on his car. See what headway you can make.'

'Of course. Good luck, sir.'

When she returns to the flat, Jenna is stretching with a

massive yawn, hair in a tangle, a warm smile on her face.

'Morning, you.'

'Morning.' Astrid points to the mug. 'Should still be warm.'

'Star. Wow, my head.' Jenna takes a sip, winces.

'Want some paras?'

'Go on, you've twisted my arm.'

Astrid retrieves a blister pack from the zipped pouch in her handbag, pops them out. 'I feel like a cult leader.'

'Or communion. Same thing, I guess. Cheers.' Astrid washing hers down with the dregs of her tea. The pills barge down her throat and it's like her head lightens instantly. Psychosomatic.

'You were on the phone out there?'

'Yeah. Listen.'

Jenna tugs a hand through the tangle of her coal black hair, reads her face like she's reading lines of a screenplay. 'Let me guess. You've got to go back early?'

'I'm covering Smithes for the day. Late notice. I'm sorry, but if you can get your arse in gear, we could squeeze in a quick breakfast at that place you were raving about last night.'

Jenna gathers up her hair and ties it, springs to her feet. 'You know what, Detective? I'll take it.'

'Jesus Christ, I love you.' Astrid plants a kiss on her lips. 'You're the best of your kind. If you were a broccoli, you'd be a tender stem.'

'Outrageous.'

Astrid throws Jenna's her jeans, wondering if she'll make the 10:45 or the 11:02.

Breakfast delivers. A stack of bubble and squeak patties: potato, spring onion, bacon, and spinach, with a poached egg on top, drizzled with hollandaise sauce. She washes it down with a Virgin Mary and two hastily drunk coffees.

By the time Astrid sticks her head into the MI Room 2, her

hangover has all but retreated.

'Just you?'

Sarah Gardner looks up from her work station. 'Collins is doing his Fire Safety. Horley's gone to grab some lunch, ma'am, and the rest are out in the field I think.'

'So… the email last night, about Pemberton's Volvo? It appeared near the Kitteridge Practice during the death window, correct?'

'Right. Want to see?'

Astrid stands behind as Gardner brings the footage up.

'The Volvo appears on Church Road at twenty-five minutes past seven, disappears off camera. Then Mr Pemberton is back on camera disappearing into a Thai restaurant. He emerges eight minutes later with what looks like a takeaway.'

Gardner fast forwards, switching cameras. The Volvo is there, but the next time his car appears is five minutes after eight.

'So that's what, thirty-two minutes in the camera's blind spot? How far is it to the Kitteridge Practice from there?'

'According to Google, two point eight kilometres.'

'Could he have got there and back on foot in that time?'

Gardner leans her head one way, then the other, weighing it up. Shrugs. 'Five point six kilometres. Very doable for an athlete.'

'Our man's no athlete. Does a lot of walking though.' Astrid gnaws on her lip. 'Fancy getting out of here for a bit?'

'I'm going through MK's finances.' Gardner points at the screen.

'Come on,' Astrid says. 'It's good to have a break from the screen, do some real detective work.'

Astrid enters the Thai on Church Road, holding the door open for Gardner. A little bell tinkles above the door. There's a fish tank with a few colourful specimens in, and a lot of bamboo and fake leaves.

'Hello, table for two?' A waitress picks up two menus.

The scents of lime, coriander, and chilli, waft through from a kitchen. Despite her large breakfast, she can't help but feel hungry.

She flashes her warrant card. 'DI Van Doren, this is my colleague Sarah Gardner. Could I have a word with the manager?'

After a brief exchange in the kitchen, a pretty middle-aged woman appears. Gardner shows the manager the CCTV footage of Austin Pemberton.

'Yes. Mr Pemberton. He is a regular. Spring rolls, fish cakes, and a red beef curry. Always the same.' She smiles.

'So, you can confirm he had an order, waited for it, and left?'

'Over there, yes.' She points to a coat-stand and three chairs. 'Five minutes maybe and he go.'

'Thanks for your help.'

Astrid leads them out.

'That went as expected,' Gardner says.

'We have to check everything. Even the givens. On the train down, I had this crazy theory.'

'Oh?'

'I thought, what if the snake was kept somewhere in the restaurant? Pemberton goes in, smuggles it out in takeaway bags, pegs it over to the practice and lets it loose.'

'Wow!' Gardner laughs, 'That sounds pretty… I don't want to say far-fetched, but…'

'It's a crackers theory,' Astrid admits. 'But it isn't impossible. Well. Maybe it is. That's what we need to find out now.' She strips off her jumper and hands it to Gardner. She's wearing her sports top, having got changed at Sussex House before they set out.

Astrid jumps up and down on the spot trying to get some warmth into her calves and checks the route she has to run on her phone.

'Right, you ready to time me?'

Gardner's lively eyes take her in, 'Oh, I'm ready. But are you?'

'Alright, off I go.' Astrid takes off, not at a sprint, but a fast jog. Austin Pemberton's running speed was a tricky variable to predict. He'd walked Lucky every day for God knows how many years. He certainly wasn't unfit, but he was no bolt of lightning either.

She cuts through the car park of an apartment block, skirting the building and connecting up with a footpath. Then she's on the parallel road. Right. Round a dog walker, her breath still light. She's reminded how much she hates running, the compression of joints, the erosion of her anatomy. Cycling is much more fluid.

Hot armpits, cold face, complaining lungs. She rounds a corner, running at a good jog and reaches the Kitteridge Practice. She runs over the chessboard path, taps the bright front door, turns, and begins the return journey.

Jenna's trainers are rubbing. Any longer and she'd have a collection of blisters to attend to later.

Gardner waits, and presses the screen of her phone theatrically to stop the timer. Astrid plants her hands on her knees, taking in delicious gulps of air.

'Well?'

'Twenty-nine minutes and forty-eight seconds. Pemberton had two minutes longer.'

She stands straight, hands on hips, and wipes a bead of already cooling sweat from her brow. 'I wasn't leathering it, either. But would that be enough spare time?'

'Actually, I've watched some videos on YouTube. Experts can catch cobras in less than forty seconds. But to have time to release it, to let it bite and then capture it? Unlikely, but not impossible.'

‘Mr Pemberton’s still in the frame then, with some serious questions to answer.’

‘Like his thirty-two minutes in the camera blind spot to account for,’ Gardner says.

‘At the exact time Martin Kitteridge was murdered.’

36
Melody

'Auntie Mel, come look at our guinea pigs!'

Melody dabs her mouth with her napkin.

'Go ahead, if you're finished?' Ally says, picking up the dish of the last few uneaten potatoes, and the gravy boat.

'I've finished,' Melody says. 'The chicken was a little overdone and dry, but the rest was fine.'

Tristan snorts into his wine. 'Excuse me?'

'Duly noted for next time,' says Ally, smiling. 'Dessert in five. Pavlova.'

Melody accompanies Lucy and Samantha up to their bedroom and meets Pip and Squeak. Their tank is big and clean and the guinea pigs are in fine condition. One is a real scrabbler and scratches her forearm with its claw when she handles it. Of the two, it's her favourite.

After dessert she observes bath time as an uninterested social worker might. The excitement, the yelling, the constant refereeing by Ally. What was it that drew people to parenthood? Statistically it was irrefutable that more people wanted to do it than not. Ally often talked about the burning glow of love for her children, but for her, Melody, there was nothing but a clearing where that fire of love should be.

'You can be my sounding boards,' Melody says, once the kids are asleep. She takes the Manilla folder from her backpack, eases off the stretchy string and places her documents on the coffee table. Organising them into distinct piles.

'And this is what, exactly?' Ally asks.

'My plan.' Melody shows her the printout of her list of suspects, now transformed into a spreadsheet. 'It's my list of suspects and material gathered to date.'

Tristan reaches for one of the stacks. 'You know, Melody. I don't know if you've heard about this, but there's this organisation that does all this work for you. It's called the police.'

'Is he being sarcastic?' she says to Ally.

'Why is my name on here?' Tristan asks, jabbing his finger at the list. 'Me? Really?'

'I put everyone I know with a connection to Martin. Don't worry, you didn't get a tick in any of my columns.'

'Marvellous!'

She gives them a moment to leaf through her supporting work.

Tristan holds up the newspaper clipping of Martin and Kathy from seven years ago, 'Pretty spurious.'

'I know. Poor Kathy couldn't hurt a fly. Still. It's my method.'

'Are these Sheridan's snakes?' Ally says, holding up the photos of the inside of Olaf's van. 'Pretty damning, no?'

'Okay, let's say it was Sheridan. Is there anything you know, substantive, here?' Tristan asks.

She points to the printout containing Martin's account summary of the withdrawals leading up to his death, all neatly highlighted in bright green marker. 'This shows his gambling problem.'

'The statements don't prove anything. How can you show that he owed them money?'

'I have two pieces of proof.'

Tristan looks through the file. 'Where? I can't see anything.'

'One, they murdered Cleopatra as a warning when I didn't meet the payment deadline. The detective saw it with her own eyes. And two, you knew about the debt, Tristan. You've been to these gatherings with Martin. You could give testimony; dates, rough amounts spent, all that.'

He leans back in his chair. 'That's why you invited yourself over.'

'It wasn't for the chicken.' Melody looks at Ally. 'Though the rest was perfectly adequate, as I said.'

'I've got two girls and Ally to think about,' Tristan says in a low voice. 'These people have a reputation.'

'Martin is dead, Tristan. He was your friend.'

Ally reaches over and squeezes his hand. 'Babe. Just hear her out.'

'Did you know she was going to ask me this?'

'No!'

'You're a piss poor liar, Al.' Tristan reaches for the bottle but finds it empty. 'Fuck. Go on then, gang up on me.'

'It's not about ganging up,' Ally says. 'What sort of role models are we to the girls if we can't stand up to the likes of Sheridan?'

Melody leans in. 'There's a clear narrative here, Tristan. Martin owed money to morally bankrupt criminals who use exotic snakes in their sick betting circles. It just so happens Martin was killed by a venomous snake. You think that's a coincidence? I want the police to look in the correct place, for which I need to be taken seriously, and not as some neurotic wife.'

'I'm not a miracle worker.'

'But you'll do it, Tristan. I really must insist upon that,' Melody says. 'Confirm that these events are real. That you witnessed Martin racking up debt to his eyeballs. The truth, nothing more.'

'Would I get in trouble, for going along to an illegal event like that?'

Ally shakes her head. 'Surely not if you were co-operating.'

'Squealing. Grassing. Call it what it is.'

'Don't be such a child,' Melody says.

Tristan squints into the bottom of his wine glass, rolling the stem across his palm this way and that. He points at the folder on the table. 'If I talk about Sheridan to the cops, we need to be sure he's going down.'

'Chicken and egg. They will need something to go on.'

'Tris,' Ally urges.

He frowns. 'Fine. If the police happen to ask, they'll hear the truth from me, okay?'

'I won't thank you for simply telling the truth, Tristan. You and I would start to have problems if you didn't.' She holds his eye until he looks away, to Ally for help, who holds up her hands in a *Don't ask me* sort of way.

Melody gathers up the papers and starts stacking them back into her folder.

'Sheridan is not going to know what hit him.'

37
Astrid

A call from the control room brings her back to Sussex House.

Hugh Forrester wants to go on the record.

Excited, she returns Gardner to her duties and scoops up a bored-looking Collins from the Operation Windbourne room.

'How was the fire safety training? I'm due next month.'

'Don't get me wrong, it's important stuff,' he says. 'But do they really need to make it so bleeding tedious?'

She laughs, in a good mood. 'You ready to have a run at Mr Forrester?'

'Chomping at the bit.'

Mr Forrester is chatting to a lawyer when they enter the interview room. The lawyer's one she's dealt with before, a reasonable enough woman from memory. Hugh Forrester is wearing a dark navy suit with a fitted cream shirt. A prim gentleman, proud of his clean appearance. Astrid makes the introductions, and gets straight down to business.

'So, Mr Forrester. There's something you'd like to tell us?'

The lawyer puts up a staying hand to her client. 'I'd like my client's willingness to co-operate on the record, and we'd like your assurance that what he is about to share can be kept in the strictest of confidences.'

Astrid leans forward. 'The co-operation is noted and welcome. I give no assurances until I understand its impact upon the case.'

There's a pause.

'Come on, you know how it works,' she says to the lawyer. 'We can't promise anything.'

'It's fine,' Hugh says, in a low voice. 'She'll understand.'

Astrid shoots Collins a look, for theatre more than anything. 'What will I understand, Mr Forrester?'

He clears his throat, clasps his hands together on the table and looks into space as if reading off an invisible teleprompter.

'I realise now that I may be under suspicion and would like to clear my name. It's about my whereabouts, at the time of Martin's death.'

'You said you were walking into Brighton, to go to meet friends in a pub?'

'I did say that yes. It wasn't exactly true.'

Collins foot is tap tapping. 'Go on.'

'During the hours of Martin's death… I was at an…an establishment in Hove for gentlemen to… be with other like-minded gentlemen.'

I see. 'The Boiler Room?'

He looks into his hands. His shame irritates her.

'And you can prove you were there, Mr Forrester?'

'The establishment will. I had to sign in and sign out. I have a receipt too.' He offers it.

'And once you've confirmed it, Detective, my client would like the utmost discretion. What he does in his private time is his business as long as he is operating within the law.'

'We're hardly going to notify the *Argus* about it,' Collins says.

But she's far more irritated. 'When you aren't forthcoming, you slow the investigation down. I'm glad you've finally found the backbone to come in, Mr Forrester.'

He plants a palm down on the table. 'Backbone? How d–'

'I think we're done here. We'll see if this checks out.' She stands and indicates the door.

When Mr Forrester passes, she catches his arm.

'Where's your pride in who you are?'

He yanks his arm away, brushes down his suit in two stiff sweeps of the hand. 'The relative freedom and understanding you enjoy now, Detective, had its price. I'll take no lectures from those who didn't have to foot the bill.'

Stunned, she watches them leave.

Collins whistles.

'What?' she snaps.

'Just to check… the Boiler Room… is that like a–'

'Christ, Collins. It's a gay sauna! You know, where men go to fuck each other silly.'

She'd said it to shock, but Collins lets out a short hoot of laughter.

And Astrid can't help but crack a smile either. 'Well… good for them, I suppose.' She runs a hand through her hair. 'Christ, Collins. Not my finest moment. Slight hangover, it's turning me into a grouch.'

'You might still catch him.'

'You're right. We wouldn't want any complaints now, would we?'

Astrid catches up with him in the car park. It's dark, lit by the reversing lights of the first few cars heading home.

'Mr Forrester, a moment, please.'

He waits, stony faced. 'The type who needs to get in the last word? Save it.'

'I came to apologise; I shouldn't have said that back there. It was rude and wrong.'

Something passes over his face, a stab of anguish perhaps. 'Why say such spiteful things?'

'I had no right. Martin Kitteridge's killer is still out there. When I found out you were holding something back, I got annoyed. Got personal. Went instinctively for where it would hurt.'

'Look I–' He rubs the back of his head, stares at his feet. 'There was something else…'

'No more secrets, Mr Forrester. Let's be open, respectful.'

'It's about Martin.'

'What about him?'

'He was having an affair.'

It takes her a second to process… nothing had come up from his e-mails or phone records to suggest an affair. 'With you?'

Hugh lets out a mirthful smirk. 'Oh, please. Martin pointed straight north.'

'Why now? Why not say anything when we first spoke with you?'

'Melody. I know she looks like she's armour-shelled, but losing Martin must have been bad enough, can you imagine–'

'Stop. Grab your lawyer if you still want her present. But we need to get this down on the record.' She grasps his shoulder. 'You've done the right thing in sharing this information, Hugh. Let's go back inside and do this the right way.'

Thursday morning. Astrid relishes the moment of peace. The quiet. The bare, leafless beech trees and evergreen shrubs, the neatness of the grounds. There's a message from Jenna, saying she's thinking of her and apologising for not being there. Astrid pulls on gloves and gathers the bunch of tulips from the passenger seat.

Two figures stand by a gravestone in the distance. Her mum, and Ian. She's surprised Adam, her step-father, hasn't come.

Ian clasps her hand warmly. 'Good to see you again so soon, Astrid.'

Mum gathers her into a hug. 'Come here, poppet.'

'No Dad, then?'

'He's got a stinking cold; thought he'd give us a bit of space you know. Still funny about it after all these years. Tulips! How lovely.' Mum cups the petals of one with a gloved hand.

The tulips are a little nod to her father's Dutch heritage. A tad gauche, perhaps, but at least it wasn't clogs and pancakes. 'I'll put them down here.' Astrid places them by a six pack of beer and a bunch of lilies.

'Beer, Ian? Not planning on cracking them open here are you? I might have to arrest you.'

Ian Goodworth looks pleased with himself. 'We used to drink those after shift together back in the day, sitting right on the bonnet of the patrol car, looking out to sea. Different time then, course. Nope, these ones are for Sandy, or the elements.'

The tramps more like.

'You look tired, poppet.' Her mother links an arm through her own. 'I know how that organisation works, they take and take. Don't give them everything you have.' A warning stare, a nod to the tombstone.

The engraving is a little mossy, but still legible.

Sanders Van Doren
1949-1990
Loving Father, Husband &
Dutiful Copper

She rests a hand on stone. It's funny. In every memory of her father, he is always in his uniform.

'You know, I had dozens of partners over the years, but none ever came close to him,' Ian says. Tears well in his eyes. 'I'll never forgive myself for what happened to him. I should have…'

Not all this again. She's heard versions of this self-recrimination before. 'It wasn't your fault, Ian. There was nothing you could have done.' Astrid rests a hand on his shoulder.

Respects paid, they walk back to the car park together, her arm still linked to her mother's.

Leaves whisper under their feet.

'You off back to work now, poppet?'

Astrid checks the time. 'Another busy day ahead.'

Ian asks, 'How's that case going?'

'A lot of promising leads.'

'Good. You know I saw that lot yesterday at a retirement dinner. Smithes brown-nosing the Chief Constable. Burrows pumping the flesh.'

'You were there? I had to cover for Bill.'

'That is what you are at the moment, Astrid. Cover for Bill. In every sense.'

A blackbird swoops from a branch, pecks at the ground and takes off with a worm in its beak.

'I wonder if you should try something different, Astrid.'

'Mum!'

'It doesn't have to be out the force necessarily, but there are plenty of roles where you can make a difference without putting yourself in harm's way.'

'Bringing people to justice does make a difference, Mum.'

'Justice?' Ian gives a derisive laugh. 'I thought that once. You think Sandy got any justice? The years beat it out of you. You see the innocent locked up, the guilty walk enough times, enough bloody unsolved cases to stuff a sports hall… justice.' He shakes his head.

'Ian, don't,' Mum says. 'Not today, please.'

'You think I'm naive. But without the hope of justice, what else is there? What peace for the victims and their families? There has to be a reckoning.'

'A reckoning.' He nods. 'For what it's worth, I hope you're right. Just try not to become like me.'

'Oh, I don't know Ian. You've not done too badly for yourself.'

But the light comment falls flat, the pain behind his eyes overwhelms his sparkle. And she hopes, badly, that she can heed his advice.

*

At Sussex House, she sticks her head in the MI Room 2.

'Anyone seen DCI Smithes?'

Heads shake.

Critchlow appears. 'Ma'am? Do you have a minute?'

'Of course.'

'We've checked out the address listed for Olaf Gudmundsen in Bexhill.' Critchlow holds up his phone. The screen shows a photo of a boarded-up bungalow. He swipes, showing her more. 'Mountain of mail through the letterbox. We've spoken to the neighbours. Seems nobody's been there for at least six months.'

'Vehicle?'

'I've got an alert issued on the ANPR to notify me if it turns up. Nothing yet. He's probably driving with fake plates.'

'Keep me posted. Thanks.'

Astrid pulls up a chair next to Horley and writes down a name on a Post-it. She doesn't want anyone to hear yet, not until she's spoken to Smithes. 'I want you to pull up all correspondence between Martin and this name, do a manual read through.'

Horley barely glances away from the screen. 'Manual? That'll take longer. Can't we just keyword it?'

'I'm okay with longer. But do it as a priority, please. Flag anything that jumps out, as soon as you have it.'

He stops typing. She has his full attention now. 'Am I alright to touch this paper, or is it red hot?'

'Get on it, Horley.' She makes a zipping motion across her mouth.

'Yes, ma'am.'

She moves on to the next thing on her mental to do list. Pemberton. She finds a quiet spot, and dials his number.

He picks up on the eighth ring. 'Hello?'

'Mr Pemberton, I hope I'm not disturbing? It's Detective Van Doren.'

'Detective. All well, I hope?'

'There was a detail from our interview I wanted to go over with you, if you can spare a minute?'

'Please, by all means.' He sounds at ease; she imagines him in his armchair, a mug of coffee in hand. Or perhaps a glass of rosé. It is ten a.m. after all.

'On January the tenth, in your statement you said you were at home all evening?'

'Yes, that's right.' He sounds a little less sure of himself now.

'Mr Pemberton, we have CCTV footage of you and your Volvo in Hove during the two-hour period in which Martin died.'

'Really?'

'Yes, really. Going into a Thai restaurant on Church Road.'

'Blimey, yes! Of course. I completely forgot. I picked up a takeaway. I'm dreadfully sorry, I thought I'd done that on the Thursday, but yes, by George it must have been the Friday.'

So far, so acceptable. Now for the trap. 'And, then? You drove straight home and tucked in front of the TV, I imagine?'

'Not exactly,' Pemberton side-steps. A pause. 'I was rather peckish. Please don't think ill of me, but I scoffed the whole lot in the car. It's all better when it's hot, especially the spring rolls and fish cakes. They go soggy otherwise.'

'So, you sat in your car and ate it all? Why not eat in the restaurant?'

'It is a sad man who dines alone. If I must do it, I'd rather be in the privacy of my car or house…'

'I see. Thank you for clearing that up for me, Mr Pemberton. I won't take up any more of your time.'

She rings off, sensing that if he is lying, he's very good at it. But then, murderers often are.

Through the gap in the slatted blinds she spots a Smithesesque shadow passing. She rushes, pops her head out. It's him, walking with someone. 'DCI Smithes, sir!'

He turns, and so does Burrows, the Chief Super, and she

curses inwardly.

'Excuse me for interrupting. Sir.' She gives Burrows a deferential nod.

The guru keeps his expression calm. Inclines his head towards the lift. 'Walk with us.'

'When you have a moment, we have a possible breakthrough in the case.'

Burrows raises an eyebrow. 'Care to join us in the lift, we're on our way to a meeting. If you don't object to a curious eavesdropper?'

Sweat gathers in the small of her back. They wait for the lift to empty, then the three of them enter. The doors close.

'Hugh Forrester, the receptionist, suspected the victim was having an affair.'

'Who with?' Smithes asks.

'Kathy Spellerman, the vet nurse.'

Burrow's lets out a whistle. 'The jilted lover? Or maybe the wife knew?'

'Mr Forrester doesn't think Mrs Kitteridge knew.'

'Let's confirm it definitely took place,' Smithes says. 'Bring in Spellerman now, under arrest if necessary,' he says, pointedly. 'We'll interview together at say,' he checks his watch, 'anytime from one onwards.'

'What made this man come forward?' Burrows asks.

'Bridge building, sir.'

'Good police work more like. Detective. Keep it up.' Burrows nods. The lift doors part. The two men leave, off to their important meeting. Astrid remains in the lift, stuck in her box. What did Burrows make of her?

She fires off a message to Critchlow to bring in Spellerman, hoping he's not off on another task already. Arrest might not be necessary, and she'd bet Kathy would come in voluntarily. She'd come across as the meek, goody-two-shoes sort.

Though looks could be deceiving.

Ground level. At the coffee machine she feeds in change, chooses to take it black. It hums in a monotone. Thank Christ her normal desk isn't within earshot; this buzzing would drive her crazy. She takes a sip, burns her lip. Then sees a face she can't quite correlate to the familiar office environment.

It's Melody Kitteridge.

Collins is a step behind her, struggling to keep pace. Has she found out about the affair? Mrs Kitteridge has a folder tucked under her arm and a determined air that screams that this will be a pain in the arse. Damn, why hadn't she insisted, *insisted* on her using Baqri? She was an excellent FLO, trained for it.

'Mrs Kitteridge. You've come all the way to Hollingbury to see us, when you could have just called.'

She practically thrusts the folder into her hands. 'We need to talk, somewhere quiet.'

Collins looks apologetic. He must have signed her in.

She sighs. This was all she needed. 'You'd better follow me, then, Mrs Kitteridge.'

38
Melody

The drab interview room is presumably decorated to drain interviewees of their fight.

'Is he going to Colombia to fetch the coffee himself?'

A smile tugs at the edges of Detective Van Doren's mouth. 'Here he is. I hope you're ready to be disappointed.'

Detective Collins puts a coffee down in front of her in a disposable cup with a sugar packet and a stirrer.

'Not very environmentally friendly, is it?'

'So, what can we do for you, Mrs Kitteridge?'

'I have a theory about who killed Martin.'

'We're listening.'

Melody leafs through her pages of the bank statements, points a finger to the highlighted amounts. 'Martin, well, *we,* as it transpires, are in a horrendous amount of debt.'

The detective doesn't look surprised. *This much she knows.*

'He was gambling at illegal events. I had no idea to what extent until a man came to threaten me and said the debt was mine now Martin had died.'

Van Doren leans towards her. 'Name? When was this?'

'The day after Martin died. This thug, I don't know his name. I call him Pug because he looks like one. Bald. Arms like tree trunks. A little scar, here, and a sleeper ear-ring.'

'We know him,' Collins says. 'Have you ever heard the name Richie Sheridan?'

'Yes. That's who Martin owes the money to.'

DC Collins looks confused.

'So, the five grand was some sort of pay-off.' Van Doren says.

'A show of good will. It's a fraction of what we owe.'

'And your cat…'

'If you hadn't arrested me, then Cleopatra would still be with us.'

'Mrs Kitteridge,' Detective Van Doren says, 'while that was extremely regrettable, you didn't help yourself. Why couldn't you have come to us with this earlier?'

'Surely that's obvious? This brute said he would "do me in" if I talked to the police. But now, Tristan Campbell, a friend of Martin's, can confirm that Martin went regularly to these illegal gambling events and that he racked up lots of debt there.'

Van Doren is scribbling something down.

'Martin practically cleared us out. He couldn't pay and that's what got him killed.'

'I can see a potential motive there, Mrs Kitteridge.' There's something cautious in Van Doren's tone. 'Proving it is another matter entirely.'

'That's your job, isn't it?' Melody takes a sip of her coffee. It's dreadful.

'Mrs Kitteridge, Sheridan is organised crime, and using a snake is not his normal MO.'

'Then you're badly informed.' Time for the hook. 'Do you know the nature of these gambling events? Live animals in fights and races, including snakes. That's why Martin first went there. He didn't just gamble at these events. He *worked* there.'

She can tell they're shocked. 'In what capacity?'

'He was their so-called "dark vet". He tended to their illegal animals, put down injured dogs after fights. He was the unofficial doctor too, stitching up wounds if the clientele brawled. Anything to avoid contact with hospitals or the police, where real questions might get asked.'

'Snakes? Illegal Gambling? How do you know all this, Mrs

Kitteridge? From this…' Collins checks his notes, 'Tristan Campbell?'

'Tristan will confirm it, yes, but I've seen it with my own eyes too. I went to one.'

'You infiltrated one of these events?'

'On Tuesday, in fact. You're looking at Richie Sheridan's new "dark vet". I must say I wasn't given much choice in the matter; it was either that or they paint my walls again, only this time with my blood.'

'Mrs Kitteridge,' Van Doren says, angry. 'Again! Why didn't you come to us sooner?'

'My way is better.' Melody takes out her phone and shows the detectives the photo she took of the hay barn with the lights spilling out of it. 'Now, in here was where they had the snake race and the dog-fight.'

'You could've got yourself killed.'

'Don't make the mistake these people have, Detective. They think they've got a scared, pliable wife. Someone weak to do their bidding and line their pockets. But they've let a parasite in, and I'll eat them inside out, you see that I don't.'

A look passes between the detectives.

She slides her finger to the next photo. 'Now you'll find this particularly interesting. This is Sheridan's snake handler, Olaf, tending to the snakes in his van.'

'A snake handler?' Collins leans over the photo. 'Dark blue T3 Transporter. Did you get the plates?'

'And are those snake tanks inside?'

'I did get the plates and yes, those are snake tanks.'

'Go back to the beginning, minute by minute. Tell us everything you saw that evening, Mrs Kitteridge.'

Typical. She presents them with the highlight reel and they want to toothcomb the lot. She sighs, and recounts everything she witnessed that evening.

'You can have everything in my folder, all my research. I

have my own copies.'

'And these registrations?' Detective Collins holds up a sheet of paper.

'All the cars at the event, a few of the names I managed to pick up. Our favourite farmer George Dapper was there, by the way. You'll find my other research; my list of suspects and their ranking against my criteria. Supporting evidence such as bank statements and newspaper clippings.'

'Mrs Kitteridge, I can say with confidence that I've never seen anything quite like this before,' Van Doren says, uselessly.

'I've done my part here, Detectives. Now, it's time for you to do yours. These reprehensible people killed Martin. They killed Cleopatra. And they're torturing animals. We must stop them.'

'Mrs Kitteridge…' Van Doren begins, closes her eyes and when they re-open, they have an icy focus. 'Are these people likely to need you as their "dark vet" again?'

'That's why I'm here, Detective. I'm going tomorrow night.'

39
Astrid

In the back of an unmarked car in a lay-by off the A27, Astrid fights her nerves. An orb of light curves from the Amex stadium, a vibrant torch to the black sky above. Brighton & Hove Albion have a game on that evening.

She couldn't give two fucks about football, but from the back seat half-listens to Smithes and Collins talk about the manager, the slim possibility of Europe this season. Her phone rests in her palm, waiting. As soon as Melody Kitteridge gets the location, it'll automatically forward to her own device.

A roar goes up from the crowd.

'One-nil Seagulls. Get in,' Collins says from the driver's seat.

'Bill?' she asks. 'What's the feeling up top on the information provided by Mrs Kitteridge?'

'Are you worried that the wife's gift-wrapped us a lead and put it on our laps, how it makes the investigation look?'

'Yes,' she admits, and touches the window. An insistent chill presses back from the glass, thirstily sapping her body heat.

'It's like football. People only really remember the result.'

Astrid checks her tactical tablet. Horley had set it up to display the location of Melody Kitteridge's Defender, using the same tracking software her husband had used. The dot throbs at her house in Medina Villas. For the op, Melody's codename is The Lioness.

She runs her hand under her undercut, softer now. She'll get

Jenna to run the buzzer over it again tomorrow when she gets home.

'Come on,' she says, impatient. In the seat next to her are their jackets and body armour, a reminder that they don't know what they're walking in to.

Another minute passes. Then her phone vibrates. GPS co-ordinates.

'Incoming.' Both men turn. The map takes a moment to load up. Not what she expected at all. 'Shit.'

'Where?' Smithes demands.

'Newhaven, looks like the industrial estate near the harbour. Am sharing with the team now.'

'Urban? We need somewhere to convene near the site.'

'Three Ponds Holiday Park in Tarring is on the outskirts. They've got space.' Collins offers.

Smithes nods to her to make the call and she reaches for the radio.

Collins pulls off the A26 into the Three Ponds Holiday Park. The lights of mobile homes and motorhomes make the tarmac glisten with recent rain.

The first Tactical Firearm Unit is already there. Astrid checks Melody Kitteridge's progress. Twenty-five minutes away. She steps out and greets the sergeant, finding it hard to speak. The air is cold.

Curtains twitch from the mobile homes

Excepting the team starting in Washington, all are there within ten minutes, but there's no time to waste. One of the sergeants holds a torch. She spreads an enlarged map over the bonnet.

'It's this spot here, a lorry depot in one of the warehouses. There's only two road exits, here and here.' Astrid marks them with a pen.

'Sergeant, you will go in first, ideally we'll contain them in the depot and pen them in there. The primary target is the driver of a dark blue Transporter van: Olaf Gudmundsen, he'll be the one to actually get us Sheridan if we can get him to talk. Arrest Sheridan and any of his lieutenants if they're there. Anyone else present, we need name, ID, reg, and a brief statement before we let them leave.'

'And if they make it out of the depot?' the sergeant asks.

'I just spoke to the control room,' says Smithes. 'Newhaven is providing patrol units to create road blocks at these two spots.'

'It's a second layer of containment,' Astrid says.

'Yes, ma'am. I understand there may be armed people on site and, potentially, attack dogs?'

'That's a very real possibility.'

Smithes clears his throat. 'We have authorisation to use taser guns and rubber bullets, Sergeant, on animal or human; though it goes without saying, the cleaner the better.'

Astrid puts on her own body armour and feels like a beetle, and is grateful to shrug on a POLICE emblazoned jacket over the top.

She checks the tablet. 'The Lioness is seven minutes from destination. Everyone be ready for the Go.'

She gets in the back of the car, lets out a deep breath. 'Come on, Melody. Just give us the nod.'

Then they can spring their trap.

40
Melody

The horn of the ferry reverberates around the town. Less a boat, more a collection of lights, sliding out of the harbour. Melody takes a turning to the industrial estate, dipping down, and loses the view. No sign of the police, which is good. They must be hiding well. She cuts the music. She's made a playlist for the occasion, culminating in "The Final Countdown" by Europe. It is supposed to be energising; perhaps it is, but she needs quiet now.

Off the main road, it's another world. Quiet. Apocalyptic.

The streetlights are weaker, struggling orange orbs against the darkness. Deeper, past the warehouses, chain-links and spiked fencing. Ahead; a huge industrial gate is rolled back. Her destination.

Her senses sharpen, adrenaline channelling through her body.

'You can do this, Melody. It's simple.'

This was her chance to get Sheridan back cleanly. She'd guess it'd be a half hour to an hour before all the punters arrived. Then the small army of police could descend on her signal. The sweet power of retribution, and she held the starter gun.

Melody swings the car into the forecourt. Huge doors gape open. Within, a line of headlights beams out, sharp as stars. A Jeep revs its engine and accelerates towards her.

'Wha–' for a moment she thinks it's trying to ram her but it screeches to a stop beside her.

Pug, in the driver seat, motions for her to lower the window. She does.

'Was it you?' He stabs a finger at her.

'Was what me? What's going on?'

'The pigs are coming. Get out of here, now! I'll deal with you later.'

His Jeep lurches, and is followed by another, it's a blur of tinted SUVs and then Olaf Gudmundsen's dark blue Transporter. Gears crunch as he passes.

She fumbles for her phone. Rings Van Doren.

It connects.

'Melody? You were supposed to tex–'

'They're all leaving! They know, they know! Get here, now!'

Van Doren shouts, 'All teams, Go, Go, Go!'

Cars stream out of the warehouse. It'll be too late. She turns the car around in a tight circle, the wheels whining. But why? To where? She stops the car and thumps the steering wheel.

Lights and sirens appear. A police van, then another, followed by an unmarked car with the light on the dashboard. Detective Van Doren leaps out of the back and sprints past her Defender, heading for the warehouse and is back a few moments later.

'What the fuck!' Van Doren shouts. 'What happened?'

Melody holds her hand to her forehead, thinking. 'Someone must have tipped them off. I don't know how, but they knew!'

'The snake handler! Did you see his van?'

'Yes, yes, he was here. He went that way, they all did.' She indicates the direction. 'But–'

Van Doren barks something into her radio and jumps back into the car. It takes off in a cloud of exhaust and Melody is left there, alone, once more.

One fact cuts through all others with razor precision.

Pug had found out about the sting, and blamed her for it.

For that, there would be consequences.

41
Astrid

It's not lost. Not by a long stretch. The road block had been set up instantly, the patrol cars already in position at the two exits. Sure, the cage was a little wider than she'd have liked; but the convoy would soon find themselves trapped ahead and behind.

Map spread out on her lap, radio buzzing with updates.

'West exit: the convoy is approaching. At least a dozen cars. Over.'

'Step on it, Collins.'

'The front vehicle has a steel bumper. They don't appear to be slowing down... I think.... Move, move, move!'

'Shit,' Smithes says from the front.

'Report now! What's happening?'

Static, then a voice, background shouting, *'They rammed us, shunted their way through, both patrol cars damaged. Over.'*

'Injuries? Over.'

'None. Over.'

'Small bloody mercies,' Smithes growls from the front.

Astrid squints between Collins and Smithes, straight ahead. Smoke in sodium light. Two police cars, twisted metal and battered body work, a third crumpled and facing the wrong way. The officers, dumbfounded, at the side of the road.

'Keep going,' Smithes says. 'We need that van.' The wheels crunch over debris and pixelated glass.

She radios through to the east roadblock, disbands it, and

orders them up to the main road, reading out a description of the Transporter with the registration Melody Kitteridge had provided at interview. It seemed Olaf Gudmundsen wasn't using fake plates, but had altered the reg with rectangles of black tape.

Collins shifts gear, traffic slows and eases to the hard shoulder, letting him slip past. He drives smooth, quick. The lights and siren give them an advantage.

The radio crackles. East team confirm sighting of the van. *'In pursuit, suspect heading east on A259.'*

'Yes,' Smithes says, gripping the handle above the window, phone pressed against his ear. 'Can you hear me? Yes, this is DCI Bill Smithes, EA194 requesting air support on A259 between Newhaven and Seaford.'

Collins is making good progress. Up ahead Astrid can make out the blue lights and siren of the pursuit vehicles.

Through the radio, an officer in the lead car narrates the turns and progress of the blue Transporter. She traces a finger along the map. Into Seaford or break off on a minor road to the north? Out in the darkness, squares of light funnel past; a train.

'There aren't any level-crossings ahead are there?' Collins says, as the same thought arrives in her own mind.

'The Seaford one was removed a few years back,' Astrid says, consulting the map again. 'Don't think we'll get that lucky.'

They fall in behind the patrol cars, and as they round a bend, she spots the Transporter.

'There he is.' Adrenaline courses, rushing round her system.

The thumping beat of rotor blades. A giant circle of light appears, dazzlingly bright, framing Gudmundson's Transporter.

'Give it up,' Smithes mutters. 'Don't be stupid.'

The Transporter doesn't stop. It never ceases to amaze her. In chase situations, each passing minute tips the odds further and further in their favour, and yet, too few give up to the inevitable. Delusional. Desperate.

'Stinger?' Collins asks.

'I'll see if we can set something up before Eastbourne. Let's back off a little for now,' Smithes says.

'Ease off slightly, maintain distance. Examining tactical options. Standby.' Astrid instructs into the radio. It's a good call, all too easy for pursuit dogs to get hot-blooded in these situations and force a tragedy.

Smithes is on the phone to the traffic control room when the Transporter veers to the right. Confirmation of it comes through on the radio, like a retrospective sat-nav.

'Where's he going?' Collins mutters.

'This goes back on to the A259 eventually. I don't get it.'

'He's spooked, making stupid choices,' Smithes says. 'Won't be long now.'

He takes them along the beachfront road, right past the beach, the spotlight following. It makes no sense. 'There is a minor way through at the end that cuts down to the golf course.' They shoot past a squat fortification with a cannon on top, home to Seaford museum, then down a dirt road, bumping over potholes, then back on the asphalt on a residential road.

'He's lost it,' Collins says, 'he's desperate.'

They go down a short hill and turn onto a road that skirts the bottom of a golf course. Here, the van surprises them again, briefly ranging onto the other side of the road, then turning in a sharp arc, jumping the curb, and driving onto the course.

The patrol car screeches to a halt,

'Follow him!' Smithes barks.

There's a hard jolt as the car climbs the curb at speed. Astrid's teeth knock together at the impact.

'Suspect is driving on…' Astrid takes over the narration as the lead car, and briefly consults the map. 'Seaford Head Golf Course.'

'He's tearing up the greens!' Collins shouts. The red lights of the van ahead of them go out, but the helicopter has it. It shimmies right, left, and then turns back sharply to the right, losing the searchlight.

'Shit!'

'Suspect has switched off his lights.'

'Can he get out of here? Does the course connect up to another road anywhere?' she asks, her map no good now.

'I don't think so,' Collins says. 'There might be an old droving track on the fifteenth from memory, but no way he can make it to the top of the cliff in that van.'

'Could he be going for the sea? Drive himself off?' Smithes asks.

'There!' Astrid points. Then into the radio, 'Air support, follow the headlights of lead pursuit vehicle. We have eyes.'

As their headlights swing round, the light catches a wheel suspended in the air, the van leaning on its side in a bunker.

'Stop the car!' Astrid shouts.

The car skids to a halt in the muddy grass. She jumps out, torch in hand, already lit. She leaps onto the side of the van, shines a torch through the window, expecting to see a man slumped against the steering wheel.

'Suspect not in the car,' she says into the radio, and slides down the car and out of the bunker. 'On foot. Request air support scan area to north of crash site. Get bodies out here searching, we might need the Dog Unit too.' Maybe Smithes was right, and he's heading for the clifftop.

Her legs grind up the incline. She glances back. Torch heads sweep back and forth, more patrol cars drive up on the course.

The wind whips in her ears, the helicopter's blades echo across the sky. Her breath fogs. Despite the cold, she's sweating under her body armour. She continues up the course, thighs burning with the gradient. Then it's flat. A flag ripples and snaps in the stiff breeze. There's a noise to her right, she swings the light.

Heels running.

'Stop! Police!' she yells, then into her radio, 'This is Van

Doren, I have a visual, in pursuit. Signalling now.' Running, she torch signals the helicopter. Her world lights up. It follows her as she runs.

It's him. She's sure. Long hair. Jeans.

She works her legs, cursing her body armour and jacket obstructing her running flow. She's fitter, needs be, and her legs eat up the ground between them.

Close. Close enough to hear his laboured breathing.

She dives at his legs and wraps her arms around his ankles.

He falls, planting a hand to steady himself, squirming a leg free. It smacks against her cheek, but she can feel no pain, just wet mud. She holds on to the other leg, twisting him down face first to the grass, she scrambles up with a knee in his back, and secures his arms behind his back.

She's breathing hard. He's groaning and lost his fight. She brings his wrists together and secures them with plastic ties.

'Suspect detained,' she gasps into the radio, the spotlight still on her. She wrangles his wallet from his pocket. Olaf Gudmundson. Flashlights bob, nearing their position.

She's sweating beneath all her layers, but she doesn't care. She has her man.

Once her breath returns, she reads him his rights.

Olaf sobs. If this wretch had reached the top, he just may have been desperate enough to jump.

42
Melody

Melody throws a holdall bag onto her bed and raids the wardrobes and chest of drawers for clothes.

Vet field kit from the closet.

Washbag from the bathroom.

Think.

Phone charger. Laptop.

In the closet she finds the GPS tracker packaging Martin had bought for the Defender. It had been her salvation from scrutiny. Now it could serve a second purpose. Inside the box is a second device in bubble wrap. She takes it, a plan solidifying.

Outside, a car rumbles down a street, she parts the blind. Not Pug's car.

Breathe.

The message on her phone from Pug had been short.

Humans can be animals.

Had Tristan tipped them off? Spineless idiot. And that puts Ally's house out of the question. In her bedside drawer: codeine tablets, vapour rub, and a canister of pepper spray. She bags it all and leaves the front bedroom light on.

The street's clear. She tosses her bags into the Defender, and starts driving.

She parks the Defender on a quiet residential road skirting Hove Park, loads herself up, and walks the leaf-slimed pavement, watchful for black 4 x 4's with tinted windows. She cuts through the park, keeping her eyes low when she passes an evening dog walker.

Twenty minutes later, the apartment block looms down at her. The flat numbers are meticulously labelled, and she holds her finger down on the call button.

The fumble of a handset being picked up. Then Kathy's voice over the intercom.

'Who is it?'

'Melody Kitteridge. May I come in?'

'Melody…? Of course…' The buzzer sounds and she lets herself in.

No bloody lift. The stairwell reeks of disinfectant and rubbery plimsolls.

Kathy is waiting for her on the landing, in pyjama bottoms and a jumper. The sleeves are stretched beyond her wrists. She gnaws on a thread end.

'Could you help me with these bags?'

'Of course! Sorry…' Kathy snaps into action, unburdening the heavy holdall from Melody's shoulder. The release of the weight is a relief.

Once inside, Melody goes through to the lounge and collapses onto the sofa, loosening the zip of her coat. Kathy's housemate, Alice… Alicia?... is also in pyjamas, sitting on the single seater cross-legged, a laptop balanced on her knees.

'Hello there,' she says with a stiff wave.

'Studies suggest radiation from laptop batteries can cause cancerous effects. Try putting a tray underneath, a barrier of some sort.'

'Good to know…'

Kathy drops the bag in the hallway and joins them.

'Is this because of the funeral tomorrow, did you want some company?'

'Actually, there's a gas leak at the house. I wondered if I could impose? I wouldn't need a bed.' She tests the springiness of the sofa.

‘Okay…’ Kathy says. ‘That cool with you, Alice?’

Alice is wide-eyed ‘Yeah… I mean, if it’s cool with *you,* Kathy?’

‘Me? Oh yeah, totally fine,’ Kathy says. ‘One hundred percent.’

Melody nods. ‘It’s good of you both. I’ll leave you some money towards electricity and what have you for the inconvenience.’

‘That’s really not necessary,’ Kathy says.

‘No, I insist. And you wouldn’t believe it but my car has given up the ghost. Kathy, might I borrow your Micra this evening?’

‘That old banger?’ She tucks her hair behind her ear, and gnaws on one her sleeves.

‘Kathy, you’ll ruin your jumper.’

Kathy lowers her arms. ‘The thing is, I’m just not sure because, you know, insurance and stuff.’

‘I’m an excellent driver. It’s just to run a few errands. In the remote circumstance that any damage is rendered, I’ll cover it.’

Kathy considers. Nods. ‘OK. I’ll get you the keys.’

Irritatingly, the Micra has a tape deck. Under different circumstances she could have dug out some of her old cassettes from the loft. She changes the radio station, but it is crackly, the reception terrible, so she drives in silence.

She stops at the Co-op; buys a little pack of sliced carrot sticks, flavoured rice crackers, an apple, a bottle of water and a pack of Marlboro Lights. It’s gone ten when she pulls back into Medina Villas, miraculously finding a parking spot on the opposite side of the street to her house. She turns off the engine, reclines the seat and nibbles at one of her rice crackers.

An hour passes. Then another. The windows fog with condensation and she burrows deeper into her down jacket. She yawns.

Coffee. Why hadn't she brought a flask with her?

She has her house keys, she could just risk it and run inside. It'd be five minutes tops.

No... stay disciplined.

Her bedroom light shines, the only one on in the street. A lamp on a timer would have been a better idea, but there's not much she can do about it now.

A little after two am, she is cold, needs to pee, and calls it a night.

A shadow approaches her. Faceless. There's something cold in her hand. She looks down. A gun. It glints.

Melody raises it, somehow knowing instinctively what to do, thumb disengaging the safety.

The shadow nears.

'Stop where you are,' she says through gritted teeth.

It takes another step closer.

'I mean it.'

Another step.

'One more step and I swear...'

It doesn't stop and she squeezes the trigger, once, twice, finger pumping but nothing happens. She lowers the useless gun, takes a step backward from the approaching figure.

The gun wriggles in her hand.

She looks down. It's a snake coiled and twisting around her wrist, it rears its head and hisses.

She wakes with a start, gasping for air.

'Melody?'

Where is she? Unfamiliar shapes take form.

'Are you okay?'

Kathy. She's in Kathy's lounge. She rubs her eyes, Kathy's outline haloed by the hallway light.

Melody sits up, gathering the duvet around herself. 'What time is it?'

'It's a quarter to five. You shouted out… are you okay? Bad dream?'

Melody reaches down, finds the glass and takes a big gulp of water. 'Yes, I do believe it was.'

'About Martin?'

She lets out a little breath. 'Do you miss him, Kathy?'

There's a silence, Kathy stares. 'Yeah… Don't you? I miss everything, the practice, the job, it's all, like enmeshed together into this thing that disappeared with him.'

'Yes.'

'Maybe I should get back to bed, at least try and get *some* shut-eye, not that I will. I never liked funerals. Who does? At least we can sort of, you know, say goodbye.'

The funeral... yes.

'And you? You must miss him. Obviously. Dumb question.'

'The hardest thing is the empty space lying next to you in the morning.'

'Yeah… I guess that must be weird.'

'Very strange. It's not Martin, *per se*, just the absence of a previous constant. Like the sun suddenly not being there in the sky. There and then… not.'

Kathy clasps her hands together, fingers squirming, interlocking. 'Melody, I'm just so sorry.'

'You've no reason to be sorry, Kathy.'

'No… I, just you know, feel sorrow. The whole… God… look, I'm just going to…' she points back to her bedroom.

Melody reclines again, pulls the duvet over herself. 'Good idea. We all need our beauty sleep, don't we?'

'Night.'

'Oh, Kathy.'

'Yes?'

'I hate to ask you for another favour, but I left the house in a bit of a hurry. I didn't bring anything to wear. Do you have a black dress I could borrow?'

43

Six months prior to the death of Martin Kitteridge

It is becoming increasingly hard not to hate Martin. As the Vet of the Year awards approach, Martin expects a First Lady-type effort from her; flyering their customers with voting instructions, helping Hugh ring around the digitally challenged clients, and assisting an online vote for Kitteridge's.

It is work she is ill-suited for.

'It's not about me, this is about all of us, the Kitteridge brand,' Martin says, too regularly.

The staff go along with his whims, but if they have any sense, they'll be poking fun at him behind his back. Yes, victory would bring some benefit, but the *Argus* has already featured their nomination. Would the additional benefit of winning really justify the considerable effort and expense?

The Kitteridge Practice foots the bill. The marketing budget has been overspent six times over; flyers, online adverts, and worst of all, the tickets to the award ceremony. Two hundred and fifty pounds per ticket. And all the staff are going to witness an event they probably won't even win. Before the Oscars, did all the Hollywood A-listers have to shell out for their seats at the table? She thinks not. Perhaps it would all be easier to stomach if there were an actual prize worthy of the title Vet of the Year. But no, besides the bragging rights and a pound shop trophy, the sponsor – a pet insurance company – would give a special 25 per cent offer on their insurance products to the clients of the winning practice.

'Fierce competition, this year,' Martin says, as if they'd been contenders every year. 'There's Wendover, Derby, Stoke-on-Trent, Truro, and the one in Swansea that won a few years ago.'

The week before the ceremony, she borrows Martin's laptop and sees an e-mail receipt from a company in China. A quick search reveals itself to be an online voting service with packages of five hundred, one thousand, even going up to the tens and hundreds of thousands of votes. The receipt amount suggests he has opted for the thousand vote package.

'Purchasing votes, are we, now?'

'Don't be so bloody naïve, Moody, they'll all be doing it too! We need to do this just to keep pace.'

There could be no winning with him. 'I understand. But just a thousand votes? Is that all? I mean, some of those other practices are large. Where's your ambition? If you're going to…' she nearly says *cheat,* '…give us a boost, you should at least do it properly.'

He strokes his beard. 'You think I should get more? Ten thousand? That wouldn't be over-egging the pudding, would it?'

She shrugs. Perhaps the fool will expose himself for the vainglorious cheat he is to the competition adjudicators.

Alas, it doesn't work. No disqualification e-mail arrives citing an unusual spike in votes from China. Nothing. When the day of the ceremony arrives, Martin produces a bag from an acceptable clothing store: Mango, characterised by its strikingly bold colours and cuts at mid-range prices.

'Open it, Moody.'

Inside is a flowing sequined gown, not something she would ordinarily have chosen, but it's glamorous and unexpectedly thoughtful. The colour is hard to pin down, but at her best guest it's Vardo underneath, with the sequin shimmers something like Inchyra Blue, both by Farrow & Ball. She'll have to consult the colour charts later and confirm. 'Thank you.'

'Sorry if I've been a bit insufferable.'

'No more than usual. Come here, let me help you with your tie.'

On the train, they secure a table. Martin looks dashing in his tuxedo, as does Hugh. Kathy's in a suitable, understated outfit, a high cut dress with purplish Pitch Blue by Farrow & Ball, which reminds her of Dairy Milk wrappers. Lydia would have benefited from a dark colour, but wears a dress is an unfortunate Tangerine Twist by Dulux. It is hideous.

Melody is nervous about the ceremony. Not at the prospect of victory exactly, but that Martin's head will be too large to fit in the train carriage for the return journey if they do. Ally gave her some of her old Valium tablets, "to take the edge off" if she needed it, and as the train rocks them back and forth, she slides a 2 milligram tablet into her mouth, runs her tongue over its smooth surface and takes a swallow from her awful tin of gin and tonic.

The hall is fancy, reminiscent of her few formal Cambridge dinners. They each pluck something fizzy from a tray on arrival and take their appointed seats at a round table. There is a welcome speech while efficient waiters tong bread rolls onto side plates. It all feels strangely pleasant, like in a film.

Martin keeps wiping his hands on his trousers.

'Did I pre-order the goat's cheese tart with caramelised onions for the starter? I can't remember.'

'How's my hair?'

'To Kitteridge's!' says Hugh, raising a glass of red. Melody looks down and has one too. What happened to the champagne?

'Cheers!' She raises a glass. 'To Martin, thanks for letting us ride your coat-tails, darling.'

They don't so much as laugh as guffaw, like at a cracker joke. Glasses clink, wine is drunk.

Her starter turns out to be a cold Salmorejo soup which she would never have ordered, but the Valium is having a nice, neutralising effect. Martin has a duck pâté.

'Blush by Little Greene.' She points at the wedge of pink paste with her knife.

He raises his eyebrows in a humouring type of way. 'Tastes fabulous. Worth every penny.'

The low lights and the low murmur of conversation around the hall are comfortable. Between the starter and the main, there's a speech from the insurance sponsor, and even that doesn't seem as dull as it ought in the Valium glow.

Martin has his head down, staring between his legs.

'Are you okay?'

He folds something and tucks it into his breast pocket. 'Just checking the speech. You know, just in case.' He suppresses a belch, but the pâté afterdraft is enough to have her reaching for her napkin in case she's suddenly sick.

'Sorry, Moody.'

The main arrives. For her: pork belly with an apple jus with roasted carrots and fondant potatoes.

'I thought I ordered the salmon?' she whispers to Martin, who waves her away.

It looks impossibly heavy, like the table might buckle. There's no way she'll finish it. Martin has a confit of duck. He really has got it in for ducks this evening. But it doesn't matter. Everyone seems happy. Kathy, rosy cheeked, a little tipsy. Lydia snorting at something funny. Hugh is checking out the bum of a waiter. Would it really be so awful if they won?

Feedback. The tap of a microphone. A throat clears.

'Ladies and gentlemen, it's time to announce the award.'

Martin straightens his jacket, touches his hair.

They draw it out, taking forever to open the bloody

envelope. Martin's nails are digging into his forearm.

'This is it.' He says.

Her napkin drops to the floor and she bends to pick it up. There's a round of applause. She's missed it.

'Who? What?'

They're all on their feet.

'Yeeeeees!' Martin cries, yanking her up to her feet. He pats his pockets.

'Breast pocket,' she says, hating him.

He hugs Lydia and Kathy. She leans in. 'I need to tell you something.'

Martin nods towards the stage, smiles, shakes Hugh's hand, and he's off. He tries to gather himself in front of the microphone. The Valium must be wearing off – or she hasn't taken enough – because in that moment, he looks so insufferably smug she wants to throw her bread roll at him. He raises the trophy aloft, leaning down into the microphone.

'Wow… thank you, thank you. This really is a special moment for the whole team.'

Oh, the faux selflessness.

'I'd like to thank everyone who voted for the Kitteridge Practice.'

'They can't hear you, they're all in China,' she mutters into her wine glass.

'Shhh!' someone says.

'We're extremely lucky to have such loyal customers, and privileged to have such amazing staff.'

'Wahey!' Lydia yells.

'He doesn't mean you,' Melody says, but nobody seems to hear.

'And thank you to my wife, Melody, our number two at the practice, this is for you too, darling.'

Two? That wasn't even the right nomenclature! It was *second vet*!

Martin returns to the table. Why he'd needed to write those few lines of codswallop was beyond her. He holds the trophy aloft and pumps his arms twice, thrusting it in the air as the applause rains around them.

He gives an *aw shucks* smile and takes his seat, placing the trophy down in the middle of the table. As predicted, it really is a cheap piece of crap.

She leans in again, right to his ear. 'I've been meaning to tell you, Martin. I went to the fertility doctor.'

'What?'

'The doctor. They had a cancellation and I got an earlier appointment.'

'When? What did they say?'

'I'm afraid it just isn't biologically possible.'

He's smiling, confused. 'What? There must be some sort of mistake.'

'No, Martin. It's definite. I can't have children.'

44
Astrid

It's a little after eleven when Astrid lets herself into her flat. She's dog tired. Thankfully, Smithes made the decision to interview Mr Gudmundson the following day. A good call. Taking a run at him when they were sharper and rested made the world of sense.

The TV is on low, Jenna sipping at a cradled mug.

'Hey. What you watching?'

Jenna stretches, yawns like a cat. 'Sofia Coppola's most recent masterpiece.'

Coppola was a director Jenna really rated, though Astrid had little sense for what made something good, only whether she liked it or not. Whatever plot insights or cinematography analysis Jenna offers, Astrid absorbs and accepts like a student receiving a lecture. Film held secrets for Jenna to plunder, but for Astrid it was enough just to have an escape from the day job for a couple of hours.

Astrid flops on the seat next to her, plants a kiss on Jenna's head. Jenna's absorbed in the screen and for her sake she tries to get into it, but it's too far in, and asking Jenna for a detailed run down would only piss her off.

'What's good about this one?' she says.

'The way she uses space and silence. Like a character in themselves... What happened to your face?'

Reflexively, she touches her cheek where Gudmundson had kicked her. Had Jenna really not looked at her all this time? 'It's nothing.'

Jenna pauses the movie. 'Come on.'

'Alright.' She inclines her head. 'Raid in Newhaven. Someone tipped them off. Car chase. Air support, sirens. The guy we're chasing loses it, goes off road across a golf course, crashes his van into a bunker.'

'Get out.'

'I'm serious!'

'So how did you get that shiner? Wouldn't want people thinking the wrong thing about me.'

'The guy in the van made a run for it. I chased him down, caught a boot in the face as I made the arrest.'

Jenna nods. 'You want me to get some ice on that? Probably a bit late, but it might control the swelling.'

'Hell no, I want it to look bad for the interview tomorrow. Psych him out. We'll stack charges, he'll freak out, and hopefully co-operate for a lighter sentence.'

'Sounds like you've got it all figured out.'

'Yeah, actually, I do. Which reminds me, I'd really like to take you out to Cuckmere Haven for dawn one day. I cycled it the other day and it was breath-taking, the light… you have to see it.'

'Sure.'

Astrid sniffs. 'Fuck, I really do need to take a shower though. You be up for a bit?'

Jenna zaps off the TV. 'I'm beat actually. I'm going to bed.'

'Come on, I only just got back. I can watch the rest of this thing with you if you like?'

Jenna winces at the word *thing.* 'I hate to throw a film quote at you, but the world doesn't stop and start at your convenience.'

She squints, thinking. '*The Big Lebowski?*'

'Cha-ching, another point for Astrid Van Doren. Night, babe.'

Jenna moves like a cat, dissolving away. Must be tired.

Astrid gets in the shower, letting the arrows of water pelt her face, pricks of pain on her bruised cheek. She washes her hair and steps out, feeling clean and purified.

She wraps a towel around her head, wipes the condensation from the mirror with her palm and stares at herself.

Jenna said she had offbeat good looks, whatever the hell that meant. She wasn't classically pretty, handsome perhaps, with high cheek bones, but now they are distorted in a house of mirrors sort of way. Puffy, discoloured. Bags under her eyes. She has looked and felt better.

She can't stop herself smiling. Damn, it was worth it. What an arrest!

The next morning she's out early with a Thermos of decent coffee sitting in the drinks' holder. Jenna's liquid drum 'n' bass comes on the stereo. She cuts it. She's given it a fair go, but she likes what she likes. The Boss, Courtney Barnett, The War on Drugs and Kurt Vile. She voice-activates a mix, and her mood instantly rises, singing along to the lyrics.

'Gudmundson is in with his lawyer,' Smithes tells her, when she gets into Sussex House. 'He's appointed Tabitha Matheson.'

'That's all we need.'

They talk tactics. Illegal animal breeding doesn't tend to draw much heat, legally speaking. Fines for the most part and any prison time pitiful. Assaulting a police officer is possibly the most they have to hit him with. Smithes is rightly concerned they haven't got enough meaty charges to force Gudmundson's hand into co-operating with them. On the other side of the equation is Sheridan and his reputation for dealing with grasses in a brutal and uncompromising manner. Astrid's springy mood starts to retract. No easy wins to be had here.

'So, we need to have something more compelling. Something to make the cost of not co-operating outweigh the threat of Sheridan.'

'The way Gudmundson was driving last night, he was

desperate. My read is that Sheridan could have paid Gudmundson to kill MK.'

'Highly plausible, sir.' She admits to the logic. It doesn't feel quite right, but there is little tolerance for gut hunches in Burrow's culture. 'We have no alibi for him yet. He's a snake breeder, plus there's a loose connection to the victim. It would fly. Not sure even Matheson could deny we have grounds.' She's starting to see where this is all going now.

Smithes nods thoughtfully. 'Good.'

'Question for you, sir. Say Olaf Gudmundson committed the actual act… would we be willing to do a deal with him if he gave us Sheridan?'

Smithes appraises her, lowers his voice. 'Impossible to say at this stage. It *would* be a big scalp.'

'Good to know our options, if it plays out that way,' she says.

With the additional line of questioning, Matheson asks for another hour to consult with her client before the interview, a reasonable request which Smithes grants, not wanting to get combative with the notoriously prickly Matheson. Then, at eleven fifteen, Astrid and Smithes sit down in a boxy windowless interview room.

Olaf sits, slumped, hands in his lap. On seeing her bruising, he looks away. Disgusted with himself? His lawyer, Matheson is calm, like she knows something they don't. It's discomfiting.

'We've got quite the list to get through.' Smithes' pen hovers over a bulleted list of charges. 'We'll begin with the most pressing and most serious.'

'Please do,' Matheson says, with confidence.

Before Smithes can lead, as they'd intended, she rests a hand on his arm. 'May I?'

He raises an eyebrow and nods.

'Olaf,' she says. 'Before we begin in earnest, I'm sure you're worried about your snakes. They're all alive and well, and are being looked after by Clive Wilson from the RSPCA.'

No thanks to your off-road driving, she thinks.

'Thank you for telling me and… I'm truly, very sorry about…' he points below his John Lennon glasses, to his cheek.

'No,' Matheson snaps to her client. 'You were jumped by someone in the darkness, anybody would wriggle and seek to get away.'

Astrid, incredulous, opens her mouth to say that she had identified herself. That Olaf wasn't jumped down a back alley on the way home from the pub, he'd been tailed for miles by the police and the helicopter, for Christ's sake. Who did he think it would be? But, somehow, she manages to bite her tongue, though it galls her to let Matheson get away with this sleight of hand, this little knicker-flash of what her defence would look like in court. Smithes often said there was a time for sledgehammers and a time for chisels. This, undoubtedly, was the latter.

'Apologies, go ahead now, Bill,' she says, hoping to have unsettled Matheson's groove.

'Mr Gudmundson, where were you on the evening of the tenth of January between the hours of four thirty and eight p.m.?'

Olaf looks up. 'I was in Hull, on business. I stayed the night in a Travelodge. I arrived there about five in the afternoon.'

'What were you doing in Hull?' Smithes does a good job at hiding any disappointment.

Matheson shakes her head. 'Nowhere near your crime scene, Detective Chief Inspector. He has receipts and the hotel will have security cameras.'

'We'll have it checked out.' Astrid rests a hand on the table. They'd lost their biggest piece of leverage. Time to play with what they had left. 'These other charges are stickier though, Olaf. Now, while you might have been in Hull the night of Martin Kitteridge's murder, you do breed snakes illegally.'

She waits to see if he'll say anything, then continues.

'Have you bred and sold any venomous cobra snakes, Olaf?'

He looks at his lawyer, 'Yes. I had one, an adult male.'

'Until recently?'

'Yes. I sold it.'

'To whom, and when?'

Olaf opens his mouth, but as expected, Matheson holds up a hand and stares her down.

Smithes gives her the tiniest of nods.

'Now, I'm sure your highly competent lawyer has spelled out the best and worst case scenarios for the remaining charges against you, which stand little chance of being successfully defended. A skilful advocate Mrs Matheson may be, she's not a miracle worker.'

'Flattering, I think? But get to the point.'

'If you have material evidence of who you sold or provided a cobra to in the last year, then we may be able to do something about all these other charges.'

Matheson doesn't bite just yet. 'Material evidence? How about an affidavit from my client? Would that suffice?'

Astrid defers to her superior.

'Would he be willing to take the stand?'

Matheson, in turn, defers to her client, who gives a curt nod.

'So, who did you supply cobra snakes to, Mr Gudmundson?'

'Not snakes. Snake. Just one. And–' Matheson silences him with a gesture.

'Nice try. Now. Let's have it all official before my client talks. Call me sceptical, but let's keep the motivation strong on both sides of the table, shall we?' She turns to Olaf. 'Until I've read it and okayed it, you don't say a word. Got it?'

He bobs his head up and down twice, still looking into his lap.

Astrid can't help but like Matheson, adversary that she is. A real old goat of a woman and if she was ever in trouble, exactly the sort of person she'd want in her corner.

45
Melody

She must have got back to sleep eventually. Right now, it doesn't feel like it. Her neck feels like a sumo wrestler had been kneeling on it all night. She tips her head this way and that to soothe it. No good. She must upgrade from the couch soon, for all concerned.

She retrieves her phone from the floor where it had been charging, and plugs Kathy's lamp back in. She listens. The flat feels quiet. Empty. Once this is all settled, she could work as a locum vet. Begin again. Kitteridge's already feels like a lifetime ago.

Coffee. But first she has to pee and maybe take a shower. Melody opens the door to the bathroom and instantly realises her mistake. Kathy shrieks, her towel drops from around her body to the floor.

'You could have knocked!' Kathy snatches up the towel from the floor.

'You could have locked,' Melody retorts. She stares at Kathy.

She has a meandering tattoo of a cobra winding up from the curve of her hip to the back of her shoulder. 'Kathy… what is that?'

Kathy pales. 'Oh God, Melody. It's just a tattoo, okay?' She turns, lowers the towel slightly so Melody can see the snake head a bit clearer. The detail of the forked tongue. 'Look how it's starting to fade. I got it years ago, it's just a horrible coincidence–'

'Kathy.' Melody draws on years of surgical and emergency

experience and maintains a level head. 'I know you'd never do anything to hurt us. It's just a tattoo.'

Kathy fans herself with a hand. 'You don't know what a relief it is to hear you say that.'

The shower head drips, drips, drips.

'Right...'

'OK, then.'

'I'll just...'

'Yes.'

Kathy's squeezes past. Almond and honeymilk on clean, taut, young skin.

Melody closes the door, slides the bolt over and rests her back against the door.

A cobra tattoo? Strait-laced Kathy? Never in her wildest dreams could she have imagined that. Melody showers, unable to think of anything but the tattoo. It was so fluid, beautiful.

She monopolises the bathroom, applies foundation, and black mascara. The effect darkens her brown eyes, which normally are a Red Earth number 64 by Farrow & Ball, but today are a darker Spanish Brown by Little Greene.

She pulls her hair up into an austere bun that pulls at the skin of her face, tightening it, making her look and feel younger. In the lounge there is a simple black dress, that she just about squeezes into, and a black shawl, which she drapes over her shoulders. Her ensemble is completed with smart black flats and the biggest sunglasses she owns.

The crematorium is packed.

Ally and Tristan, and Howard and Susan share the front row with her. Ally squeezes her hand.

'You know I don't like that.'

'Sorry. We're here for you, that's all.

'I know. Listen. This morning I walked in on Kathy in the bathroom. She has a tattoo of a cobra.'

'Get out! You're kidding?'

Melody scours the room, catches Kathy's eye and gives her a nod. 'It was most unexpected.'

'Hi, Melody,' Hugh holds up a hand. Austin sits towards the back, the other rows packed with Kitteridge family friends, Martin's godparents, clients, present and former, some of Martin's old Cambridge friends. Betsy had come too; they hadn't spoken in years. At the back she sees Detective Van Doren. Their eyes meet. They give each other a curt nod.

Just let this be over with.

Martin wasn't a religious man, but Susan has arranged for a preacher to lead the service. Not a word goes in.

On the dais, the coffin is a tasteful teak. Martin's final home.

Suddenly she hears: "The Power of Love" by Huey Lewis & the News. The priest stops, and a murmur passes through the congregation. It's her ringtone.

'Christ!' Ally hisses, 'turn it off, Mel.'

She removes it from her clutch. Unknown number. She silences it.

Susan is leaning forward, trying to catch her eye, ready no doubt to shoot daggers; but Melody isn't playing.

Howard is invited up to the lectern, notes trembling in his hands.

'No father should ever…' he begins, then stops, a sob caught in his throat. 'My boy,' he says, looking at the coffin, and then shakes his head and returns to his seat.

Melody feels a single tear roll down her cheek, and she catches it with her index finger. Her in-laws haven't asked her to speak, rightly guessing she would have declined.

Then they rise to sing – and she can barely believe it when she sees the crib sheet – the jaunty schooltime hymn, "All the Animals I Have Ever Seen".

She keeps her mouth clamped shut throughout.

Then it is time.

The light hum of machinery, the faint suggestion of flames in the gaps as the coffin lowers into the oven.

She mutters a goodbye to her husband under her breath.

And that is it.

He is gone.

The congregation pack into the pub, filling the bar, the seating areas, even spilling outside to brave the late January cold to vape, smoke, and tell stories. She stands with Ally and Tristan, nibbling at a salmon sandwich. Kathy comes and gives her a big, unwelcome hug. She accepts it with rigidity.

Kathy's face is raw. 'I can't bear it.'

'Here, have this. It'll help.' Melody hands over her double vodka on ice. 'I'm not going to drink it. No hope of getting a proper drink in here.'

Kathy runs her wrist under her eye, accepts the glass. Sniffs it, and pulls a face.

'Kathy. Get yourself on the books of an agency, pick up some locum work.'

'It won't be the same.'

Susan pushes past, not meeting her eye, talking to her husband in tow, '...and would you believe she didn't even have the common decency to turn off her phone.'

Ally snorts at her drink. 'Wow.'

'Was that *the* most blatant attempt at passive aggressiveness in the world?' Tristan says.

'What?' Melody says.

'I wouldn't worry about it. The priest only mentioned about turning off your devices twice before starting,' Ally says.

It does remind her though. She checks, and sees there is no voicemail, but there is a text message.

You can't hide forever.

A chill plays over her spine. Martin might be gone, but his legacy still has its hooks into her.

Kathy gasps and squints into the bottom of her now empty glass. 'That was horrible.'

'I'll have you over sometime, Kathy. I make a Bloody Mary to die for.'

'She really is an artist,' Ally says.

Someone clears their throat. She turns. It's Detective Van Doren. There's an ugly bruise on her cheek.

'Fancy a smoke?' She offers a pack of Marlboro Lights, a single cigarette popping its head up in invitation.

Melody pauses, then accepts the cigarette. She trails Van Doren through the crowd by the bar. Austin's there, with an enormous glass of rosé, looking at pictures of his wife and Lucky on his phone.

'Austin?'

He's slow to turn. 'So much loss,' he mumbles.

'Yes, well…'

'They say it comes in threes.'

'Austin. Tell me you're taking a cab home.'

'What? Yes, of course.'

'Promise? Or do I need to confiscate your keys?'

'Scout's honour.'

Outside, it's a pleasant but breezy day. Seagulls gather on the mossy roof of the pub, Van Doren sits on her hands on a damp-looking brickwork wall.

'Poor Austin.' Melody lights up, hands the lighter back to Van Doren.

'Are you close?' Van Doren asks.

Melody exhales. 'He was Martin's friend. But I know him from our Cambridge days. Austin's exceedingly clever, perhaps one of the most intelligent people I've ever met. Here.' Melody hands back the packet.

'Keep them. I only smoke socially. When my girlfriend quit, so did I.'

'The power of partnership.' She taps ash into the shrubbery. 'It was good of you to come today.'

The detective runs her hand under her undercut, a habit, it must feel nice. 'Important to pay your respects. Plus, on a police officer's salary, you can't say no to a free spread.'

Melody doesn't quite laugh, but lets out a little puff through her nostrils. 'As long as you don't try and hug me and tell me how sorry you are, you're welcome here.'

'I appreciate that. Hopefully you won't be seeing too much more of me. I think we're getting close. Olaf Gudmundson's ready to co-operate.'

'And give up Richie Sheridan? I hope you have a good witness protection programme.'

She considers confiding in this young detective, about her fears for herself. It is tempting. She is earnest, would try and help.

'Detective, I'm…' Out to sea, the waves are rough. A Jeep is stopped on the road, its engine running.

'What is it?'

'That Jeep,' she murmurs, and the window lowers, a beefy arm leans out. Then she sees the bald head.

Van Doren leaps up, and is reaching into her pocket, for a gun? No, her identification.

The tinted window rises up. Tyres squeal, and the Jeep takes off.

Van Doren gives her a quizzical look. 'Was that him? Is he stalking you?'

Melody grinds the cigarette out with her heel. 'I need to go back inside.'

No, being wrapped in a blanket of protection would only stymie her own ability to act.

Her phone beeps. Unknown number.

Like a piggy led to the slaughter

It's dark. Melody requisitions the Micra for a second night of surveillance, armed with a Thermos of coffee this time.

Her parking spot isn't as good as the night before, but she can still see her house. The estate agent must have switched off the bedroom light because the whole house is in darkness. Melody has one headphone in, eighties synth pop keeping her company in the long hours of cold and dark. She sips coffee, heart jumping at each car that passes down the road. At one in the morning she has to pee.

Reluctant to go back, Melody gets out and crouches behind the Micra. The air is bitterly cold on her buttocks, the first brushes of frost gather on the windows of the adjacent car. This is what she's been reduced to. Baring her behind to the tarmac in the early hours of the morning.

Relieved, she returns to her stakeout spot, pours another coffee and continues her vigil. She will return every night if she has to.

A little before three in the morning, she senses, then hears the low rumble of the engine. She resists the temptation to clear the condensation from the window. The smudged light passes, first white, then red, and halts, stopping outside her house.

Her heart rate quickens.

It's them.

The clip of doors opening, the engine still running.

She can't bear it. She wipes a streak in the window.

Pug. The swarthy one is with him too, jemmying the front door with a crow bar, while Pug watches the street.

They enter.

She softly opens the door of the Micra and runs at a crouch, scampering to the Jeep. She lies on her back and pushes herself half under the car. Dampness, oil, exhaust. The car continues to judder above her, she fishes in her pocket for the device. The underbelly of the car is too dark, all black tubes, metal and unknown shapes. The torchlight on her phone?

Voices.

Footsteps.

She scrambles fully under the Jeep, lying flat on her back with the wheels on either side and holds her breath.

'…a runner or what?'

'That bitch'll be back. And I'm going to gut–' Pug's voice is cut off by the door slamming shut.

Melody thrusts the device up. Stick! To something! It drops and rolls onto the tarmac. Her icy fingers spider walk, searching the ground. There! The pitch of the engine changes. And she thrusts the device up. The magnet connects. The chassis passes inches from her nose.

Sky.

Stars.

The fog of a long-held breath finally released, rising to meet them.

She doesn't move. Not until the engine is out of earshot.

Slowly, she gets up, brushes down her coat. The neighbours' windows are all opaque with curtains and blinds.

In the Micra she huddles over her phone. The red dot shows the Jeep heading west.

'Gotcha,' she says.

46
Astrid

Collins is waiting for her outside the boxy Magistrates court in Brighton, which is all concrete and rectangular windows. She'd pointed it out to Jenna once, who'd declared it 'Brutalism colliding with Cubism'. Functional, she'd replied, a little protectively.

She's been here plenty, particularly earlier in her career. Nowadays, the heightened seriousness of her work means that when she is summoned, it is normally to Lewes court, where the so called 'First Class' cases are held. Today is an exception. A throwback. An aggravated assault she'd closed four months previously.

'Didn't expect to see you here?'

Collins checks his watch. 'Smithes has called an urgent meeting. Sent me to get you.'

Astrid gets in the passenger seat, belts up, and fires off a message to the patrolman who had given her a lift in, and was due to give testimony himself shortly. As lead investigator in the case, she had taken the stand for the prosecution, and been cross-examined by the defence. She was sure they had the right man, but the grainy CCTV footage and inconsistent witness testimonies were making it hard work for the prosecutor. Mostly, for her it had been a lot of waiting, then going over the facts on the stand. All a little diminutive compared to what she had been dealing with recently. But she owed it to the injured lad and his family to be on her game, and she'd done her job.

'So, what's the fire? I heard legal are really short right now, and heel-dragging on everything to make a point. Is there a problem with getting the deal together for Gudmundson?'

'No, I don't think so. Last I heard, we should have something this afternoon. Actually, I didn't *just* come here to get you. We had to get a magistrate to sign off the extension on holding Gudmundson.'

'I doubt that was a hard sell. Last time we tried to bring him in, we needed three cars and a helicopter.'

'Yeah, piece of piss.'

She checks her messages again to see if there's anything from Smithes. 'So, what's the urgent meeting about? You know anything?'

'They're keeping it pretty tight, but Horley looks like he might be about to burst. My bet is he found something.'

'Horley? I had him manually going through years of e-mails between MK and Spellerman… but then it was all hands on deck to prepare for the op.'

'Maybe he's finally found something?'

'Maybe.'

Ten minutes later and they're at Sussex House and in MI Room 2. Everyone's present.

'Settle down,' Smithes says, cutting the low murmur of chatter. 'Let's get started.'

The morning in court has numbed her brain and she's ready to dive back in.

'A few things to update you on. First, we're putting together a legal agreement for Olaf Gudmundson in return for his co-operation. He's in the clear for the murder itself, but we believe he did supply the snake, for cash. We've also had a couple of breakthroughs. Gardner?'

Gardner snaps to attention. 'Sir. I went through the information Mrs Kitteridge had compiled. Mostly useless conjecture and information we already had… but there was one thing.'

A newspaper clipping appears on the screen, showing Martin Kitteridge and Kathy Spellerman holding snakes up with smiles on their faces.

Astrid purses her lips, trying to skim-read the article.

'This was in the *Argus,* seven years ago,' Smithes says, 'It contradicts the idea that MK had no connection with snakes. The girl in the picture is Kathy Spellerman. We've received a tip-off that these two were having an affair. Keep this image at the back of your minds a moment.'

Smithes pauses. There's quiet but for the faint buzz of the coffee machine outside. *What's he's got? Something good to be taking centre stage.*

'Officer Horley? Come up here.'

Horley pushes his glasses up his nose and shuffles to the front, taking the clicker from Smithes.

'Sir. I conducted a read through of correspondence between MK and Spellerman.' Horley talks to a space in the distance, clearly nervous. 'And I've compiled the following e-mail exchanges. All originated from the same two IP addresses between MK and Kathy Spellerman. All were sent over the same network identifier.'

'Meaning?' Smithes prompts, for the benefit of the room.

'They were e-mailing each other from within the Kitteridge Practice. The messages were technically in the trash, but backed up on a cloud server. I managed to–'

'Horley. Please just show us,' Astrid says.

'Yes, right, of course.' Horley clicks, and the screen lights up with a mail. What strikes her at first is the sparseness, the lack of text.

M. Kitteridge.
Subject: *That thing*
To: KMS

Need to see you.
Tonight?

M. Kitteridge.
Subject: Re: That thing
From: KMS

Yes!!

Then at the bottom, there is an emoji of a hooded snake.

'Holy shit,' Astrid says when she sees the sign off, then covers her mouth, realising she'd said it aloud.

'Why didn't we catch this before on the initial scan?' someone asks.

Horley rubs at the back of his head. 'He had over thirty-two thousand e-mails archived. We were keyword searching the official list, it doesn't look for emojis... we didn't ask it to. It was only when DI Van Doren got me to do a manual read-through that we caught it.'

Smithes gives her a nod that seems to say, *good work.* Horley clicks on.

'The messages stretch back nearly three years. They tend to be short, logistical in nature. They fall into two camps. The planned ones, i.e. let's meet tonight at eight, or tomorrow at seven. Or, more commonly, they are spontaneous.' He clicks on, showing examples. 'Like this one which simply reads: 'Now?' Sixty-eight percent of the exchanges fall into this category.'

'Have you done us a nice 3D pie chart to show us the split? Opportunist screws and planned nooky,' Hussain says, earning a laugh from a few of the team and a scowl from Smithes. 'No disrespect meant, this is good stuff, man.'

But Astrid is thinking. 'These spontaneous messages? Horley, have you done any timestamp analysis?'

'I have. Almost all were sent between 4 p.m. and 7:30 p.m., every day of the week except Sunday.'

'The only day Kitteridge's is closed,' Gardner says.

'There was an increase in frequency both years between January and March.'

'Very clever,' Astrid says.

'An insight to share, guv?' Horley says.

'Cross-reference the times of the messages with Melody Kitteridge's call-out logs from the vet practice.' She feels a room of eyes on her. 'It's lambing and calving season. Melody is the call-out vet and that's her busiest time of year. I'd bet anyone here a three-course dinner that Martin and Kathy snuck away when Melody was on call-outs.'

Nobody takes the bet.

'Do any of these messages indicate where they meet? It must be somewhere close, right?'

'Nowhere specific,' Horley confirms. 'This is the only message which hints at a place. From Spellerman to MK,' Horley clicks on. Astrid looks at the date.

Her mouth is dry.

The date is the day of Martin's death.

10 Jan

I'll be waiting for you after work. Come up.

Please, please come.

'Come up?' Astrid asks. 'Up where? And the begging? Why the change in tone?'

'The tenor, if you can call it that, changed five weeks before MK's murder. It's her, asking to see him. Him refusing.'

'This is excellent work, Horley.' Smithes assumes the floor once more. 'I've sent out a patrol car to bring her in. Questions?

Ideas on next steps.'

Astrid's eyes wander over to the board. SNAKE AS SYMBOL. A new admiration for Uzoma burrows into her chest. She speaks up. 'Kathy Spellerman has a shaky alibi, that final e-mail suggests she wasn't with Lydia Gregorivic at all. She's covering for Spellerman, we just need to prove it.'

Gardner raises a hand. 'I'll see if I can dig anything up.'

'We may need to grill them both separately in interview on the alibi, look for inconsistencies in timings and details to see if they trip up.'

Smithes hums, considering. 'No. Not yet. We've already got enough interviews to conduct for now. Let Gardner do her thing. If we don't get any joy, then we'll bring Gregorivic in later, kick the tyres on the alibi.'

'Sir,' she says, in acknowledgement of this little reminder that this was his show, not hers.

He claps his hands together. 'Good. Now, let's get to work.'

Gardner lingers. She tucks a strand of hair behind an ear.

'Sounds like we're getting close.'

'Let's hope so.'

'When this is over, think we'll go out for a drink or something?'

Astrid plays it safe. 'I can't think about it right now, not with all this going on.'

'Right, of course.'

She shakes her head, 'But yeah, we'll all do something sure. Get the team together, blow off a little steam.'

'Right,' Gardner nods. 'The team. Sounds good.'

'Let me know if you dig up anything on that alibi.'

'Will do, ma'am.'

47
Melody

Melody cycling.

The path runs alongside Hove Lawns. It's been years since she's been on a bike. Now she recalls why. Bloody hard going. The unforgiving wind leans against her. It is as if she is on an exercise bike, pedalling for all she wants yet remaining stationary. Quicker cyclists on quicker bikes slip past her. Each a little insult. The pannier bag adds a lot of weight. That must be it; she isn't unfit.

The bright side: tailwind on the way back. The helmet, the sunglasses, offer anonymity. Best of all, no number plate.

Under the whipping wind she picks out the jaunty opening of "The Power of Love" by Huey Lewis & the News. She brakes, pulls the bike onto the grass, letting the other cyclists and electric scooters pass unhindered.

'Yes?' she says, shoving the phone underneath her helmet.

'Melody. It's me. Susan.'

'I know. Your name comes up on the screen when you call me.'

'I dread to think what name *you've* put in.'

'Bitch-face Susan, if you must know.' In the gaps between beach huts, columns of sea churn like reacting test tubes.

'Charming as ever!' There's a pause, some muttering at the other end. 'Look, the estate agent called. We've had an offer on the house.'

'How much?'

'A million and a half.' Mathematics. After paying off her

share of the mortgage, she'll be left with nearly two hundred and eighty grand.

'I accept.' She hangs up.

She could have paid off Sheridan after all, but they were beyond that now.

She refers to the tracking app. It shows Pug's Jeep is still in the location where it had been overnight. Another ten minutes in the saddle and she'll be there. She zips her phone back into the strap across her chest, checks that the path is clear, and leans her weight into the pedals, urging the bike forward into the wind once more.

The red dot blinks. Here? Smooth white walls curve. Well above head height, no getting over that without a ladder. Two security cameras cover the door and every angle. It is an odd location for a house, sandwiched as it is between Hove lagoon and the power station. Luxury seafront living, just within the postcode magic of Hove and yet… The high fences and nearby bunker yards give it an industrial air. Opulent and rough at the same time. Power station chic.

The set-up is discouraging. Stealth would be required, more than she possesses. The front door, then. Still, it wouldn't do to be recorded on camera. She leans the bike against the wall on the other side of the road, out of the camera's periphery. In her pannier, Melody rummages around, finding a bottle of Evian, still slightly chilled. The trickle of it down her throat is divine.

Next, she retrieves a tub of Vaseline and a cloth. She wraps a scarf around her like a Bedouin, and on tiptoes, smears the jelly liberally over the camera lenses.

She experiences a moment of doubt. Crushes it. She recalls Pug as a boy shaking out a tea towel full of shattered glass for the cat. The kittens. Then Cleopatra. The snakes, the dog-fighting, the violence she witnessed at Plum Tree Farm. No. These people know no other language than violence. She's tried, hasn't she, to do it the right way? And now they are after her. It was strike, or get struck.

A lorry passes. Then a moment later, a dusty white van. Clear. She removes the tranquilliser gun from the top of the pannier. Loads it with a pre-pressurised dart. The feathery stabiliser is a bright pink Fuchsia Lily by Dulux. Pretty but conspicuous.

A car approaches and she hides the gun, squeezes the back tyre as if testing the pressure.

She waits. Pedestrians in the distance, a group of four cyclists pass, a dog walker. A break will come. She is patient, tries to visualise it.

When he answers the door, she will shoot and bundle him backwards. The element of surprise will be on her side. It would take a few crucial seconds for the ketamine to take effect. She could hold out a few seconds, couldn't she? But what if there was someone in there with him?

The gun is single fire, but she could quickly load it with another dart. She readies two more darts, pockets them. Then, for a precious moment, all is quiet. She puts the pannier bag over her arm, the gun concealed between the bags, finger ready on the trigger. Back pressed against the wall.

You can do this.

She swallows.

Heart pounding.

Sirens.

She stuffs the gun in the bag, uprights her bike. Fool! Probably just an ambulance passing, spooking her, but louder. Louder still. She climbs on, as two police cars appear, tyres screeching as they take the bend and skid to a halt metres from where she's standing.

How did they know? She is frozen to the spot. Open-mouthed. An officer jumps out of the car and points at her. 'Madam!'

'I…' she's going to be sick.

'Clear the area! Move!' The officer yells. The officers knock on the door, only waiting five seconds before using a bright red battering ram. They hammer on the door. *Whack. Whack.* The door splinters. An officer kicks it open.

She cannot tear her eyes away.

'Move, now!'

She pedals a metre or two. Loops around to watch from the other side of the road. The police swarm in.

They weren't here for her.

They didn't know what she was planning. It's OK, it's all OK.

The crackle of a car radio.

'What's going on?' someone says at her side. A middle-aged woman with a border collie on a lead, pinching the top of a poo bag.

'I've no idea. They battered the door down.'

'Look!'

Pug is being marched forward by two officers, his hands behind his back. One puts a steadying hand on Pug's bald head, easing him into the car.

'I don't understand why they do that. If they don't know how to duck to get in a car then they deserve to bump their heads,' the woman says.

'Quite,' Melody manages.

The dog walker is filming it on her phone.

The police car is unfeasibly small for Pug's bulk, his jacket pressing against the window, like a black airbag had erupted inside.

Then their eyes meet.

He scowls. Then he mouths something for her to lipread.

You're dead, bitch.

'Do you think they'll pay me anything for this? The *Argus,* I mean?' The dog walker says.

But she can't drag her eyes from the car.

'To think they've finally got him.'

'Him?'

'Richie Sheridan. Are you not from around here? Tourist?'

'That…' she points to the car disappearing down the road, 'that man…the bald one. Is Richie Sheridan?'

'So you have heard of him. I'm going to call the news desk. Might get a few bob for this.' She waggles the phone. 'Toodle-oo.'

48
Four months prior to the death of Martin Kitteridge

Sitting, bare-bottomed, on a sea urchin. Breaking her arm. Standing, pinned in by a dense crowd of jostling people. Shaving off all the hair on her head. Drinking a litre of apple cider vinegar in one go. Being robbed at gun or knife point. Getting slashed superficially by that knife. Having the scar anywhere but her face. These are all the things she would gladly accept if it meant she didn't have to go on holiday with her in-laws.

But when Martin insists upon something.... He practically bundles her into the car and locks the doors, as if she still might make a break for it.

She tries the handle. Testing. Half-teasing.

'Just stop this bullshit, Moody, seriously.' He's red-faced, exasperated.

He won't have this cheap. He's had to do all the packing – hers included – clean the house, and arrange the cover at Kitteridge's.

'I don't know what you mean.' She opens the window, lights a cigarette.

'Not in the car, Moody, for fuck's sake. You'll make the upholstery stink.'

She chain-smokes the whole way to Newhaven, until her lungs feel like they've been through a meat grinder. Howard and Susan are on the same four-hour crossing but – heaven for small mercies – are at least in their own car for the drive down.

‘Where’s the vet of the year?’ Susan says, giving Martin a too-long squeeze. Then, ‘Melody,’ she inclines her head.

‘Susan. Howard. Anyone have any change for the cigarette machine?’

‘You’ve started smoking again? I thought…’ Susan says.

‘Don’t.’ Martin gives her a *I’ve tried but she won’t listen* look.

‘If you need me, I’ll be on deck, leaning precariously over the railings.’

When they berth in Dieppe, Martin asks if she’ll share the driving. In response she takes two five milligram tablets of Diazepam and reclines her seat as far as it’ll go.

‘Wake me when we get there.’

When she wakes, it’s dark. They are at the villa. A monosyllabic, bleary-eyed Martin carries in the cases. The air is warm and sweet with pine. Cicadas pulsate. Water gurgles in the pool filters.

While the rest of the party stumble to their beds, Melody is so well rested, she can’t possibly sleep. Instead she takes a midnight dip in the pool. The sub-surface lights create bright orbs of colour; a soothing Teal Touch by Dulux, deepening to a Regal Blue by Crown in the patches farthest from the lights. She easily swims a hundred or so lengths in the stubby pool, and it feels like enough exercise to offset the day’s travelling and sleeping. Then she lies on a sun lounger, letting the disturbed pool lap as it calms itself.

Headphones: she listens to a new mix that begins with “Message in a Bottle” by The Police. This is superb.

If she stays up all night and sleeps during the day she won’t have to talk or see anyone. The perfect holiday.

She rises, having missed lunch, and spends the afternoon trying to make a passable cocktail with Orangina. It isn't possible.

Any thoughts of passing the entire holiday in this fashion are quickly dashed. Her presence, Martin informs her, is expected, particularly on the night of his parents' fortieth wedding anniversary; the trip's *raison d'être*.

On the day itself, they pack into Howard's Range Rover and drive north to visit a vineyard; a picturesque chateau surrounded by a besieging army of rowed vines. Melody manages to keep an air of bonhomie by micro-dosing herself with Diazepam every three hours. After being shown the swollen grapes outside, they and a group of six Germans are dragged through the process of wine creation. She doesn't care about the temperature, when it moves from the enormous stainless-steel urn to the barrels, or how they're coopered or what wood they're made from. Alchemy be damned, she was here for the gold.

Finally. Wine tasting. It's such a relief to have the glass in her hand. While the sommelier witters on about tasting notes, she downs hers. It is a crisp, cold white. The warm weather, her dry thirst, and her relief at the tour being over, all help the different vintages slip down her neck. Howard is ruddy-cheeked and suitably impressed enough to buy three cases of the wine.

'That'll do us for the rest of the week,' he possibly jokes.

In the evening, Martin mans the barbecue. Her offering: a warm goats cheese salad with caramelised onion dressing. Her mother-in-law must be feeling a little misty-eyed about her anniversary because she compliments her on the salad.

All in all, Melody feels a small sense of achievement. No arguments. A magic combination of medication, night owling, and drifting through the social engagements produce a passable time.

The sun browns her skin pleasingly. They lunch on delicious bread and cheese, one day she picks a pomegranate from a tree. The seeds are a bright Volcanic Red by Dulux but it lacks any sweetness or flavour.

One day they venture out to Aix-en-Provence, amble the hot streets and all four of them drink strong brown beer at a street café; Susan flaps herself cool with a tourist map, Howard and Martin discuss the strange fizziness to the beer while she checks the Kitteridge Practice inbox. Earlier in the week she'd hoped for some disaster that would drag them home, but as the finish line nears, it is more out of boredom that she checks. All is under control.

Friday, the last full day. Martin and Howard have walked into the village to the boulangerie, she is having a smoke and a coffee by the pool, contemplating a swim, when Susan appears from nowhere, like the angel of death.

'Mind if I join you?'

'It's a free country.'

'I hope you don't mind me saying, but you've been in that dress all week, would you like to borrow one of mine?'

Susan has never been so kind to her in her life. Something is up. 'The Vet of the Year did the packing. Not Packer of the Year, unfortunately.'

Susan gives a thin smile. 'It's been a nice holiday, hasn't it? You've enjoyed it, I hope?'

She's suspicious, lowers her sunglasses, sucks in her lips, and goes for the truth. 'I wasn't looking forward to it. But I've not hated it.'

Susan scoffs. Or laughs. 'We all wanted you to be comfortable.'

'Why, exactly?'

'After your news. You probably don't realise it Melody, but you've been grieving your faulty womb.'

Faulty womb? She pushes the sunglasses back up her nose. *So, Martin's told you.* Things suddenly make sense; Martin's unnatural acquiescence, the lack of conflict, the easy atmosphere. They've been tiptoeing around her.

'It's raw, for you, for Martin, even for us. We've wanted a

grandchild for years. And Andrea… Let's just say, Martin was our main hope.'

Martin's sister's sexuality was always talked about in euphemisms. She's living with *a friend* or, Melody's favourite, her *female companion*. Martin had told her the truth: Andrea was ensconced in Melbourne, happy with some singer/songwriter, away from her toxic mother. *Good for her.*

'Disappointment all round then,' Melody says.

Susan moves her head from side to side as if to say *maybe, maybe not.*

'Could you imagine coming here every year, and having a little one running around, leaping into the pool in armbands?'

'Not really, no. It's not the sort of thing an infertile person would imagine, Susan.'

She sips her coffee, it's cold, bitter, creamy, and just enough to leave her wanting another.

Susan's eyes narrow in thought. 'Have you spoken to Martin about adoption?'

Melody pinches the bridge of her nose. 'Good God.'

'Have you?' Susan presses.

'No.'

'Look, I know this is hard, it must be particularly difficult for you given…'

'Given what?'

'You want me to speak frankly? You didn't know your biological parents and were passed from pillar to post as a child. It's no surprise you're reticent about being a mother, but what you don't seem to realise, Melody, is that you are in a different situation now! You have a stable, loving husband, a good life. Willing grandparents to help out. A child, your child, wouldn't have the upbringing you had.'

'But adoption?'

'Is it the biological connection? I understand you might have some misgivings…'

'Susan, just don't.'

'But where do you stand on surrogacy, Melody? I have some literature to share with you.'

'Where do I stand on surrogacy? On its windpipe until it stops twitching, Susan! I suppose I should be grateful you left it until the end before ambushing me.'

She holds her hands up. 'Ambush? Melody! Calm down, please.'

Melody's on her feet, fuming, fumbling with her cigarette packet.

'It's no wonder you don't function properly when you poison yourself!'

She lights up, blows smoke in Susan's direction. Susan waves at it, and fake coughs.

'You know, Martin deserves the chance to be a father. I think you're being very selfish.'

'And what about what I want? Where does that fit into your little masterplan?'

'It would make you both happy. I've been a mother, *I* know things that you possibly couldn't until you've held your own baby in your arms.'

'Why does everyone assume I want a fucking child? Has anybody ever thought to actually ask?'

Susan looks genuinely perplexed. 'But it's the life-giving nature of our sex as women, as carers, as nurturers.'

Melody shoots her the most venomous look she can muster, barges past her, and into the villa. She chucks her toiletries into her wash bag, packs her clothes and shoes into her suitcase. She takes the car keys. Martin will have to sit between the cases of Chateau de Seuil and suffer the company of his parents for nine hours.

For her, the peace of the open French roads, her music, and best of all, those disgusting people in her rear-view mirror.

49
Astrid

On their way to the interview room, Smithes pulls her aside.

'A moment.'

'Sir?'

He keeps his voice low. 'Just so you're aware of the bigger picture. The fraud squad has just moved on Sheridan, arrested him.'

'Without consulting us?

'That's right.'

'For God's sake Bill, what were they thinking?'

'Power play.'

'But what if Gudmundson gives us Sheridan as the murderer? I know we like Spellerman for it more, but it's still on the table.'

'Then we just stack the charge on him.'

She sees it now. 'But Fraud get the collar. Their timing with the arrest is… interesting… to say the least.'

Smithes gives her a rueful smile. 'Perhaps I was too open about my hopes for this interview with Gudmundson. Everyone wants to be Burrow's golden one.'

'Did they find anything in his house relevant to our investigation?'

'Too early to say. I've sent Hussain to liaise with their team.'

'Right.'

He rests a hand on her shoulder. 'Let's just do our thing,

Astrid. Karma will take care of the rest.'

She raises an eyebrow. 'It bloody better.'

Tabitha Matheson looks pretty pleased with herself, the ghost of a smile on her face which Astrid feels the need to check.

'The deal is contingent, your man's not out of the woods yet.' Pleasingly, the lawyer's smile shrinks a little.

Smithes glances at the clock, states the time, date, and all the necessary preliminaries.

Olaf Gudmundson is still, eyes watchful behind his circular glasses.

Astrid takes out enlarged photos and places them in a line in front of Gudmundson. Melody Kitteridge, Kathy Spellerman, Lydia Gregorivic, Richie Sheridan, and Austin Pemberton.

'Mr Gudmundson. Have you ever supplied snakes to any of these people?'

'If I tell you about this how soon will I be able to leave the country?'

Astrid flashes Smithes a look. *Interesting.*

'Not until after trial, if there is one. Your deal is contingent on that, Olaf.' Smithes says.

'If your concern is for your wellbeing, there are safeguarding options.'

Olaf swallows and rests a finger on the bald leering face of Richie Sheridan. 'I supplied him plenty of snakes over the last eighteen months, for Richie's gambling events.'

'Did you ever supply him with a cobra?'

'Yes,' he pushes his glasses further up his nose. 'Richie had this idea of having a cobra versus a mongoose battle.'

'When was this?' Smithes says.

'September, I think.'

Astrid frowns. The timeline didn't fit. 'Did Mr Sheridan keep the snake? Look after it at all?'

'Never. I supplied the snake for the event, yes, but I took it back at the end of the night.'

She rubs her forehead. This is not going how she hoped. 'Did he ever borrow the snake again? Or use it?'

'Sheridan didn't, no.'

She leans forward. 'But someone else did?'

'Yes, in late November, I think. A private buyer. Cash. She fell in love with it at first sight, I knew she would look after it. Knew what she was doing, when she looked at some of my other snakes, she clearly had some handling experience.' He shrugs. 'A good home with a caring owner, cash buyer. It's more than I could hope for.'

'She? Can you identify that woman in these photographs?' She watches his expression closely.

Olaf Gudmundson scans each photo thoroughly, then nods.

'Yes. This one.' He rests a finger on one of the photographs. 'I don't remember her name but I am positive it was her.'

Her. Astrid swallows, trying to get some moisture in her mouth, then confirms the identity for the video.

'This is it, Astrid. But keep this between us for now. Tight circle. I don't want the press getting wind of this yet. She on her way in yet?' Smithes is striding down the corridor like a tiger.

Astrid looks at her phone. 'Sir… we are struggling to locate her.'

'Find her. Fast.'

'Am on it, sir.'

Gardner pops her head out of the Windbourne room. 'Sir? Ma'am? A moment? It's urgent.'

They join her inside.

Gardner tucks her dirty blonde hair behind an ear. 'Following up on the Spellerman alibi. It seems Lydia Gregorivic got a traffic ticket in Worthing on the night of the murder.'

It takes her a moment. 'Have you–'

'Yes. I've checked the CCTV.' She brings the footage up. The time reads 7:07 p.m. 'Lydia Gregorivic arrives, finds half a space, but half her car is covering a double yellow. Hence the ticket. Video suggests she's on her own.' Gardner switches cameras and Lydia strides into the Dome cinema. 'I checked the schedule and there was a romcom on. She comes out after nine, consistent with the film's run-time.'

'Great work!' Smithes says. 'This proves that Spellerman wasn't with Gregorivic. They both lied. The question is, why?'

Astrid bites a lip. 'Sir, I think we might need to go to the mobile carriers to help us locate Spellerman.'

'Agreed. Collins?'

Collins head pops up from his work station. 'Sir?'

The door opens. It's Symonds, breathless, in uniform. 'You're here. I've been trying to contact you!'

'We were in interview,' Smithes says, radiating calm. 'What's the matter?'

'I've just spoken to Mrs Spellerman on the phone.'

'Where is Kathy now?'

'No, her mother, Angela. She says she got a weird text from Kathy and she's not answering her phone. She has one of those friend and family finding apps. Kathy Spellerman's phone signal puts her at Beachy Head.'

Icy fingers run down the ridges of Astrid's spine. 'Is she… gone?'

Symonds shakes his head, 'I don't think so. Local team's been dispatched.'

'Van Doren. Collins. Let's get down there.'

'Step on it, Collins!' Smithes yells.

'I'm going as fast as I bloody can,' he replies through gritted teeth, gravel shooting from the tyres as he rounds another bend.

The road winds and cuts up to the chalk headland, carpeted with luscious green on top. They pass the chaplaincy, known for its patrols to intercept potential jumpers.

'Latest?' Smithes barks.

'Negotiator still on site. Kathy's still with us,' Astrid replies.

They park, and run at a jog past the sign for the Samaritans helpline, following the trail to the clifftop. There's already a small crowd of onlookers, dog-walking rubberneckers, ramblers, and someone with a shoulder camera. The news teams had got here before them. Vultures.

The local force, in high-vis jackets, have a cordon set up already. They are experienced, some twenty suicides a year occurring here. A terrible thing to be used to dealing with, but there it was.

She spots Kathy, wind blowing her brown hair, head bowed to the rocks below. An officer stands ten metres or so behind Spellerman, the negotiator, she presumes.

'Situation?' Smithes asks one of the officers.

'Negotiator on spot, sir. The girl threatens to jump if she gets any closer.'

'Who is the negotiator?'

'Christa Darcy.'

'Radio and see if she's in a position to come and talk to us a moment,' Smithes orders.

Darcy turns to look at them when the radio sounds and jogs down to meet them.

'DCI Smithes. DI Van Doren and DC Collins,' Smithes says. 'The girl up there, Kathy Spellerman, is a prime suspect in a murder investigation.'

Darcy nods. She's short, with sharp eyes that flick back to Spellerman every few seconds. 'I don't want to leave her for long.'

'Understood. Has she asked for anyone? Her mother?'

'Her mother's on the way, but she lives in Northampton.'

'Christ,' Astrid says.

'Could I accompany you up there?' Smithes says. 'Make an appeal with you? I'm aware of some of the reasons why she might be standing there?'

Darcy gives a small nod.

'Or…' Astrid says, 'just as a suggestion. I've actually met Spellerman before, sir. She knows my face. And perhaps… woman to woman…'

'Whoever it is, come now, I'm not leaving her there any longer.'

'Yes, good thinking. Go,' Smithes says.

Darcy walks fast, muttering under her breath. 'No judgements, be understanding. Have you had any training?'

'I have, but I defer to your experience.'

'Good,' Darcy says. 'What's your first name?'

'Astrid.'

'Astrid.'

The salty wind catches in her lungs, her palms sweaty.

'Kathy? It's Christa. I have someone here, Astrid Van Doren. Would it be okay if she speaks with you a moment?'

Kathy turns her head from the drop. 'It's you. The detective.'

'Can we talk?'

'Are you here to arrest me?'

Darcy gives a curt shake of the head.

She doesn't want to lie but the wrong word could prod her over the edge. 'Just to talk, Kathy. Whatever you feel right now, I promise it won't always feel like this.'

Kathy wipes a tear. 'How could you possibly know?'

She holds up her hands. 'You're right… I don't know exactly how you feel. But I do know what it's like to be in love, and want that person with every ounce of your being. And I know grief, Kathy. The way it settles in your bones. You can't imagine anything else, that feeling good again will ever be possible. That you'll feel love again.'

'I miss him so much.' Kathy brushes away an errant strand of hair.

'Of course you do, sweetheart. What do you think Martin would say to you if he could see you standing here?'

Kathy lets out a sound that could be a laugh, could be a sob. 'Get down from there, silly girl.'

'He wouldn't want to see you suffering like this.'

'It's what I deserve,' she sniffs, glances back at the crowd. 'Is Mum here?'

'On her way, it might be a couple of hours, Kathy.' Darcy says.

'I want to talk to Melody, then.'

Darcy shoots Astrid a look. Who?

'We can do that, we can get Melody on the phone if you like?'

'In person,' Kathy says. 'She needs to know… I need to tell her face to face'

'What does she need to know, Kathy?'

'Just get her here!' Kathy screams, the ferocity astonishing.

Astrid holds up a hand. *Christ. It had been going well.* She takes a breath. 'Okay, okay. Let me give her a call, okay?' Just… please, Kathy, hold tight. We can sort this out, I know we can. Hold tight, sweetheart, please.'

50
Melody

Melody pulls into the car park at Beachy Head. An officer has coned off a space for her. Good job too. Double parked cars and vans everywhere. A Transit pulls in behind her, boxing her car in, a news crew stream out like a disturbed ants' nest, busying themselves with equipment, hair and wires.

She taps the driver on the shoulder and thumbs to the van. 'If that is still boxing me in when I want to leave, I'll back straight into you.'

His mouth rounds into an O.

'Mrs Kitteridge is here,' an officer says into his radio.

'Send her up.'

Melody recognises Van Doren's voice on the other end.

At the top of the headland, a crowd are gathered behind a cordon, the dots of high-vis jackets.

As she powers up the path behind the officer, a strange feeling of unease nestles in her. To think. Kathy, at Beachy Head. Her vet nurse had weighed things up, and sought her escape here.

She rounds the news cameras and crowd of onlookers, ducks under the cordon, lock-jawed. Van Doren steps out of a little huddle.

'Thanks for coming so quickly, Mrs Kitteridge. This is Christa Darcy, our lead negotiator. You already know DCI Smithes, and DC Collins.'

Melody gives them a sharp nod and squints beyond them. A

figure sits, hugging her knees to her chest. A picture of misery. 'How is she?'

'Listen to whatever she has to say,' Darcy says. 'Be understanding.'

Van Doren looks uncomfortable. 'I'm having second thoughts about this. It's a lot to ask of you, Mrs Kitteridge.'

'I've known Kathy a long time. She asked for me, specifically, didn't she?'

DCI Smithes pinches the bridge of his nose. 'Look, let's not dance around it. Mrs Kitteridge, Kathy is in a confessional state of mind. You may have to hear some hard truths and we're concerned about how you might react.'

'What do you mean, exactly? Hard truths.'

Van Doren wrings her hands, 'Mrs Kitteridge. I regret to be the bearer of this news. Your husband and Kathy were having an affair.'

'Don't be ridiculous. When could they possibly have done that? Martin and I lived in each other's pockets!'

'Kathy will probably tell you about the affair.'

'And possibly more. We don't know.'

'You can't mean….'

'I'm afraid it is a strong possibility.' Smithes says, 'And right now, our main hope of finding out rests on her not jumping off that cliff.'

Her anger flares. She points to Kathy. 'That girl up there couldn't hurt a fly! She would never do anything to hurt Martin, do you understand me? Never!'

'Mrs Kitteridge.' Smithes' voice is hard.

'I'm sorry,' Van Doren addresses the others. 'DCI Smithes, your call, but I recommend that we don't send her up there. I'm sorry Melody, but this is a lot for you to take in.'

'Then what did you drag me all the way out here for, if not to help?!'

'Darcy? Your thoughts?'

Darcy thinks for a moment. Melody wonders at her job. That out of all the words in the world, her job was to pluck out the right combination and elicit a desirable outcome.

Darcy sighs. 'I tend to agree. We could go up there, point down to Melody. Maybe we can convince her to step away to talk to her?'

She's heard enough of this rubbish and takes off, sprinting up the path.

'Melody! Stop!'

But she's running as fast as she can, her legs eating up the final metres to the summit.

'Kathy! It's me!' She gestures to the trailing police officers. 'Stand back. Give us some bloody space.'

Below, shingle, rocks, and the sea. Waves crash. The drop steals the breath from her lungs.

Kathy looks up at her, the wind blows her hair over her face, and she gathers it, tucks it behind an ear. 'It's a long way down isn't it?'

'You asked for me?'

'I…' her eyes swim with tears. 'I'm just so… sorry, Melody.'

'The police tell me you had an affair with Martin. Is it true?'

She nods, buries her head between her knees.

Melody takes a breath, feels a hand on her arm.

'Melody, step away. Come on,' Van Doren whispers.

She pins the detective with a stare. 'Let me talk to her! Back off. Now. Kathy.' Melody turns to her vet nurse. 'You loved Martin?'

Her brown eyes soften and she wipes her eyes on her sleeves.

'Kathy, Martin was very charismatic and exceptionally single-minded when he wanted something. That's how he got me.'

Kathy sniffs.

'But Martin could be a bad person at times, terrible in fact. You're a bright, attractive girl. Martin would have taken advantage of your affection for him, twisted it to his own purpose.'

'No, no, it wasn't like that. I wanted it. I wanted him!' She breaks off in sobs. 'I didn't want to hurt anyone. Especially not you, Melody.'

'I understand.' And she wonders if she does. 'Now. Stand up, wipe those tears from your eyes and come here. Let's put an end to this silliness.'

'But–'

'Kathy. You know I don't like being made to wait. Now come on, there's a good girl.' She does something a little unnatural, raising her arms up, like she'd seen other people do thousands of times in her life.

Kathy gets up slowly, gives a glance behind her at the drop.

'Now, Kathy. I don't hug just anybody, don't miss your chance.'

Kathy drifts to her, stumbling, crying, falling, collapsing into her frame, slumping into her breast, chest heaving in sobs against her. Tears and snot against her jacket. Not to mind, it would wash out.

'You're okay now, Kathy,' she says, unsure of how much pressure to apply when squeezing back.

Over her shoulder, Astrid mouths *Well done.*

Fool. When would this detective stop underestimating her?

51
Astrid

She is in a sombre mood when she returns to Brighton Marina. There will be psychological assessments made of Kathy Spellerman before any interview can take place. Smithes let them off early to catch up on paperwork, though she has no intention of doing any.

When she swings open the front door, it bashes into a bag. It is full of Jenna's things. There are two hard-shelled wheelie cases, a huge blue Ikea bag filled with clothes, picture frames, sketchbooks, and paperbacks.

'Jenna?' she calls. Her voice echoes back.

Astrid takes a long neck from the fridge, pops the cap and forces a wedge of lime into the neck with her thumb. She balls up her suit jacket and launches it at the counter. She slides down to the floor, resting her back on the fridge and thumps the back of her head against it. Unbuttons her blouse, rolls up the sleeves and drinks, drinks deep.

She checks her phone to see if Jenna had left her a message. Nothing.

But everything was going so well! I was going to propose!

She finds the photo of Cuckmere Haven she'd taken on her phone. *There. I was going to do it there.*

This is all too sudden. It must be that actor. That *bitch.*

She takes another swig.

She spoke of love to Kathy Spellerman on Beachy Head. As if she had a fucking clue. Spoken to the wrong person at the wrong place and time. The case was almost over too… but then there'd be another and another. What did Jenna expect? What did she want? She knew what she was getting herself into.

She could argue her case. Beg for Jenna to stay. But like Jenna's final cigarette, she'd been given up on. Jenna didn't backtrack from big decisions.

Keys clatter in the lock.

One eye closed, Astrid squints into the beer bottle. The spent crescent of lime, puffy and useless at the bottom.

She stands upright, not wanting Jenna to find her on the floor, not to remember her like this. She holds the bottle tight to her chest, and waits for Jenna to come through.

They get the green light to interview two days later. Kathy Spellerman arrives with her mother Angela and a smartly suited man named Barber; her legal representative. In the interview prep with Smithes, he drew up a strategy to account for the mental fragility of Spellerman. It fell on the sexist trope of her being the nurturing gentle one, while he got to ask the zingers at choice moments. Typical, but she swallows it.

'Can I get you anything before we begin?' Astrid asks.

'No, I'm fine thank you.'

'And how are you feeling? Up to a few questions?'

She gives a little nod, and Astrid is reminded of a little woodland creature.

Smithes cautions her and begins. 'There's a lot we'd like to ask you, Ms Spellerman. I'd like to give you the opportunity to freely come forward first with anything you'd like to tell us.'

The open trap, a playbook classic. Please, go on, incriminate yourself.

'Why don't you ask your questions,' Barber says, clearly wise to this tactic. 'My client can clear up any confusion you have about this case.'

'No problem. Kathy, could we ask you about the night Martin died?' This tiptoeing. Not her style.

Smithes holds up her original statement. 'We have you on record stating you spent the evening with Lydia Gregorivic. But that wasn't true, was it?'

'No,' she admits. Wise girl. The lawyer had prepped her well.

'Help us understand, Kathy, why would you lie about something so important?'

'A criminal offence,' Smithes says. Thick and unnecessary. *Go hard on the big stuff Bill, not this.*

'I…'

Astrid leans forward. 'Kathy, it's not a crime to have an affair, OK? We all make mistakes.'

Kathy gets a nod from the lawyer. 'I was scared. I thought, maybe, if you knew where I really was, that you'd think I did it – killed Martin – I mean. But I didn't.'

She's lied smoothly enough in the past, Astrid thinks. 'Tell us. Where were you then?'

'I finished with Hugh and Lydia and pretended to walk home. Then I doubled back a few minutes later. I went back, hoping Martin would see me.'

The lawyer watches closely, allowing play to continue. This narrative would be her defence. Astrid pays close attention, looking for holes, contradictions.

'Why wouldn't he want to see you?'

The lawyer intervenes. 'Kathy, tell them what you told me. I think it is important context.'

'Right,' she takes a breath. 'It started with Martin nearly three years ago. It just sort of happened one day when I was there working late.'

'You were young, impressionable,' Astrid offers in the pause, 'Did you feel he took advantage of you?'

She shakes her head. 'Nothing like that. I wanted him. I knew he and Melody were trying for a baby, and I think it was a bit of a strain on their relationship that it wasn't working… and then…' she closes her eyes, 'you'll probably find this out anyway so I may as well tell you. I got pregnant.'

Astrid tries not to show her surprise. 'When?'

'Last August.'

'What happened?'

'I didn't tell Martin at first. I thought, stupidly, I could keep it a secret.'

'But he found out?'

'Morning sickness isn't the easiest thing to hide, especially when your lover is a medical professional. I was maybe eight or nine weeks pregnant when he guessed.'

The story fits what she sees in the timeline of the emails. The playful tone between the lovers had changed to one of desperation from Kathy's side. *I need to see you. Please. Nothing's changed! Let's go back to how it was.*

'How did Martin react?'

'Badly. He persuaded me it would be best to get an abortion. He arranged and paid for it all.' She purses her lips as if trying to steel herself against crying again. 'And that was that.'

'That must have been hard.'

The lip takes another gnawing. She nods quickly. 'Very.'

'And how did that make you feel about Martin?'

'I couldn't understand it. He wanted a child so desperately with Melody, and here was I able to give him what she couldn't… I didn't want to hurt Melody, but…'

'Kathy,' the lawyer warns.

'You hoped he'd leave her for you?' Astrid says.

'Did that make you angry?' Smithes asks.

Kathy shakes her head. 'Disappointed, naturally. Confused. He didn't want to see me anymore. It didn't make any sense.'

She can almost hear the cogs in Bill's brain turning. Now here is a motive. Kathy is right, they would have found out.

'Let's return to the night of his death,' Smithes says, 'now we understand the context… were you hoping for a reconciliation?'

'Pathetic, aren't I? I sent him a message earlier in the day telling him I'd be in our place. I went there and waited for him to come.'

'You need to help us out a bit here, Kathy,' Astrid jumps in. 'Where did you meet? Martin's Office?'

'God, no! Way too risky. Melody had no idea about us, we'd never have risked that. We were so careful. Martin even had a tracker on Melody's car so he knew when she was heading back from a call-out.'

You devious bastard, she thinks.

'He'd thought it all through,' Kathy glows with admiration. 'He rented us a little bolt hole. Paid in cash.'

'Where?' Smithes asks.

'Above the practice in a single bed flat.'

Astrid recalls one of the apartments was supposedly empty. And the mystery key. She desperately wants to ask, but sits on it. Best to keep on track with the timeline.

'So, you went up to the flat and waited for him?'

'Yes. I had a nap. I was so tired.'

'How long for?'

'When I woke it must have been gone half seven. I went home to spend the evening with my flatmate.'

Astrid doesn't voice it, but this feels brittle. 'Did you hear anything below? Any sounds?'

'I was asleep,' Kathy says. 'But when I left, Martin's light was on in his office.'

Smithes asks, 'Why not just go in and see him, Ms Spellerman?'

'It was one of our rules. Everything happened in the flat.'

'Ms Spellerman. You lied to us about your alibi, why should we believe a word you're saying now?'

'Detectives, I will remind you that my client is being extremely co-operative and is in a fragile state of health. We won't tolerate any bullying behaviour.'

Smithes fixes Barber with a stare. ‘That was not bullying behaviour, merely a statement of fact. Why should we believe you, Kathy? There’s something else you’re not telling us, isn’t there?’

‘No… I… I don’t know what you mean.’

‘Counsel requests a comfort break.’

Astrid whispers in Smithes’ ear, ‘Let’s have a break.’ She gives him a knowing look.

‘Granted. Interview suspended at eleven fourteen a.m.’

52
One month prior to the death of Martin Kitteridge

Melody spits bile into the toilet bowl, wipes sweat from her forehead with the back of her hand. Palms the button and the sick swirls down, like a retracted accusation.

'Holy shit, you're unfit,' Ally barely disguises her amusement.

Even in the changing rooms, the faint sound of instructions being barked over music reaches them. 'Am not. You could have stayed, you know.'

'And miss the entertainment? Only ten minutes left anyway.'

'Despite that, it was better than Zumba.' Melody takes off her sweaty sports bra, undoes her ponytail and slides the band over her wrist and stumbles into a shower cubicle. Cranked fully to blue, blissfully powerful jets lance her skin with water so cold it could be glacial meltwater.

Ally is showering in the cubicle next to her, shampoo foam flooding underneath the partition. 'Left, right, jab and kick!'

'Be saying that in my sleep tonight.' Melody wonders if she'll ever be able to lift her arms above her head again.

*

Home. Martin's cooked dinner, the table laid, a chicken breast with some sort of cream sauce on it, chips and peas. No candle – thank God, she's too tired for romance.

'How was… what was it she dragged you to? Boxercise?'

'She didn't drag me, exactly.' She slumps into her chair, pours out a generous glass of Verdejo. She's earned it. She's ravenous and saws into her meat, prongs a chip, dips it all in the pool of sauce. He's overdone the chicken a little. 'I am hungry.'

Martin raises a glass of beer. 'Enjoy.'

She gobbles down the meal, sets down her cutlery neatly together, the plate bare.

'The couch calls. I'm in the mood for something that's borderline unwatchable and bed. You?'

'Let's talk.'

She's too tired. Has he no radar for these things? Another part of her chastises herself. After all, he made an effort with dinner, even though she could deduct points for the frozen chips and peas, not to mention the chicken. What was it with him? He could competently conduct thoracic keyhole surgery in a mammal, yet timing how long to cook a breast of chicken was beyond his ken.

'Come on, Moody.'

She leans back, cradling her glass in her palm. 'Fine.'

'I'm afraid it's on your favourite topic.'

'What else?'

Martin looks up, like he's choosing his words carefully. 'Do you think it's worth us getting a second opinion?'

She stares into the wine, and longs to swim in its pleasing grass colour, something akin to the White Lead shades by Little Green; a blend between Mid and Deep.

'I've come to terms with it now, Martin. We're fine as we are. The two of us.'

'A second opinion,' Martin repeats, 'is just sensible.'

'The doctor was pretty unequivocal.'

'*Pretty* unequivocal? The modifier "pretty" meaning *quite* in this instance, just doesn't ring true for such an absolutist term.'

'I'm tired,' she says sleepily. 'Didn't realise I had to do battle with the bloody Oxford dictionary.'

'Which doctor did you say it was again? Mr Pretty Unequivocal?'

A sip of wine, seconds she squanders. 'A consultant… I can't forget his name now. Remember, I mean.'

'If you can't even remember his name, how–'

'*Her* name.' She jumps on it, something to latch on to, to go on the offensive with. 'Why would you assume it's a man, automatically? Are you a misogynist, Martin?'

He gives her an ugly smile, 'Let's stay on topic, shall we? What is there to lose in seeking a second opinion?'

'Time,' she says, petulantly.

'An hour, tops. Come on. Your boxercise class was shorter than that.'

'More disappointment. Why get our hopes up again? Can't we just be content with what we have?'

'No!' He hits the table with his fist. The cutlery and plates jump. 'This shouldn't be some great revelation to you, Moody! I told you I wanted a family.'

'I…' the force of his anger shocks her.

'Or is it that you don't want to?'

'Both,' she manages, he's taking advantage of her tiredness to trap her. The world spins a moment, she rests her hand on the table.

'Have you been deceiving me, Moody?'

Where was this coming from? She pushes her chair back, wipes her mouth with a napkin. 'I can't, OK? I threw up after the class. She absolutely beasted us, that sadist. I'm going to bed.'

He gives her a hard look, nods. 'Of course. Let's put this

off. *Again.*'

'Let's.' She places her napkin down.

'Oh, before I forget, I took a call for you today.'

Her muscles ache so much she's not sure she can even push herself up to stand. How humiliating. 'Oh? Who from?'

'Some medical company, a survey. She'll try you again tomorrow about five. Ring any bells?'

Sluggish, can't think. 'Medical company? A survey? Spam probably.'

'You look stressed, Moody.' He pushes back his chair and positions himself behind her. Hands on her shoulders, strength concealed in the circular movements of his fingers and thumbs. 'You're so tense.'

'Come on, you know I don't like…'

'Being touched?'

'Massages.' She leans, trying to make out the label on the bottle of wine, but the light's too bad. 'What percentage is this?'

'Enough.'

Her arm lifts up, involuntarily. Like she's a puppet being controlled by a string master 'What are you doing?'

Martin's grip is firm, hurts, he rolls up the sleeves to the armpit. 'You lying bitch!'

'What the–? Martin, get off!' Her wine glass tumbles, rolls in an arc and smashes on the floor.

'The medical company was the parent company of Implanon, Moody. I googled it!'

She realises, then. Her breath is too short. 'You've drugged me?' She can't diagnose her symptoms, a muscle relaxant, almost certainly, but something else too.

He runs a thumb over the little bump, squints at the tiny scar. 'Now, why would someone who is allegedly incapable of conceiving bother with a birth control implant?'

She tries to move her arm but it doesn't move, there's no power there. 'Martin, I–'

'But that's odd, right? Because you've still being having your period. Only what do I find at the back of your wardrobe?' He produces her box of Tampax and joke shop blood. 'You devious manipulative bitch!' he spits through gritted teeth. 'I agree with you on one thing. No need for a second opinion. I think we've found the root cause of our problems, darling.'

Her eyelids are heavy, the ceiling spotlights melt, converge, and split apart like supernovas.

'It's a simple procedure, I've looked it up on their website. Piece of piss actually. Hold steady. No anaesthetic handy, I'm afraid.' He holds up a serrated table knife, the metal catching the ceiling light a moment. 'This will probably work, you think?'

She tips back on the chair. There's the ceiling, the crunch of glass as he steps on her fallen wine glass. It grinds as his weight shifts. Martin leans, a shadow with curly black hair like a clown in silhouette.

'No… don't…' Flexing her fingers, toes. It's all she has.

Her arm is trapped by Martin's knee, squashing the top of her bicep, pressing the muscle into her upper humerus. His elbow jerks back and forth in a sawing motion.

Pain, hot, fiery pain. She can't scream, just gasps.

Gritted teeth, sprays of saliva. 'Bitch. Lying bitch!'

She closes her eyes, grinds her teeth through the pain. The sawing stops, the knife tingles onto the floor. The pain remains, so hot it's like someone is holding a lighter on her skin.

She opens her eyes. He's bent over her arm, fingers slicked with blood, *her* blood, invading, dislodging.

'Got it, honey, it's out now. You can relax, you're fertile now!'

He stands. A surge of blood rushes out, pulsing out of the mess of her wound. Martin tips the wine bottle sloppily over the bleeding entry point. A sting of cold. Her wine mixes with the bright red blood into a morbid rosé. He lazily ties a bandage into a loose tourniquet.

'You can sort yourself out later. Raise your arm up above your head at least, Moody, for Christ's sake.'

'Can't,' she gasps.

'Of course. Allow me.' The confusion of desire and hatred in him frightens her to the very innards of her being.

No. He won't cave in. Not ever. Neither will she.

He stands, watching her, breathing loudly through his nose, then nods. 'No time like the present.'

He yanks down her joggers, pants, parts her legs and stares.

'Beautiful. Like the folds of a rose.'

Hot tears run down her cheeks. It's not for what is happening…it's the *how*. The utter helplessness, robbed completely of her power, her will, to not even be able to bite, to kick and slap him.

The clink of a belt buckle. He's touching himself now, pulling with rapid tugs, eyes closed. 'Come on, come on,' he says to himself. He grabs her mouth. 'Say that you deserve this'

She won't give him it.

'Say that you fucking deserve this, Moody! You are mine!'

Her eyes speak for her with an iron will her body cannot match. *No.*

Martin lets out a sob, lowers his weight onto her and the air presses out from her lungs. He enters, crying, trembling, tears roll and land on her cheek. But he's not hard.

He tries a few angry thrusts punctured by sobs, but it doesn't get him going. Her cold disdain rushes to meet him. He looks away, bunches his eyes up.

'This isn't over, Moody!' Stringy mucus in his mouth. Raw eyes. He yanks up his trousers and stumbles away. 'It isn't over!'

Is he coming back? She lies. Listens. Can't tell. Some cocktail of shock and defiance rolls around her body, while her arm throbs an angry beat.

How long until she can move again?
Time.
Time to think. To plan.
Martin’s right.
It is not over.

53
Astrid

'You want one?' Smithes fishes in his pocket for change.

'Please.'

Smithes feeds coins into the coffee machine. Astrid contemplates the evidence bag she holds, containing the mystery key. 'Tenner says it's the one to their lovers' nest.'

Smithes stabs a button with a finger. 'I'm not taking that bet. She's on the hook, let's reel her in.'

Back in the interview room. Astrid presents the key to Kathy.

'Looks the same.' Kathy takes out a set of keys, and wriggles one from the ring.

'May I?' Astrid holds it up to the light, overlays it with the mystery key. 'Identical.'

Smithes nods to the door. She ducks out and instructs Collins and Hussain to get a forensics team together to go through the apartment.

When she returns, Kathy is reading one of the sheets of e-mails they'd recovered.

'Can you confirm that you wrote these emails to Martin Kitteridge?' Smithes says.

Kathy Spellerman drains of colour. 'No comment.'

'We've traced them to your IP address, Kathy,' Astrid says gently.

Spellerman nods twice, tears suddenly welling in her eyes.

'Could you confirm for the video and audio please?'

'Yes,' she gasps.

Astrid tugs a tissue from the box, hands it over.

'And this snake symbol?' Smithes points at the circled snake emoji on every page.

The lawyer waves her on to answer. 'It was Martin's pet name for me.'

'A snake?' Astrid can't help but exclaim.

'Cobra. He said I had sexy curves… God, it sounds so stupid now.' She bunches the tissue in her fist, holds it to her nose.

'How much do you know about snakes, Kathy?'

'Nothing, really.'

Astrid places more photographs in front of Kathy. The first, the newspaper clipping of her with Martin Kitteridge handling the snakes from the *Argus* article.

'But that was just a little thing for school, years ago!'

'And this?' Astrid places a photograph taken from Kathy's Facebook account showing the tattoo of a recently minted cobra, red raw around the edges.

'Two years ago! It's just a tattoo.'

'This is all highly circumstantial,' the lawyer says. 'None of this would hold any water in court.'

'Okay, then let's firm things up, shall we? Do you recognise this man?' Smithes places a headshot of Olaf Gudmundson in front of her.

'Never seen him before in my life.'

'Interesting. Because he knows you, Ms Spellerman. He claims you bought a venomous cobra snake off him in November.'

'He must be mixing me up with somebody else…'

'Was that when you started planning all this, Kathy? Late November, after your abortion?'

'Don't answer that.' Barber, the lawyer is scribbling a note.

'But… this is utter crap!' Kathy says.

'Your prints were found on the whisky bottle that was spiked with sedative found in Martin's bloodstream.'

'Don't a–'

'But I've told them already. I only picked it up to look at the label to see what sort of brand he liked!'

Astrid can barely breathe. With each word, Spellerman incriminates herself further.

Smithes must sense it too, because he says, 'Martin treated you terribly. Anyone would behave out of character, when treated like that.'

She joins the attack. Softly, softly be damned. 'You must see how this all looks, Kathy? Martin ends your affair; makes you have an abortion. Martin, this man you loved, called you a cobra in bed, your little secret name for one another. You're not a bad person, you just wanted to get him back for what he did to you, didn't you, Kathy?'

Tears roll down Kathy's cheeks. 'No… I… loved him.'

'She's already said she didn't do it. Unless you have any real questions, I think we best leave it there, Detectives,' Barber says, a little wild-eyed.

'Then let me just say this.' Smithes stands and Astrid's heart is beating out of its chest, knowing what's coming. 'Katherine Spellerman, I'm arresting you on suspicion of the murder of Martin Kitteridge. You do not have to say anything, but it may harm your defence if you do not mention when questioned something which you later rely on in court. Anything you do say may be given in evidence.'

Astrid snaps on her gloves. She looks up at the Edwardian house, at the coveralled people moving about in the top window. All along, it had been just there. There is just a stain where the Kitteridge sign used to be. Now a For Lease sign is tied with wire to the front gate.

She follows Smithes around to the side entrance, and up the stairs.

Pete Wade from forensics squeezes past them down the

stairs, nodding to them.

'Pete,' they both say.

'So, this was where they met,' Bill says when they reach the top.

It's a simple apartment, with a sloping roof; lounge, diner, and kitchen all in the same room. A bathroom. A double bedroom.

'It's in here,' someone calls.

'I still can't quite believe it,' Astrid says. 'She just seems so.... meek?'

'It's the quiet ones you have to watch out for. Now would you look at that.'

Astrid takes in the cheap, wood-framed, neatly made, double bed, and a chest of drawers on which the snake tank sits. The plug hangs down, the tank is dark, empty. A bed of bark, an imitation branch.

'Spellerman conveniently forgot to mention this.'

Astrid cocks her head to one side imagining a snake in there. 'Maybe they liked doing it in front of snakes?'

'I've heard of weirder things.'

She exhales, every surface covered in forensic dust. 'This was the perfect place to keep it.'

Smithes grunts, rests a hand on her shoulder. 'You did well, Van Doren. The CPS are swimming in evidence; Olaf's testimony, the pathologist's report, the bloody tank right in front of our eyes. A jilted lover with a cobra tattooed on her body. I hope for her sake that Barber's a half-decent lawyer.'

'I actually feel sorry for her. Just a mixed-up girl.'

'Have you seen the tabloids?

'Sex, snakes and murder. Hope she can tough it out.' She means it too. Kathy Spellerman will be a high suicide risk wherever she's held. She'd probably get life, but that didn't actually mean life. No previous, the psychological scarring of her affair and abortion could all be taken into account. With good behaviour, she could be out by her mid-forties. A lot still to live for. To hope for.

She taps her gloved finger on the glass of the empty tank.

'Funny that Spellerman still won't tell us what she did with it. Even after everything,' Smithes says. 'She must have an almost spiritual connection to it, to protect it so.'

'I wonder where the snake is right now? What is it seeing?'

54
Melody

Melody dangles the thawed mouse down through the small hatch at the top of the tank. Drops it onto chips of bark.

The cobra watches. Doesn't move for its prey.

'When's he coming?' Ally asks. 'It's been here too long already.'

The shed at the end of Ally's tiny garden is stacked with folded patio furniture, a broken strimmer, and rigged up with heaters.

'Soon. You know I drove past the practice on the way here. Police and forensics were up in the flat. They'd have found the tank by now.'

'I still don't' see why you had to do that. It just seemed like too much of a risk, Mel.'

'You'll see. Everything has its purpose.' She closes the hatch, wipes her hands on her jeans. 'Will you come with me to see the flat later? Think it's the one.'

There's a double rap on the doorframe, and Olaf comes wearing a broad-brimmed hat, a large cardboard box in his hands.

'Did you check you weren't followed?' Ally asks.

'Of course. I'm not an idiot.' He puts the box on the floor and opens the flaps. It's empty and easily big enough to house the tank for transportation to his van.

Melody hands him the envelope. He glances inside.

'Count it if you like.'

He pockets it. 'No need.'

She understands. He's the only one who could ruin her. She wouldn't short-change him.

'When are you off?' Ally nibbles on a nail.

'I get my passport back after the trial. Then I'm gone for good.'

'Any news on Sheridan?' Melody asks.

'Looks like he'll get some time but I'm not hanging around to find out. Are you going to be at the girl's trial?'

'Of course,' Melody says.

Olaf wrings his hands. 'And you're sure she'll be cleared?'

Ally raises an eyebrow. 'As long as nobody is looking our way, I'm not sure it matters.'

'Of course it does, Al!' she reprimands. 'Her trial is punishment enough. And if Kathy's barrister is moderately competent, she'll walk.'

Olaf unplugs the tank. 'I don't like it. That poor girl.'

'She'll go free. Just you watch.'

Olaf grunts. 'You want to say goodbye?'

Melody crouches, presses her nose to the glass.

The cobra darts, lightning-fast, and takes the mouse in its jaws, its mouth stretched and rubbery.

Deadly.

The sea is a teal Air Force Blue by Little Greene, the sky a lighter Baby Blue by Dulux. It's a view she could get used to. Above, dense formations of lenticular clouds, mottled like giant blister packs of white tablets.

'What do you think, then?'

Ally leans on the sink and gazes out. 'Wow. I mean, this is the view from the kitchen, *the kitchen!*'

'Have you stepped out onto the balcony?' The estate agent says, teeth gleaming in a perfect smile and she opens the lock, slides the door back.

A blast of briny air envelops her, a cold kiss. Melody leans on the railings. Pots of soggy soil and dead foliage. 'Bless them. That was optimistic. Growing anything in the salt air is a waste of effort.'

'Plastic plants are the way to go, they really can be rather good these days, you can't tell the difference.' the estate agent says, and reads the look of distaste on her face. 'Are you moving in together?'

'No, I'm just a friendly second opinion.' Ally says. 'But I'd be tempted to leave the husband and kids for this view! You know, I can really see you living here, Mel.'

The pier is to her east, the i360 viewing platform like a round donut being threaded on a stick. To the west is Shoreham Harbour, the power station. Straight ahead; a seemingly limitless horizon. Uncluttered. Perfect.

'I'll take it, on one condition.'

The estate agent stifles a smile at what must be an easy commission. 'What's that?'

'I'd like to redecorate the whole place. I'll do it myself, pay for the paint.'

'Let's see…' She consults her clipboard, 'It was redecorated throughout in magnolia when the last tenant moved out. You can almost smell the paint, it's that fresh.'

Melody shakes her head. 'Magnolia. Well, you go and tell Mr and Mrs Bland that it will look one hundred times better once I'm through.'

'Sorry,' Ally says to the estate agent, and Melody smacks her friend lightly on the arm.

'Don't you dare apologise. It's the owners who should be apologising to us. It's a crime to ruin such a beautiful apartment with magnolia.'

'I'll ask.' The estate agent flashes a tight smile. 'And be sure to let you know.'

55
Astrid

'DI Van Doren.'

'Detective Inspector Astrid Van Doren.' She puts the warrant card down on the dresser and stares at herself in the mirror. Applies bright red lipstick to a mouth that feels incapable of smiling again. Daubs black mascara to lashes that surround pained eyes. She could always just go for one or two, feign a headache, come home.

The Globe is packed, but some of the team must have been here a while already because they've got a table and it's covered in half-drunk beer bottles, vodka-mixers, and empties.

'Wahey! Here she is!' Collins yells, and they all stand, offering handshakes, hugs and congratulations.

'What are you having?' Hussain asks, removing his wallet from his pocket.

'Heineken. Cheers.' She looks around. 'Smithes not here yet?'

Astrid sits, chats, drinks, as they relive the case blow by blow and for the moment, she can push Jenna somewhere further into the back of her mind.

'So, how does it feel to be the youngest female DI in Sussex Police?' Gardner asks. Sarah looks pretty tonight. A low-cut top with a butterfly motif, hair straightened and shiny.

'Unworthy? I'm just pleased we got a result.'

Gardner lowers her voice, leans in and Astrid catches a whiff of a little too much vanilla perfume. 'You know, everyone knows it was you who drove this. Bill… he's a lovely man, but he's a bit useless, isn't he? Without you we'd have never gotten there.'

Astrid flushes. 'You can't say things like that, Sarah.' And she wonders if it's true. 'Bill's an enabler… not an autocrat. He gives us room to flourish. We're lucky. There's not another SIO like him.'

Sarah gives her a knowing grin. 'I see. Loyal. But without you, his star…' She mimes something rising in the air then crashing into the table.

'Drink? I'm sure it's my round.'

Smithes puts in an appearance, typically while she happens to be at the bar.

'Congratulations, Astrid.' He raises his half-pint. He must be driving.

'You too, sir.'

'We're in a pub. Bill is fine.' He pulls at his lapels. 'Officially DCI now. How about that? Both of us together, Astrid. Quite the team.'

'Entangled fates,' she says, meaning it as a joke, but it just sounds weird.

'Good to show the face, but it doesn't do to over fraternise. Now you, you can still just about get away with it. Not for too much longer the way things are going, enjoy it while you can.'

She gives him a weak smile. 'I'll do my best, sir. Bill, sorry.'

He rests a hand on top of her own. 'You know. Sandy would be very proud of you.'

She nods, but Bill doesn't have the right to say such things.

The best venues in Brighton are gay clubs, but she can't persuade them to give it a go. They end up on West Street with the stag dos, bad music, testosterone and sticky carpets. Van Doren hovers at the bar, swigging a beer. Music pounds. Awful, with a heavy beat. Horley is on the dance floor, dancing a pretty good Robot.

'Come on!' Hussain yells, beckoning her over, but she isn't

drunk enough to dance.

‘Hey,’ Gardner takes her hand. ‘Come with me.’

‘No, really,’ she protests, ‘I really don’t want to dance.’

But Gardner doesn’t lead her to the dance floor but to a quiet spot and eases her back against the wall, and presses lips onto her.

For a moment she doesn’t respond and Gardner separates. ‘Is this okay?’

Yes. No. Does it matter anymore? She strokes Sarah’s hair, then pulls her in, lips soft and wet.

‘Oh! That is so hot! Look Dal, look!’

Astrid cocks her head to one side to see an audience of leering boys.

‘Fancy a threesome, love?’

‘Idiots.’

‘Let’s get out of here,’ Gardner says.

Instinctively she doesn’t offer to go to her marina flat. They go back to Gardner’s, a block in Furze Hill. They paw at each other in the lift on the way up. She pulls up Sarah’s top, kisses her tits, takes a nipple in her mouth, flicks it with her tongue. Hard as a bullet.

Astrid thrusts her hand down and slides in the tip of her finger. It’s wet and hot. Sarah eases herself down deeper to the hilt and lets out a muffled: ‘Fuck.’

The lift dings. They freeze. The doors part. Nobody there.

Sarah giggles, grabs her by the hand and pulls her out.

Astrid wakes early. Mouth tasting dry and horrible. Sarah’s hair is fanned across the pillow. The swell of her naked breasts under the sheet. *Feel something.* But it isn’t Jenna.

She dresses quietly, zips up her boots and eases the front door closed behind her. She’ll explain. Later.

She can’t bear the thought of her flat. Astrid pulls her leather jacket across tight for warmth, and heads for her mother’s house

56
Melody

It's a crisp, late spring day.

Lewes Crown Court is a film set; grey stone facade, steps, and corpulent pillars. The bombast of justice. Press corps, a nall army of them, swarm, encircling her.

Do you think she did it, Melody?

What sentence are you hoping for?

How do you feel about Kathy Spellerman now?

Did you know about the kinky sex games, Melody?

Nothing to say. Shades to hide behind.

Inside, she puts her sunglasses on top of her head. Scours. .lly is mid-call. Her friend has been here for the first day of the ial and is here now, on what could possibly be the final day of . While Ally has topped and tailed it, she's stayed the course. A :oic presence in the audience.

A sip of water from her bottle. A nibble on a cereal bar while ıe waits for Ally to finish.

Howard and Susan are huddled together in a corner, ɔsorbed in conversation or perhaps pretending they haven't ɜen her.

Kathy's mother is in a whispered huddle with their lawyer, ands clawing nervously at each other.

'Have you heard?' Ally says, pocketing her phone.

'Heard what?'

'Richie Sheridan's trial got postponed.'

'Oh.' She sets her jaw. 'Will he get bail?'

Before Ally can answer, Hugh joins them. He's in a smart

navy suit with red tie that he fiddles with. 'Strange day.'

'Quite.'

'Apparently they offered her a plea deal.' Shakes his heac 'Didn't want to take it, stubborn thing.'

'I'm sure she is doing what she thinks is best.' She turns t Ally, 'Shall we?'

Melody takes her usual seat in the third row. The oppressiv wood panelling, wood everywhere, the room stinks of it. Sh eyes the jurors, the clothes, the glasses, the age, the haircut Surely there is only one way to lean.

The trial was late into its third week. There had been surre moments; like hearing her own emergency call to report th discovery of the body and hearing Kathy describe her sexu encounters with Martin. There had been slow moment Detective Smithes' performance as the lead investigator. Th minutiae of forensic and pathology reports, the exhibits, th testimony and cross-examination. Her own turn on the stand a least, had been mercifully brief.

The courtroom artist is here again in the row ahead of he She stares intently at Kathy as if burning the image on to he retina. Earlier in the trial, Melody had seen her on the floo outside the courtroom during a recess, pencil-sketching Kath from memory. Not even allowed to draw within the courtroon Now there was a thing.

In a way, it is why she is here. As per UK law, there woul be no camera recordings of events from within, even the drawin was an impression of a memory. Emancipation from Marti Punishment for Kathy. Her own freedom. They were all itemise on the same bill, and she mustn't flinch from paying it in full.

They rise for the judge, Her Honour Constance Holt. Th court is in session and after a few words from the judge, th prosecution is invited to give their closing statements.

The robed prosecutor, Durham, is a serious, thin man, a fe strands of grey hair poking out from his horsehair wig. A voic steeped with gravitas. 'Ladies and Gentlemen of the jury. Over the last three weeks you've heard a tragic story. Martin Kitteridge, a husband and veterinary surgeon in Hove, was murdered in extraordinary circumstances. He left a bereft wife, a sister, parents, and a community of friends behind.' He waves a hand towards Kathy, who is staring downwards.

'Here's what we know. Irrefutably, Ms Spellerman and Martin Kitteridge had an affair that ended five weeks before his murder. You've seen the desperate emails sent by Ms Spellerman demanding a reconciliation, increasing in pitch and desperation. Here was a young woman, who fell in love, fell pregnant, and envisioned a life for herself with Martin Kitteridge. In the dock you heard her admit she harboured these hopes. You heard her admit she was bitterly disappointed. You also heard her claim that she didn't do it.

'So, could she be lying to you? To us?' Durham pauses for effect. 'Of course.' He holds up a paper, and jabs a finger at it. 'The defendant lied in her first statement to police. She lied about her alibi, she lied about being able to handle snakes. She looked her good friend and employer Melody Kitteridge in the eye every day for more than two years, while secretly sleeping with her husband! By any measure, it is a prolific track record of lies and deceitful behaviour.'

Durham sips from a glass of water, in no hurry. 'Martin Kitteridge nicknamed his lover, the defendant, The Cobra. The defence may try again to convince you that the choice of murder weapon, a venomous snake, was a coincidence and had nothing to do with this pet name.' He lets out a mirthful laugh here. 'I wish my esteemed colleague the best of luck with that endeavour.'

The courtroom hangs, rapt. Each accusation produces a short shake of the head from Kathy. Durham is good. Convincing.

'Martin Kitteridge was drugged with Midazolam, a sedative Ms Spellerman used routinely as a veterinary nurse at the

Kitteridge Practice. Fact: she had a key to access the pharmaceuticals on site. Fact: Midazolam was found inside a whisky bottle. Fact: the defendant's prints were found on the bottle.'

He scratches under his chin, letting the facts stack and settle in the jurors' minds. 'The defence will no doubt point out the multiple sets of prints on the whisky bottle. True. However, every set on that bottle has been identified and eliminated by a proven alibi or meticulous investigation. Except the defendant's.'

In the parallel trial occurring in her own mind, Melody savours this particular detail. It was truly divine. Of all of them, her own alibi was the most perfect.

Though it hadn't been entirely random. Ten days before the murder, she visited Coppell's, Bradshaw's and Dapper's farms and found the cows who were already at or approaching full term, and injected them all with a corticosteroid hormone. The hormone triggered a slow inducement of labour that can take over a week to effect. Across the three farms, she had all but guaranteed call-outs for that Friday afternoon.

'Strands of the defendant's hair, fingerprints and DNA were found in abundance at the crime scene. So where was the defendant when Martin Kitteridge was killed? Metres away, in the flat above the practice where she engineered her shady liaisons. And what was she doing? She claims to have been asleep. How convenient. In the annals of excuses, it might rank close to *my dog ate my homework.*'

A couple of jurors let out a little laugh at this.

'And then… the police discovered a snake tank in that very same apartment. Perhaps some far-fetched conspiracy theory will be offered by the defence. I urge you to remain within the realm of fact.'

Kathy probably had been asleep. Melody had dosed Kathy's cup of tea that afternoon, disguised it with sugar. Enough to make her a little drowsy.

'Then we have the testimony of the snake breeder Olaf Gudmundson. He identified Kathy Spellerman to police as somebody who purchased a venomous cobra in late November. Ms Spellerman claims to never have seen this man before in her life. Again, we have Ms Spellerman's word butting against the clear testimony.'

Melody keeps her face placid. Olaf's testimony cost a pretty penny, but he had been worth it. What really happened, was rather elegant. The snake tank had been in Martin's room all day, hidden away behind a stack of files at the back of Martin's office before anyone had arrived to work. The hatch opened on a timer at seven p.m. Then the ghost appeared. Ally, in forensic coveralls, to recapture the snake, remove the tank and lock the door.

'Nobody else could have done this. Detective Chief Inspector Smithes, the Senior Investigating Officer on this case, stated that all other suspects were investigated thoroughly and eliminated by CID. Ms Spellerman had the motive, the means, and is the only suspect without an alibi. Evidence suggests the murder weapon was in her possession at the time of the murder. Make no mistake, ladies and gentlemen of the jury, this was a carefully planned pre-meditated murder. Returning with a verdict of guilty on all charges isn't just the obvious conclusion, it is a responsibility, to bring justice to the family and wife of Martin Kitteridge, a man taken well before his time.

'The prosecution rests, Your Honour.'

57
Astrid

Bloody typical. She's late. She'd had to show her face at a career fair at the university. Pump hands, hand out some leaflets, answer questions. Fine, the force was looking for new blood and she had to build up some new credit after her latest promotion. Oh yes, the young, gay, female Detective Inspector – another poster-child for diversity. She knew why she had to do it; it didn't mean she had to like it. It was using who she was to make some sort of political point. What's more, could she trust her promotion was based on her abilities or because it looked good? And today, there was the drain on her time – missing the closing arguments in the Kitteridge case.

She skips up the steps, past the security check and slips into the courtroom, taking a spot at the back. Next to her, a reporter scribbles notes in Teeline shorthand on a little pad.

'Order,' the judge, Holt, says, banging the gavel. In her experience, Holt was a reasonable judge, but sentenced hard.

'What's happening?' she whispers to the hack.

'Prosecution gave closing arguments. Slam dunk.' He returns to his scribbles and the defence barrister rises, tugging at his gown as if for strength. The barrister, Barber, adjusts his glasses on his nose.

'Ladies and Gentlemen of the jury,' he says in his rich, low baritone. 'The prosecution would have you believe that Ms Spellerman was so distraught and twisted by her affair and lost baby that she sought revenge on her erstwhile lover. She couldn' have him, so nobody else could!' He makes a face as if smelling something unpleasant. 'Nothing could be farther from the truth. Kathy Spellerman was deeply in love with Martin Kitteridge. She wanted him back.' He holds up a sheaf of papers, and shakes them. 'She never, ever threatened him in any of the emails. Not once. She loved him and harboured hopes of winning him back. I repeat. She loved him. You do not kill something you love.'

Astrid spots Melody Kitteridge in the third row, sitting next to her friend, face as expressive as a mannequin.

'Now let's address the so-called evidence. I put it to you that virtually all the evidence presented by the prosecution is circumstantial, the evidence gathered by investigators flawed and incomplete. The life of a young girl is in the balance. Circumstantial just won't cut it. Yes, her DNA and hair samples were found in Martin's room, of course they were. It was her workplace, in her role as veterinary nurse she supported both Mr and Mrs Kitteridge hopping regularly into their treatment rooms throughout the day. It would be odd if they weren't evidence of her presence in the room.

'As for the whisky bottle, which had at least four sets of fingerprints on it: think about it. If you were planning on murdering someone in the premeditated fashion the prosecution suggests, first by spiking a drink, wouldn't you at least use gloves? Or clean the bottle afterwards? Ms Spellerman is a qualified veterinary nurse, an intelligent woman. There isn't a shred of proof that she put the drugs in that whisky bottle. Nothing. Perhaps somebody else did, even Martin Kitteridge himself. It is wild conjecture at best and categorizes the hopeful nature of this conviction.

'This case was managed by an inexperienced Senior Investigating Officer, and an inexperienced deputy. It was characterised by procedural errors, mistaken arrests, missed opportunities and the mishandling of evidence.'

Astrid feels herself shrinking. It was all part of the game, but she hates it nonetheless.

'For example, Mrs Kitteridge, though no longer a suspect in the case, was allowed to leave the crime scene for a bath to wash off crucial evidence on the night of the murder!'

Damn Tom Weston.

'Then, there is the frankly bizarre appearance of a snake tank in the apartment where Ms Spellerman and Mr Kitteridge conducted their love affair. And when I say "bizarre appearance" I choose my words carefully. Forensic teams found no prints or DNA traces on the tank. I repeat. No physical evidence. Nothing. Not Mr Kitteridge or Ms Spellerman. Nothing on the feeding hatch, nothing. Why? Did it appear by magic?'

Astrid holds her breath. What was this about the tank having no traces on it? It was the first she'd heard of it.

'She probably wiped it clean, the prosecution said. So, we have a suspect who leaves her prints on a whisky bottle and physical evidence in Martin's office and their lover's meeting spot…. yet wipes this one thing clean? Wholly inconsistent. The prosecution can't have it both ways. If that doesn't trip the alarm of your doubts, I remind you of the forensics report which states that dust particles found underneath the tank were consistent with the dust on top of the chest of drawers. Meaning it had been planted there very recently.'

'Mr Barber,' the judge warns.

'Placed there, very recently,' Barber backtracks.

Astrid, too, bristles at the implication. But then, when she'd asked Smithes about the forensic report on the flat, he'd fobbed her off with generalities; *It was all fine, as expected.*

If the defence barrister is right… but Bill wouldn't have… would he?

Barber paces in front of the jury. 'Ask yourselves, how and why would a snake tank appear in the flat, after the date of the murder? The key piece of evidence on which the prosecution rests is the sworn testimony of the snake handler Ola

Gudmundson. An unlicensed snake oil salesman, sorry, snake breeder. A man who cut a deal with police to save his skin, a deal that specifically stated that he give testimony in this trial.' He points to the floor as he says this. 'He was *incentivised* to testify. On the stand he was hazy on specifically where and when he and Ms Spellerman were said to have met. Evasive. Uncomfortable. Why? Because it didn't happen. Mr Gudmundson did supply snakes, that much is true. But to a criminal organisation with a brutal retribution for dealing with snitches. No wonder Mr Gudmundson was so keen to cut a deal and point a finger at a poor young woman caught in the wrong place at the wrong time. An easy fit-up job.'

He waits a beat, letting this sink in. Damn lawyers, he was even convincing her.

'So, let's step back and ask, if not Ms Spellerman, then who? Bank statements and witness testimony prove that Martin Kitteridge was in significant debt to criminal entities in the Brighton area from gambling on illegal events. Significant cash withdrawals were made leading up to his death, almost cleaning out the entire account. This had nothing to do with Ms Spellerman. No corresponding sums landed in *her* account. This was a desperate man scrambling to pay off some very dangerous men. And I think he ran out of time.

'Professional criminals know how to cover their tracks. Is it possible, that while Ms Spellerman slept upstairs, these hardened gangsters could have killed Martin Kitteridge?' He raises his two index fingers up as if framing his words. 'Remember: these criminals have a documented relationship with Olaf Gudmundson, who once supplied a venomous cobra for their illegal betting operation, where Martin Kitteridge racked up his debts, a fact glossed over by the prosecution as an irrelevance.'

She wants to yell "Objection!". There wasn't a shred of physical evidence to suggest Sheridan or his crew had done this. No matter how good someone was, they always left something.

'Mr Kitteridge's murder was a professional hit and a warning message to anyone owing them money. And irony of tragic ironies, they used the very snake Martin Kitteridge gambled on to kill him. This isn't mere hearsay; the police were actively pursuing Sheridan for a time in relation to this case… until they bungled the sting operation. Pressure to get a result, embarrassment at their botched operation, they needed a name fast. With the big fish off the hook, they pinned it on the next best fit: my client, Ms Spellerman.'

Barber was a complete and utter bastard. That was *not* how it went down.

'The evidence against Ms Spellerman is at best circumstantial, at worst, desperately coerced. The most likely perpetrators were not satisfactorily investigated. There is no trustworthy, material evidence in this case. Not a shred. This poor woman has been through enough, and should not be sitting in this courtroom today. Ladies and Gentlemen of the jury, etch the words *reasonable doubt* into your minds as you deliberate. This young woman made mistakes; she fell in love with a married man. But that is not a crime. You can and must clear Ms Spellerman of all charges for which she is accused and put an end to her ordeal.'

He nods up to Judge Holt.

'Your Honour, the defence rests.'

Bloody hell.

The reporter whispers, 'Didn't see that coming. Any comment to make, Detective Inspector?'

She shakes her head. But wasn't this what always happened? Perception, and therefore judgement, were always at the mercy of clever advocacy.

The jurors file out. She'd better get back to work, four cases on the go, a busy team under her. She spots a custody officer she knows, asks him to drop her a text when the jury have a verdict Could be hours. Could be days.

Melody Kitteridge stands, fanning herself with something, talking heatedly to her friend. Then, as if sensing her, their eyes meet briefly across the courtroom. Astrid raises a hand in acknowledgement. Mrs Kitteridge mirrors the gesture.

Either way. It would all be over soon.

58
Melody

The sea shakes up and down.

Melody wipes a bead of sweat away with her forearm. "Love Will Tear Us Apart" by Joy Division plays on the Bose. Strangely good to run to. Must be the drum beat. The digital display ticks from 11.9 kilometres to 12 kilometres and she presses the down arrow to lower the pace for the warm down.

Outside a seagull soars on a thermal, as if pinned there. She steps off her Reebok GT30 Lite treadmill and grabs some Evian from the fridge. The cold liquid wells beautifully in her belly. The gull rises, disappearing from her plane of vision.

She checks her phone. Still nothing. A clerk from the CPS has been keeping her up to date with proceedings. The jury had been unable to reach a unanimous verdict, a majority verdict of no less than ten to two would be deemed acceptable.

The trial is pleasing, the world sees two options: Spellerman or Sheridan. Martin has been dealt with, Kathy is receiving her punishment and she, Melody, is beyond suspicion. Free.

Melody runs a bath, hot, with a splash of Dettol. She washes her hair with soap and a jug of water. After, she stands at the kitchen window staring out to sea, conveying carrots from plate to hummus pot to her mouth in a triangle.

Her phone blinks into life.

Finally.

*

The press is out in full force. The court room is packed, straining at capacity.

Melody wears a smart suit, the shade a purifying Skimmed Milk White by Farrow & Ball. Ally clears her throat. 'However it goes, shall we get a drink?'

'There's only one likely outcome. We'll celebrate after, I know an excellent cocktail lounge.'

'Wherever you like, Tristan's going to pick the kids up from school. I'm yours all day if you want.'

The courtroom rises. The stage is set. The judge, the jurors, the defendant, the gallery, the prosecution and defence teams nervously waiting. There is only one question in the minds of everyone in the room, and at this moment, the only people who know are the twelve jurors.

Kathy's head hangs. Melody recognises it, she sees it often enough in animals. It is suffering. It should be over soon enough. The words *not guilty* will pivot her suffering to joy.

Judge Holt asks the foreperson to come forward. She stands. Plays with the buttons on her cardigan.

'Have you reached a unanimous verdict?' Holt asks.

'No, your honour.' The foreperson replies.

Melody tries to swallow, but her mouth is arid.

'Have you reached a majority verdict of at least ten to two?'

'Yes, your honour.'

'Very well.'

'On the charge of Grievous Bodily Harm with Intent, how do you find the defendant?'

There's a pause for a beat, breaths collectively held.

'Guilty, your honour.'

Melody rocks back into her seat, stunned. Kathy gasps out a 'No'. There's a collective release of energy from the gallery, disbelief, satisfaction, all mixed into one. Howard rubs Susan's shoulders, who is nodding vigorously. Everyone knows that the outcome of this lesser, though serious charge, will mirror the greater one.

'Order!' Holt barks, with a snap of the gavel, 'Order!'

The noise subsides. Holt gathers herself.

'And on the charge of the Murder of Martin William Kitteridge, how do you find the defendant?'

'Guilty, your honour.'

'But I didn't do it!' Kathy sobs. 'I didn't! I swear!' Custody officers pull her to her feet, cuff her, and lead her away.

The court is adjourned for sentencing. Everyone is up on their feet, the barristers shuffling papers, muttering to each other. Barber is straight over to Kathy. The poor girl is a ruin. Susan and Howard are hugging.

'Er… Mel?' Ally whispers.

'Are they simpletons?'

'Who?'

'The jury? I mean, it was obvious! Wasn't it?'

Ally looks back to where Kathy had been sitting. 'Maybe she'll appeal, or get a light sentence?'

Melody worries at her knuckle. They're taking Kathy, Melody turns away unable to stomach the image.

'Don't look now but…'

At the back of the courtroom Detective Van Doren is watching them, arms crossed. The detective looks about as pleased as they do about the outcome.

'Let's get that drink. You need it.' Ally is on her feet.

On the way past, Melody pauses in front of Van Doren.

'Detective. Congratulations on the result, got you a promotion, I understand?'

Van Doren cranes her head and gives Ally a little wave. 'I see that you brought your partner in crime with you.'

The detective's choice of words is unsettling. 'You don't seem very pleased with the outcome.'

'Neither do you, Mrs Kitteridge.'

'I said on the stand that I didn't believe Kathy would kill Martin.'

'She's looking at a long stretch.' Van Doren looks tired, jaded even. 'Take it from me, women's prisons are horrible places. Overcrowded. Violent. She'll get eaten alive in there.'

A hand pulls at her jacket.

'Come on, let's go,' Ally says.

'I–'

'Come on.' Ally tugs her away.

'You watch yourself, ladies. Take care now!' Van Doren calls after them.

Melody feels Van Doren's eyes on her back as she leaves. 'Are they really as bad as all that? The prisons?'

'Keep walking.' Ally says.

On the steps, cloying reporters. Susan is giving a statement, but some of the press see her, and jump over to her, surrounding her and Ally.

She had prepared a brief statement, but it was for Kathy's acquittal. She is unprepared, unsure what to say.

Ally pushes a path through. 'Move please, move!'

'Are you pleased with the result Mrs Kitteridge?'

'Do you feel justice was served here today, Melody?'

The question checks her. She gives a little shake of the head, no and Ally pulls her past the flashing cameras and into a waiting taxi before she can say anything else.

'Relax, Mel, please. Try not to stress about it. She was guilty of *something*,' Ally says fanning herself.

Melody takes a diazepam from her purse. 'We need to fix this.'

'Not now.' Ally holds her gaze. 'Let's get a drink. Talk. Calmly. Let's process this.'

Melody cracks her fingers into her knuckles one by one, waiting for the pill to take effect.

A half hour later and they are sat at the bar in the cocktail lounge. Ally pocking a square black napkin with straw holes.

Melody waves at the girl behind the bar, who indicates to

give her a minute.

'Can I tell you something?' Melody says. 'Sheridan and I, as children were in the same foster home together. We scarred one another, were split up and took our separate paths. I do believe it was his hand that inadvertently pushed me towards being a vet.'

'Why didn't you say something? Does he know?'

'I don't know. But I wish it was him who got sent down today and not Kathy,' she shakes her head. 'I misjudged it.'

'I know. But you must have known that this was always a risk, right? There aren't any absolutes when you do what we did. Failure of the justice system aside, I'd say it couldn't have gone any better.'

The bartender comes. They order, their conversation pauses while the bartender tongs two discs of ice in pre-frosted Copa de Balon glass. A generous glug of speciality gin with hints of Cape gooseberry. A dash of vermouth. Premium tonic water. Limequat zest sprinkles the surface, and a lemon spiral.

Ally lifts the glass. 'Salut.'

'This better be strong."

It chills her lips, her tongue, teeth, and gums. It's surreptitious. Astringent. Blissfully alcoholic.

Ally lowers her glass, a question in her eyes. 'So, what do you want to do?'

59
Astrid

The traffic is snarled up into Brighton. Astrid seethes, smacking her hand against the steering wheel.

'Fuck!'

She's been played. They all have. She knows it, bone deep.

She drives to Ian Goodworth's, as if brought by some internal satnav. He is up a ladder, scooping moss from the gutter. He descends, smiling, but it fades the nearer he gets to the car.

'Astrid? What's wrong?' The car door opens and he's there.

Her knuckles are white, still gripping the wheel.

'Come on. I'll get the kettle on.'

She sips at the sugary tea. Ian, in the armchair by the fireplace watches her, his cup rattling a little on the saucer. In a silver frame, there's a photo of her father and Ian shoulder to shoulder outside the police station. In the shade of his helmet, his eyes are sunken, hidden, watchful.

Ian squints. 'Was it today the trial finished?'

She grips the handle cup like a railing in a storm.

'I haven't had the radio on. Did she get off, then?'

Astrid drains the tea, puts it down on the table. 'Oh no. She got sent down, but she didn't do it.'

Ian's eyebrows shoot up, a leg crosses over the other. 'You're sure?'

'Now that it's too bloody late. It was the wife. I've never felt so sure about anything in my life. When Spellerman got sent down, Mrs Kitteridge had guilt wracked all over her, I could smell it on her.'

'You have actual proof?'

She tells him about her suspicions being raised by the snake tank. Too much didn't add up; the dust signatures under the tank suggested it had been planted. The fact it had been wiped with bleach.

'It's not enough. You must have investigated her?'

'Of course. But it was her alibi, Christ, it was perfect. Suspicious enough that we'd check it. We chased it to death, witness statement, got her on CCTV, even a tracker on her car puts her miles away the whole time.'

'I see what you're saying. Too perfect. So… she had an accomplice?'

Astrid snorts. 'Ian, if you'd met Mrs Kitteridge, maybe you'd understand. She's just not… what's the term? Neurotypical? To imagine her working with an accomplice just felt impossible.

'We eliminated her early, and had other suspects we couldn't strike off: Pemberton, Sheridan, and then we got blinkered with Kathy Spellerman. And there was Melody protesting Kathy's innocence the whole time! Christ, she might as well have been waving a flag in our faces saying "It's me! It's me, you blind fucks!"'

'Astrid,' he stands, rests a hand on her shoulder. 'This isn't on you. Smithes should have picked this up. A more experienced SIO would have.'

She sends him a weak smile. 'Cold comfort, Ian.'

'I imagine you want to burst into Smithes' office and tell him you've made a dreadful mistake? Or perhaps Burrows, even?'

'That's where I was going.'

'But you diverted yourself to my doorstep.'

'I did.'

'Wise. What stopped you?'

'I don't know.'

'Instinct,' Ian says, 'You were thinking ahead. What would

Smithes have said?'

Once upon a time she would have thought the best of Bill Smithes. But a quiet cynicism pervades her thoughts.

'He'd remind me that both of our promotions were founded on the Spellerman case. A climbdown now would be an embarrassment to the force.'

'And?'

'He'd probably threaten me with a transfer to keep me quiet.'

'I think you're entirely correct.'

'This isn't me saving myself either Ian, I'd give back my promotion in a heartbeat to put this right.'

'But you know it doesn't' work like that, Astrid. There's no undo button. You're more likely to influence things from a position of power.'

She can't sit any longer. She stands and paces in front of the empty hearth, hands jammed in her pockets.

'I know this case cost you a lot, Astrid. Your mother told me about Jenna. I am sorry. The job takes its toll.' His fingers rub at the pale edges of the armrests. Worn fabric. A habit. 'You should take some comfort.'

'In what?' she's incredulous.

'That you're the only one who knows, you alone figured it out who really killed that man. It might not feel like it now, but it isn't nothing.'

He's wrong. It is nothing.

'You experience cases that haunt you over the years, Astrid. And you have to learn to make peace with them or it'll eat you inside out.'

Christ. Make peace? He almost sounded like Smithes. 'But *how*, Ian?'

With a shaky hand, his cup and saucer rattle as he places hem down on the side table.

He looks apologetic. 'I never figured it out, sweetheart. But hat doesn't mean you shouldn't try. You'll have a lot worse than this one, believe me.'

Her heart breaks for him. The photo frame is in her hand. Impossible not to compare this younger, fresh-faced Ian standing next to her father, on the side of the good and just. Naïve no doubt, as she has been. Now diminished, red-eyed and with red capillaries spidering over his skin, like an over-ripe grape about to burst with little else than bitter advice to give.

'I'll find a way,' Astrid says and places the frame back on the mantelpiece. Her watchful father holds her stare.

She had always thought it the height of unfairness that her father had been the one murdered that day, all those years ago. He, with the family had died, and Ian, without a family had survived. But looking at Ian now, perhaps her father had been the luckier of the two after all.

60
Three months later

Melody can feel the back of her neck burning. She swats away flies, takes a drink from her water bottle and wipes her mouth with the back of her hand.

'Thoughts?'

Kathy chews a lip, makes a humming sound, something she always does when she thinks. 'Closed fracture, should he not have splinted it in the first place? Would it be better to get him on a trailer to avoid the fulcrum effect?'

Melody is pleased at this response, but tilts her head one way, then the other. 'It's a judgement call. Generally if it's below the midtibia and midradius, temporary stabilisation or a cast can be helpful. The idea of a splint isn't wrong *per se…*' she doesn't give any more of a clue.

'Well, Dapper's made a right hash of the splint, then.' Kathy crouches down, patting the flank of the calf. 'These splints are too small, the angle isn't right.'

'What else?'

'More padding?'

'Precisely. So-' she shields her eyes against the sun, a figure is emerging over the horizon. A walker being pulled by a dog.

'Who's that? George doesn't have a daughter, does he?'

'Wait… isn't that…' Kathy is shielding her eyes too. The walker is close enough now. Out of place. 'It's the detective.'

Is she here to arrest me? But the clothes… the dog…

Kathy waves. 'Morning.'

'Beautiful day, isn't it?' Van Doren says. She is in rock band

T-shirt, darkened with sweat patches, and khaki shorts; in a soothing Bath Stone by Little Greene. Kathy explains about the injured calf at their feet.

Melody bends down and ruffles the head of dog. 'Beautiful Border Collie. I didn't realise you had a dog, detective?'

'Got her a couple of months ago while I took a few days off. She's a rescue. Gets me out and about on my days off, some company in the evenings.'

'Good for you. She's adorable,' Kathy says.

'I spoke to Hugh Forrester, he said you had just set up again.

'Ah, so that's how you knew we were here.'

'Well we fancied a walk, didn't we Bella?' she fusses over the dog. Melody inspects the dog's teeth, eyes and ears.

'She looks in fine good condition. Beautiful coat. Don't give her too many scraps and leftovers or you'll ruin her teeth.'

Van Doren smiles, and gives Kathy an affectionate squeeze on the arm, 'I was so happy to hear you'd been released, Kathy.'

She snorts. 'Not as happy as I was. Thank you though, Astrid, for visiting me in there. My lawyer said you were my secret weapon.'

'I don't think it would have mattered if Olaf Gudmundson hadn't recanted.'

'Well I don't know how or why, and frankly, I don't care. I'm going to get on with life, make like, much better choices. I'm going to train to be a vet.'

Van Doren has a knowing smile. 'Good for you, Kathy.'

'Kathy, could you go and get George to bring the trailer over. We'd better move this bull calf, get him X-rayed.'

'Of course. Nice to see you, Astrid, and to meet you Bella.' Kathy sets off at a brisk pace towards the barn.

Van Doren shifts from one foot to another. Maybe it's the heat. The flies. Her presence. The sun lotion stinging her eyes from her sweat, but she's uncomfortable.

'You clearly want to say something. So, say it.'

Astrid lets her stew, fiddling in a backpack and gets out a bottle and container, and fills it, placing it in front of Bella. She laps it up greedily.

Kathy is out of earshot now. 'You think you got away with it, then?'

There's a twitch in Melody's cheek, her jaw set. 'Got away with what?'

Astrid laughs. 'Oh, you want to play it like that do you? Fine. You know, it's all been bouncing around my brain ever since that day in court. The more I thought about it, one thing came into sharper focus. The snake tank.

'It was a deliberate mistake. You thought you were being so clever. You were careful enough that it couldn't be linked to you. You did it to get Kathy off. But it was too cute. The jury didn't see it. And it didn't work. The guilt on your face told me what you'd done. And you know what I think?'

'I have a feeling you're going to tell me.'

'You didn't feel bad for what you did to Martin. It was because Kathy was wrongly convicted.'

Melody lets out an ugly smile and shakes her head. 'I suppose you're recording this somehow, detective? Turned up all disarming with your Border Collie. Try and catch me with my guard down?'

Astrid shakes her head, lifts her top, shows her phone. 'I understand your paranoia. But no. We're just two women having a chat, okay?'

Mrs Kitteridge looks doubtful.

'You had some deal with Olaf Gudmundson to identify Kathy, to keep the spotlight off yourself and Ally Campbell. But when Kathy got convicted, you realised it had worked t*oo well.* You got him to recant, and the case against her fell apart.'

'Let's indulge this for a moment. Saying you are correct, just hypothetically. What would be your next move?'

'That depends.'

Melody crosses her arms. 'On what?'

'Why you did it.'

'As if you really care.'

'Actually, I do, Mrs Kitteridge. You've shown you can forgive cheating, at least to Kathy.' Astrid points to Spellerman, nearly at the barn now. 'But not your husband. Why was that?'

Mrs Kitteridge looks off into the distance, possibly weighing up whether to be straight with her or not.

'I loved Martin. He was the first man to really see me. I mean really *see* me. We really were rather good together, and for a long time too.'

'Until?' She prompts.

Melody takes a deep breath, and rolls up her shirt. There's an ugly scar on her inner arm by the bicep.

'Did he do that?'

'Martin wanted us to have a child, to the point of obsession. I couldn't imagine anything worse. Motherhood is just a burden of agonies. I would not endure it for anyone. Even him.'

'Did you know–'

'–And yes, I knew Kathy was pregnant. For a while I was hopeful, he could have his extra-marital child as far as I was concerned and leave me out of it. I was more than happy to play along. It seemed like a fair compromise. So I pretended I didn't know. But no,' she gives a pained sigh, 'Evidently it had to be with me or not at all.'

'And "not at all" was what turned him violent?'

'It was complicated. I pretended to be infertile.' She points at the scar. 'When he found out, he drugged me, cut out my birth control implant with a dinner knife and... well, tried to inseminate me, forcefully.' Even as she says this. Melody Kitteridge seems hard as a stone.

'You're not cattle, Mrs Kitteridge, and Martin was no bul stud. What you're describing is called rape.' Astrid fights th urge to tell her she should have gone to the police. 'That must have been incredibly traumatic.'

'So now you know.'

The calf makes a guttural noise and Melody stoops to soothe it. The tractor is coming. The giant wheels kick up loose grass and cow pats, the trailer leaping and crashing behind it.

'Back to work.' Melody offers a hand.

'That hand's not been up that cow has it?'

'Leg fractures don't usually happen in their intestines, detective.'

Astrid takes it. 'I appreciate you sharing the truth with me. It doesn't make what you did right, it makes it understandable at least.'

'If you come, I'll fight tooth and claw.' Melody says.

Astrid sucks in her cheek. Nods. 'I know.' She crouches down, runs her hand between Bella's ears. 'Come on you.'

They walk a few paces, then she turns. 'You know. Now I've got Bella, I'm in need of a good vet.'

'Well. You'll be able to find us, I'm sure.'

'Always,' Astrid calls back. Bella is strong, insistent and pulls her across the field, back towards the rippling pastoral greens of the Downs.

There she can run free.

What did you think?

Thank you for reading *Dark Vet.*

Reviews are the oxygen books live by.

90% of us use reviews to decide what to read next. If you enjoyed this one, pass the love forward with a review – I'd be much obliged.

For updates on the next book, discounts, and exclusive offers you can join my mailing list at **cjhannon.com**

Acknowledgements

I'd like to thank my beta readers, particularly fellow author Shaun Baines, and my wonderful wife Beccy– not just for her insightful feedback, but her support and encouragement. My parents for their unfaltering support, SGH's sharp eye for detail and AH knowledge of nature! Louise Walters, for her sharp editing and Nick Castle for his work on the creepy cover. Thanks also to my ARC team for your speedy reading and support.

About the Author

CJ Hannon writes YA fiction and Psychological Crime Thrillers in front of snow-capped mountains to the soundtrack of frogs and crickets (and the odd barky dog). A recent convert to through the year sea swimming, CJ also has a side line in avocado and chirimoya cultivation.

Other Titles by the Author

Psychological Crime Thriller

Beachcomber (Short story)

Young Adult

Perry Scrimshaw's Rite of Passage
Orca Rising
Orca Rogue Agent
Orca Divinity Fix (2021)

Printed in Poland
by Amazon Fulfillment
Poland Sp. z o.o., Wrocław